Vigil for the Dead

A Yorkshire Murder Mystery

Tom Raven Book 6

M S MORRIS

Margarita Morris and Steve Morris have asserted their right under the Copyright, Designs and Patents Act 1988 to be identified as the authors of this work.

Published by Landmark Media, a division of Landmark Internet Ltd.

M S Morris® and Tom Raven® are registered trademarks of Landmark Internet Ltd.

msmorrisbooks.com

ISBN-13: 978-1-914537-32-5

CHAPTER 1

The ball landed at his feet with a wet splat and rolled to a halt. Tom Raven looked down into the expectant eyes of his dog, Quincey, who was clearly hoping they would continue playing this game for a few more hours. At least.

Labradors, Raven was quickly discovering, were practically inexhaustible.

'One more go,' he said, bending down to retrieve the soggy, sandy tennis ball, 'and then we're going home for our supper.' He threw the ball as far as he could and Quincey bounded after it with a happy bark, his paws skittering across the sand. Life's simple pleasures. If there was such a thing as reincarnation, Raven wanted to come back as a dog.

He thrust his hands into the pockets of his jacket – it was finally warm enough in Scarborough to ditch his black winter overcoat – and strolled towards Quincey, who was now scampering about in the wet sand at the water's edge. Almost midsummer and the days in North Yorkshire were noticeably longer than at this time of the year in London. Raven liked to make the most of the light evenings, taking

Quincey out after picking him up from the dog minder's.

They were on a stretch of Scarborough's North Bay in the lee of the headland where dogs were permitted all year round. The more touristed South Bay was out of bounds during the summer months to canine visitors, a restriction that Raven quite understood as someone who, until very recently, had never owned a pet in his life. Now he found himself a member of the dog-owning community and his life had changed forever. He had undergone a steep learning curve in the past few weeks, akin to bringing a baby home from the hospital for the first time, and it hadn't stopped yet.

It turned out there was a whole industry devoted to healthy dog food, free of colourings, additives and preservatives. A carefully balanced nutritional regime was required, unlike the convenient ready-meals, takeaways and fast food that Raven was happy to shovel down his own gullet. Quincey, it seemed, enjoyed a far better diet than his owner.

Yet what to feed the animal was just the start of it. There were medical matters such as vaccinations and worming treatments, not to mention daily exercise and behaviour training. Raven really wanted to be a good dog owner. As a father, he'd missed too many milestones as his daughter Hannah was growing up, leaving most of the parenting to his ex-wife Lisa. Now he was on his own and Quincey relied on him. It was a lot of responsibility. He hoped he was up to the job.

'Quince!'

Raven called to the dog by his nickname, keen to get home and put today's refrigerated ready-meal in the microwave and Quincey's gourmet recipe into his bowl. *Quincey* wasn't a name he would have chosen himself, but it had been given to the Black Labrador by his previous owner, a murderer now safely put away in a high-security prison.

But for once, the dog didn't seem to be in a hurry to bring the ball back. An old man in a scruffy green jacket was shambling across the beach in the dog's direction and Quincey was eyeing him with curiosity. The dog hadn't yet learned not to speak to strangers, and Raven, feeling an unexpected surge of protectiveness, set off to intercept the old man and rescue Quincey from an undesirable encounter.

As Raven approached, he realised the man wasn't as ancient as he'd first appeared. He was perhaps not much older than Raven himself, in his late forties or early fifties. But life hadn't treated him kindly. He looked like a down-and-out. Frayed combat trousers, dirty black boots, matted hair and a weathered complexion beneath a military-style cap. And there was something off about him. A wild gleam in his eyes. A soft muttering, not to the dog but to himself, although Raven couldn't make out any coherent words in his mumblings.

Quincey also seemed to be having second thoughts about the stranger. He ran to Raven's side and offered him the soggy tennis ball without the usual expectation that it would be thrown again. It was time to go home.

Raven clipped the lead to the dog's collar and held it tight.

The man came a few steps closer before juddering to a halt. He shifted his attention from Quincey to Raven, revealing a weather-hardened face lined with deep furrows. He stood lopsidedly, shouldering his heavy rucksack unevenly as if compensating for some kind of injury. His eyes darted about, unable to fix on Raven for longer than a second.

'You don't know me, do you?' He was about ten feet away and Raven hadn't expected him to speak. The accent was local, the tone of voice expressing disappointment.

'No.' Raven certainly didn't recognise the man, but there was something about that voice that made him pause.

'And yet I know you.' The man shuffled forward on unsteady legs. Raven instinctively recoiled at the sight of a vodka bottle poking out of the rucksack. He loathed alcohol and the effect it had on people. The man was obviously a drunk. But where had he heard that voice before?

'You're Lance Corporal Tom Raven.' The stranger looked him up and down, as if it were Raven who had let himself go, not this vagrant with his worn and tattered outfit and his reek of vodka and stale sweat. 'Or you were.'

It came back to him in a flash.

A vision of a group of young lads who, just like Raven, had signed up with the Duke of Wellington's Regiment straight after leaving school. They'd been comrades in arms, boys playing at being soldiers, thinking they were men. They'd been kitted out and trained up and shipped off to the Bosnian War in the nineties. War had made men of them soon enough. The ones it hadn't left dead.

'Private Sean Collins.' How could Raven have failed to recognise him?

Bosnia was a lifetime ago. Raven hadn't seen or heard from Collins or any of the other lads in nigh on thirty years. It would have been a miracle if he had recognised him, so changed was Collins from the fresh-faced soldier he'd once been, full of bravado, quick with a joke, and always keen to impress his kid brother who was still living back home in Yorkshire.

Collins grunted in acknowledgement of Raven's delayed recognition. 'So you haven't forgotten everything.'

'How could I forget?'

The war had hurt them both, in Raven's case leaving him with a wounded leg that had never completely healed. Collins had also suffered an injury, which explained the way he leaned slightly to one side under the weight of his backpack. But as Raven regarded the other man's haggard expression and looked into those haunted eyes that darted left and right without ever seeming to rest, it became plain that the damage it had wrought upon Collins had reached far deeper beneath the skin. Raven avoided asking the obvious question of how he was doing. It was clear he was doing terribly.

'Got a light?' Collins rummaged in his pocket and

retrieved a crumpled packet of cigarettes. He offered one to Raven with dirt-streaked fingers.

'I gave up when I left the army.'

'Too bad that.'

Raven couldn't tell if Collins meant giving up smoking or leaving the army, or merely the fact that Raven no longer carried a lighter.

Collins pocketed the cigarettes with a shrug and reached into his rucksack to take a swig of vodka instead. Beneath the layer of grime that cloaked his skin, his hands were calloused and worn. Old man's hands. He offered the bottle to Raven and, when it was refused, shoved it into one of the deep pockets of his cargo pants. He cast a glance over his shoulder as if he feared being spotted. His eyes flitted left, then right. He shuffled closer until he was no more than a foot away.

Raven felt revulsion at the stink of alcohol on his breath and the ripeness of an unwashed body. His instinct was to step back but he rooted himself to the spot out of some lingering sense of duty to his former colleague.

No, not his colleague. His brother. A bond forged in battle could never be broken.

The regimental motto had been *Virtutis Fortuna Comes*. Fortune favours the brave. Well, it hadn't favoured Sean Collins, that was for sure.

Without warning, the man shot out his filthy hand and grabbed hold of Raven's sleeve. Quincey growled, low in his throat.

'What do you want?' demanded Raven. 'Money?' He would happily give Collins enough to get himself a bed for the night even knowing that it would most likely be spent on booze, but if the man turned violent he'd find he'd met his match soon enough. Collins had been a strong man once, but now he was a wasted mess.

But it seemed the man had neither violence nor money in mind. His arm returned to his side and he cast another wary glance around the almost empty beach. 'Raven, I've been looking for you everywhere. You've got to listen to

5

me. I need your help.'

Raven frowned. 'You've been looking for me? Why?'

'Listen.' Collins couldn't get his words out fast enough. 'They're going to destroy everything. Boom!' He clapped his hands together, making Quincey bark and Raven jump.

'What are you talking about?'

'Traitors!' Collins spat on the ground. 'That's what they are. Nothing more, for all their fancy words. Traitors to their country!' He grew more agitated, waving his arms about. 'You've got to help me stop them, Raven. Or else we'll all be dead.'

Raven furrowed his brow, trying to follow the man's logic. 'Who are these traitors?'

Collins leaned in closer. 'I can't tell you yet. Not until you agree to help me. But they're the enemy, I tell you!' His eyes grew wilder, flashing in every direction.

Raven was losing patience rapidly. Collins clearly needed help, but not the kind he was asking for. He had a serious mental health problem that only a professional could begin to tackle. 'Listen, Sean—'

But Collins was in no mood to be reasoned with. He lunged at Raven in desperation, seizing his arm again. 'They'll kill us all, Raven! There's not much time!'

Raven had had enough. He removed Collins's hand from his sleeve and pulled out his wallet. 'Look, Sean, you need to sober up. Go and get yourself a hot meal and a bed for the night. We'll talk again in the morning.' He counted out some notes. 'This should be enough. There's a hostel in town. I tell you what, I'll drive you there myself, just—'

'I don't need your fucking charity!' spat Collins, 'and I'm not drunk!' He drew back from Raven as if he'd been burned. 'You're just like the rest of them. No one'll listen to me. I'll just have to deal with it myself.' He stormed off, muttering to himself as he went. His boots left deep marks in the soft sand.

Raven watched as his former comrade snaked his unsteady way across the beach. The encounter had shaken him, reviving old memories he'd thought were buried deep. Memories he'd prefer to keep that way. Nothing good could come of revisiting the past.

And it was sad to see a former friend in such a sorry state.

How had Collins ended up that way? The war had treated them both badly, and it wasn't always easy adjusting to life on Civvy Street after serving in the army, but Sean Collins had clearly fared worse than most. Raven wondered where he would go now and what would happen to him. He wished he could have done something more for the man, but it was hard to give help to someone who refused to accept any.

He wondered briefly what Collins had been jabbering about. *Traitors. The enemy. They'll kill us all.* But these were surely just the ravings of an unbalanced mind. Poor bugger.

Quincey nudged Raven's leg with his nose, bringing him back to more pressing matters. Such as supper.

'Come on, Quince, let's go home.' The dog didn't need telling twice.

CHAPTER 2

The walk had been long and arduous and there were still another seven miles across dense heather moorland to go. Tomorrow, her hamstrings might seize up completely and refuse to cooperate, but for now DC Jess Barraclough was still just about managing to put one foot in front of the other. If she focused her attention on the wild, uninhabited, breathtaking moor stretching out around her, she could almost forget her aching body.

But not her aching heart.

How Scott, her late boyfriend, would have loved this walk with its spectacular views of hills and valleys, miles of lush heather and sites of ancient burial mounds. In her imagination, he was the unseen companion urging her on, mile after mile. It was strange yet somehow comforting that a dead person could be such a source of strength to the living.

This was Jess's first crossing of the Lyke Wake Walk, the infamous forty-mile hike across the North York Moors from the starting point at Osmotherley in the west to the finishing post at Ravenscar in the east. She was determined to make it to the end and claim her membership of the

Lyke Wake Club, the society exclusively for those who completed the crossing within twenty-four hours. It had been one of Scott's unfulfilled ambitions. She was doing the walk for both of them.

But this was not a walk to be attempted alone. The distance was too great and the route too treacherous. It would be easy to get lost on the moors where you might never see another living soul, save for the sheep that regarded you with mild curiosity before resuming their chomping. Jess was one of a group of four.

The leader of the group was Ronald Fairchild, a seventy-year-old retired vicar from Jess's home village of Rosedale Abbey and an old family friend. Tall and wiry with a weathered complexion and bushy white eyebrows, Ronald was an experienced walker and longstanding member of the Lyke Wake Club, having crossed the moors on many occasions and in all weathers. The club, with its somewhat eccentric and macabre traditions, had awarded him the coveted title of *Doctor of Dolefulness* for having completed at least four crossings, one in the middle of winter and one unsupported, and for having submitted a thesis on the Bronze-Age burial mounds that lined the route, visible reminders of the omnipresence of death.

Then there was Janice Sillitoe, in her mid-sixties, who had been a PE teacher at a school in Scarborough before retiring to the village of Goathland in the middle of the moors. Chatting as they crossed Wheeldale Moor and passing the standing stone known as Blue Man-i'-th'-Moss, Jess had learned that Janice had once taught hockey and netball to recalcitrant teenage girls. From the older woman's no-nonsense, upbeat manner, Jess was sure there had been no slacking in Janice's games lessons. Jess had liked games when she was at school but had been in a minority. Like Ronald, Janice was also an experienced walker and had completed sufficient crossings of the Lyke Wake Walk to be awarded the title of *Mistress of Misery*, which was ironic since Janice was anything but miserable. While Ronald kept them on the right track with his walking maps and compass, Janice kept everyone's spirits up with her cheery, can-do attitude. She was one of those inexhaustible women who organised village fetes, started petitions, and raised money for charity. A good person to have with you on a forty-mile hike.

The final member of the group was much closer in age to Jess. Twenty-five-year-old Matthew Whelan was doing a PhD in Geosciences at Newcastle University. He was currently lodging with Janice while he undertook his research into the effects of climate change on the moorland. He fell into step beside Jess as they approached Lilla Howe, a Bronze-Age round barrow, marked by the medieval Lilla Cross at its summit.

Fylingdales Moor lay all around them, a patchwork of greens, yellows and browns, interrupted only by the enormous concrete-and-steel pyramid of the radar station at RAF Fylingdales. The eighty-foot tall structure rose incongruously above the rolling moorland and was visible from miles around. Looking like an alien spaceship that had landed on the moors, the radar formed part of a ballistic missile early warning system.

Right now a ballistic missile attack was the least of Jess's worries. She was far more likely to twist an ankle on the rough ground, sink into a bog, get lost, or die from dehydration in the June heat. They had set off in the early hours of the morning and she was so exhausted by this stage in the walk she was only listening to Matthew with half an ear.

'The peat bogs are at risk from climate change,' he was saying. 'Rising temperatures affect the ability of peatlands to absorb and store carbon. If the soil is warmer, organic material decays at a faster rate and releases more carbon into the atmosphere. It creates a positive feedback loop.'

'Uh-huh.' Jess nodded. 'Very interesting.' She didn't really have anything to say in response but she was happy to let Matthew do the talking. He had a rich, warm voice that was pleasant to listen to, even though he tended to go on a bit. If he saw the ancient Land Rover she drove he might have something to say about its environmental credentials, but she didn't expect to see him again after today. He would soon be returning to Newcastle where he probably had a girlfriend – why was she even wondering about his love life? – and she would be back at work in Scarborough, solving crimes with her colleagues, DCI Tom Raven, DS Becca Shawcross and DC Tony Bairstow. Matthew's whereabouts and personal life could have no interest for her whatsoever. She tried to concentrate on what he was telling her about the peat bogs but all she could really think about was reaching the finishing point and enjoying a pint at the Raven Hall Hotel in Ravenscar.

Ronald and Janice, also deep in conversation, were about twenty-five yards ahead. Jess marvelled at their stamina and hoped she would be as fit and active at their age. As they reached the edge of the barrow and began climbing the rocky path that led to the top, Janice gave a sudden cry. Her voice, honed from years of bellowing at teenage girls on the hockey pitch, carried across the moors like an air raid siren. 'Oh, my Lord, what is that?!' She placed one hand to her chest and looked as if she might be having heart palpitations.

Jess hoped they weren't about to have a medical emergency, not out here so far from civilisation. Leaving Matthew where he was, she quickly made her way up the barrow mound and went to the older woman's side. 'Are you all right, Janice?'

Janice, speechless for once, nodded and pointed up ahead.

As Ronald comforted Janice, Jess peered in the direction of the stone cross at the centre of the barrow. Of Maltese design, it stood over seven feet tall. Ronald had explained to her earlier that it dated from the tenth century, having replaced the original seventh-century cross. Its weathered surface bore the marks of having survived for hundreds of years in an exposed spot on a wild moorland, battered by rain, hail and snow. The burial mound on which it stood was the resting place of Bronze-

Age warriors, some of the earliest inhabitants of this untamed landscape. Now, a dark object lay at the foot of the cross. A single red kite circled overhead as if keeping watch.

Jess dropped her rucksack to the ground and approached the cross cautiously, barely breathing. As she drew nearer, the dark shape on the ground took on a recognisable form. She saw with horror that it was the charred remains of a corpse, so badly burned that identification would surely be impossible.

One more body at this site of death and burial.

CHAPTER 3

It had been a busy day at the police station and by the time Raven arrived to collect Quincey from the dog minder's it was already nearly seven o'clock. Still, the evening was fine and bright and he was looking forward to heading back to the North Bay for another session of ball throwing and fetching. The dog couldn't get enough of the activity and – no point kidding himself – Raven enjoyed it too. He was also feeling the benefits of fresh air and regular exercise. It calmed him down after a day at work, he was sleeping better, and his leg was stronger and less prone to ache. Overall, Quincey was having a positive influence on him, even if solo walks with his dog tended to encourage his solitary habits.

But Raven didn't mind that. Dog and man suited each other. They were two of a kind.

A couple of days had passed since Raven had encountered his old comrade on the beach. He'd kept an eye open for Sean Collins ever since, but the poor soul hadn't put in a repeat appearance. Raven felt guilty that he hadn't done more for his old pal yet also relieved that the guy had vanished. If he'd found his way to the homeless shelter, all well and good. And if he hadn't? Well, what could Raven do about that?

Still, there but for the grace of God.

The encounter with Sean had made him count his blessings and to his surprise he had found quite a few. Numbering them on his fingers, he could reel off an entire handful: a job that was going well; good colleagues; a wonderful daughter; a house that was finally fully refurbished; and a dog.

He pulled his car over on Barmoor Lane in front of a chalet-style dormer bungalow fronted by a long driveway and neatly trimmed lawn. When he had first become the reluctant owner of his four-legged friend, he hadn't known how he was going to look after a dog while working all day, sometimes long and unpredictable hours. It was Barry Hardcastle, the builder who had demolished and then re-built the interior of Raven's house, who had come to the rescue. It turned out that Barry's wife, Vicky, looked after dogs in their home on Scarborough's northern edge. She was a minder for dogs whose owners led busy lives and sometimes worked shifts. She was delighted to add a Black Labrador to her small group of charges that included a King Charles Spaniel, a West Highland Terrier, and a scruffy mongrel. She only accepted friendly dogs, she explained to Raven on their first meeting, and drew the line at Alsatians and Rottweilers. Fortunately, Quincey had passed the "friendly" test with flying colours.

As Raven walked up the driveway, Barry's van pulled in behind him. The sight of it gave Raven mixed feelings. For months that damn vehicle had been parked outside his house in Quay Street, blocking the narrow road and causing havoc with the neighbours. He was glad the work on his house was finished, but he missed chatting to the builder who was the nearest thing he had to a friend in the town.

Barry jumped down from the cab and came to shake Raven's hand. 'How's it going, mate? No probs with the plumbing or anything?'

'Not at all,' said Raven. 'You did an excellent job.' It was strange how the passing of time had altered Raven's perception of his builder. For months, he had cursed Barry's unreliability and the mess he left in the house. There were moments when the builder's presence – or lack of it – had reduced Raven to despair. Somehow, those memories were fading from his mind. If he wasn't careful he might end up inviting Barry back to do more work on the house. He would have to guard against that. 'Where are you working at the moment?'

'Me and Reg are converting a massive Victorian place into holiday flats up near Oliver's Mount.' Reg was Barry's young apprentice who, as far as Raven could recall, had never uttered a single word in his presence.

'Are you working for Liam Shawcross by any chance?' Raven's sergeant, Becca, had a brother who was into property, particularly anything that could be rented out at inflated prices to Scarborough's tourists. It was Liam who had recommended Barry to Raven in the first place.

'Yeah, that's right. It's another of Liam's ventures.'

'He must own half of Scarborough by now,' joked Raven.

Barry didn't laugh. 'You're not wrong there, mate.'

They went around the back of the bungalow to the extension where Vicky looked after the dogs. It was basically a large space filled with dog baskets, food bowls, and rubber toys. The floor was of practical wipe-clean linoleum, the walls of bare plaster. Vicky had complained to Raven with a roll of her eyes that Barry kept promising to put a coat of paint on them but never got round to it. Builders, apparently, were notorious for not finishing jobs on their own properties.

It always melted Raven's heart to see Quincey bounding over to greet him. It was like collecting a young child from school before they reached the age when they didn't want to be seen dead with their parents. He wished he'd collected Hannah more often when she was young and eager to share her drawings and chat about her day.

But his work at the Met had prevented him from getting to the school by three o'clock, which was the middle of the day as far as Raven was concerned. Vicky was happy to keep the dogs until six or seven in the evening, but Raven didn't like to take too much advantage of her generosity. He didn't want her to think he was unsuited to owning a dog. Even though he probably was.

'Quincey's been a very good boy today,' said Vicky. She always said that and Raven hoped it was true. She was a strong, energetic woman in her forties who clearly loved dogs and didn't mind that her clothes were always covered in dog hairs. In a reflective moment she'd once confided to Raven that she and Barry had tried for years to have a family. 'But nothing doing in that department,' she said with a brave smile. 'So I decided to look after dogs instead. My friends who have children tell me that dogs are far less trouble.'

The owner of the King Charles Spaniel was also collecting her dog, stroking its long silky ears and murmuring terms of endearment into its little face. Raven had spoken to her on a couple of occasions when they were dropping off or picking up at the same time. She was mid-forties, had introduced herself as Melanie and said she worked at the hospital. She must have just come from there because she was still in her uniform of short-sleeved blue tunic, dark trousers and sensible rubber-soled shoes, good for dog-walking as well as quiet on the wards. Melanie had told Raven how much she valued Vicky's help with Lulu – the dog – because she lived alone. Just her and the dog. 'Much like you,' she'd added, although how she had become privy to that information, Raven wasn't quite sure.

He was about to depart with Quincey when his phone buzzed with an incoming call. He would have let it go to voicemail, but saw from the screen that it was work. If something had come up, then now would be the time to ask Vicky if she would keep Quincey for another hour or two, although Raven dreaded the reproachful look the dog seemed to have mastered for whenever Raven let him down. He excused himself and stepped outside to take the call.

Listening carefully to what the duty sergeant was telling him, he couldn't quite believe his ears. There couldn't have been a worse time for this to happen.

'Where did you say the body is?' He walked away from the open door, conscious of listening ears.

'Lilla Cross, sir.'

'And where on earth is that?'

'On top of Lilla Howe, out on Fylingdales Moor.'

The last thing Raven needed now was a dead body right in the middle of the high moors. He pictured the bleak inaccessible landscape. How was he even going to get there? 'And who found it?'

'Some walkers, sir.'

'All right,' sighed Raven. 'I'm on my way.' He gave the duty sergeant the names of DS Becca Shawcross and the CSI team leader, Holly Chang, and told him to get them on board. If he was going to be trekking into the back of beyond he needed a good team around him.

A body on the moors! It would take hours to get out there and set the investigation in motion. Fortunately the light evenings at this time of year would make that a lot easier. But what was he going to do about Quincey? He stepped back inside to break the news.

'Normally, I'd love to have Quincey for the evening,' said Vicky when Raven had explained his predicament. 'I do sometimes look after dogs overnight if their owner has a night shift. The thing is, it's our anniversary today and Barry is taking me out for a slap-up meal. You wouldn't believe how difficult it is to get him into a suit and tie.'

'Of course,' said Raven glumly. 'Then I'll have to take Quincey with me. I guess he won't mind sitting in the back of the car for an hour or two with the window rolled down. Will he?'

The stern expression on Vicky's face gave him his answer.

But what choice did he have? Much as he hated the idea

of leaving the dog in his car, if Vicky couldn't help, then he had no one else to turn to.

'Quincey can come home with me and Lulu,' said Melanie brightly. She had clearly been eavesdropping on the conversation and now came over with her King Charles Spaniel in tow. 'I couldn't help overhearing that you have to go into work,' she added in a sympathetic voice, lightly touching Raven's sleeve with her fingertips.

Raven could hardly believe his good fortune. 'That's very kind,' he said, 'but really, are you sure–'

She cut him off with a wave of her hand. 'Honestly, it's no trouble. Off you go and do your job. Quincey will be fine with me.'

The dog was looking from one to the other as if following every word of the exchange that would decide the outcome of his evening.

Raven knelt down and gave the dog a rub. 'Would you like to go home with Melanie and Lulu?' he asked.

'Of course he would,' enthused Melanie.

Quincey seemed less convinced, but Raven knew there was no other option. He and Melanie exchanged phone numbers and he thanked her again. He gave Quincey one last hug and promised to collect him as soon as possible. Then he left before the dog could fix him with his doleful eyes.

CHAPTER 4

Bumping across the North York Moors in a four-by-four mountain rescue vehicle was not how DS Becca Shawcross had planned to spend her evening. She had been intending to call in at the family guest house on North Marine Road and visit her parents. Living as she now did in an apartment overlooking the North Bay, she missed her mum's home cooking. Her flatmate, Ellie Earnshaw, was good fun but quite exhausting at times, constantly wanting to go out partying. And neither of them was a great cook so if they shared a meal at home it tended to be a takeaway. She had been looking forward to her mum's roast chicken with Yorkshire pudding and thick gravy.

But when the call came through she knew she was duty-bound to attend the crime scene. She couldn't let Raven down. And, if she was honest, a burnt body in the middle of the moors on Lilla Howe sounded intriguing. It wasn't your run-of-the-mill stabbing in the street after a drunken brawl.

But bloody hell, it was a bumpy ride to get there.

The routes that walkers used to cross the moor were

impassable even to the rescue team's Land Rover Defender with its off-road capabilities, so instead they were driving along rough tracks that traversed the moorland.

The vehicle lurched as its offside wheel plunged into a hollow. Becca was thrown against Raven, who sat morosely staring out of the window. On her other side, Holly Chang bounced miserably in her seat. 'All my bones are broken already,' complained the CSI team leader. 'Much more of this and my brains will be scrambled eggs too.'

'Not much further to go now, love,' said Pete, one of the two red-jacketed mountain rescue volunteers who had met them at a small parking area off the main road crossing the moor. He and Jim, who was at the wheel, appeared calm and relaxed. Becca marvelled at how confidently they navigated the rough terrain. In every direction all she could see was a bleak, treeless wilderness. The ground was covered by deep heather and criss-crossed by streams and ravines. Without the help of the volunteers, the police would have no hope of getting to Lilla Cross before nightfall.

'Glad to hear it,' continued Holly. 'What else did I have planned for this evening? Seeing my kids? Having a conversation with my husband? No, I'd much rather be out here with you folk, having the contents of my stomach turned over like butter.'

This last remark was directed pointedly at Raven who wisely refused to take the bait. Getting into an argument with Holly Chang was like stepping onto a rollercoaster without a seat restraint. The petite woman may have reached only up to Raven's shoulder, but she was treated warily by her colleagues and her long-suffering husband alike. Besides, it was hardly Raven's fault they were out on the moors when they ought to have been at home. He didn't decide when and where a body would be found.

Becca wondered what Raven had done with his dog for the evening. At least she didn't have anyone who relied on her, animal or human.

After a few more minutes of dipping and lurching along

the trail, Jim brought the vehicle to a merciful halt. 'We can't get any nearer,' he said, turning around to face his passengers. We'll have to proceed from here on foot.'

'Just as well,' said Holly, opening the door on her side. 'My poor backside will be black and blue.'

Becca followed her out of the vehicle and onto the safety of steady ground. Yet just as soon as she was out, the wind whipped her hair across her face. Back in Scarborough the weather had been warm and calm and she had felt comfortable in short sleeves, but on the high, exposed moorland she was glad of her summer jacket to protect her from the wind.

Out here, the landscape looked as it must have done in ancient times – untamed and desolate. The moor stretched out for miles, and the only sign of human habitation was RAF Fylingdales, a couple of miles to the south. Even at this distance, the enormous pyramidal structure of the radar station, so out of place in this environment, was clearly visible.

'Just watch where you're putting your feet,' warned Pete. 'The ground is very uneven.'

'Really?' said Holly sarcastically. 'Thanks for telling us.'

It was just gone eight thirty in the evening but with only one more day until the summer solstice, it would be light for hours yet. Lilla Howe was a short distance away. They set off towards the mound, heads bowed low against the wind. Becca wasn't averse to an afternoon stroll beside a river or along a forest trail, but this was more like an assault course. The heather was deep and unyielding, forcing her to lift her feet high with every step.

'We're lucky,' said Pete who had fallen into step beside her. 'The ground's nice and firm right now. It gets worse after it's been raining. You can find yourself up to your knees in the peat bog.'

His comment earned him more grouchy mutterings from Holly, who was battling valiantly with the heather.

Becca turned around to see where Raven had got to. He was some distance behind them, clearly struggling to keep up. She would have offered to lend him an arm to lean on but knew he would never accept any help. He was stubborn like that.

Instead, she pressed on, giving Holly a helping hand with her heavy bag of CSI equipment.

The four walkers who had found the body were waiting for them at the base of the tumulus. As Becca drew closer to the mound, she was astonished to see that one of them was her colleague, DC Jess Barraclough. She knew that Jess was a keen walker and was currently taking some annual leave but hadn't known what she was doing with her time.

Jess came up to her and gave her a quick hug. 'I'm so glad to see you!'

'You too,' said Becca. She looked at the large mound before her. It was impossible to see the body from the foot of the barrow. 'Where exactly is it?' she asked Jess in a low voice. There was no need to specify what "it" was.

'At the top. Beneath a stone cross.'

They waited for Raven to catch up, then Jess introduced her walking companions – Ronald, the group leader, Janice and Matthew.

Raven wasted no time getting down to business. 'What time did you discover the body?' he asked Jess.

'Six o'clock. We set off at four this morning at the start of civil twilight and were on course to reach Ravenscar by ten this evening. We hoped to complete the walk before nautical twilight.'

Becca blinked. Had she heard Jess correctly? Four o'clock in the morning? She'd been tucked up fast asleep in bed at that time like any sensible person. Yet Jess had been out on the moors and planning to walk for eighteen hours. Becca had heard that the Lyke Wake Walk was challenging but hadn't realised you had to be completely nuts to do it.

'Where have you walked from?' asked Raven.

'Osmotherley,' said Jess. 'We met up at Rosedale Abbey last night and then my dad dropped us off at the

start of the walk this morning.'

Raven nodded. 'Impressive. Were there many people out walking today?'

'Not a soul,' said Ronald. 'That's what's so wonderful about crossing the moors. The solitude.' He gave a blissful sigh.

'You're an experienced walker?' Raven asked.

'I do the crossing about once a month,' said Ronald

'When were you last here?'

'Not for a few weeks. But I know a group who came this way yesterday and there was certainly no body then, or they'd have said so.'

'And what time would they have been here?'

'Probably about the same time as us. Late afternoon or early evening.'

'You say you found the body at six,' said Raven, sounding puzzled, 'but the call to 999 wasn't made until half past.'

'There's no phone signal out here,' explained Jess, 'so Ronald and Janice walked on to the Flask Inn at Fylingdales village to make the call. Matthew and I stayed with the body and waited for them to come back.'

Becca sneaked a quick glance at her phone and saw that Jess was right. She had no bars on her mobile whatsoever. If you were stuck out here in need of rescue you'd have to send up a distress flare and hope that someone noticed it. But the only people nearby were at the radar base and they were probably too busy looking for ballistic missiles coming from far away to notice a flare signal in their backyard.

Janice stepped forward then, frowning at Raven. 'Do I know you from somewhere?'

'No, I don't think so,' said Raven, barely giving the older woman a second glance.

But it seemed to Becca that Janice thought otherwise. Her frown deepened as if she wanted to pursue the matter, but then she let it drop.

Raven seemed impatient to get on and examine the

body. 'Now, if you don't mind stepping aside?'

The walkers stayed back while he, Becca, Holly and Jess ascended the rocky path up the side of the mound. The stone cross at the top stood over seven feet tall and, to Becca's eyes, looked primitive in nature. Its rough, weathered surface was at home in this windswept landscape and it was encircled by low-lying boulders and rocks.

Within this circle lay the charred remains of a body.

Holly was suddenly all business-like, the ride from hell in the Land Rover forgotten. She donned her white coveralls and approached the body while the others stayed a little way back.

'Burnt to a crisp,' she called over the wind. 'The ground all around is scorched too. This one's going to be difficult to identify.'

Even from a distance, Becca could see that the body and the surrounding scrub were almost completely blackened. 'Any indication of the cause of death?' she asked.

Holly crouched over the remains, examining them closely. 'Nothing obvious. I reckon that's going to be a challenge as well.'

'Can you tell how recent the fire was?' asked Raven.

Holly pressed her gloved hand to the earth. 'There's still some residual heat in the embers, so my guess would be within the last twenty-four hours.'

'That fits with what Ronald told us,' said Becca, 'so the body was most likely burned last night or earlier today.'

'Hey,' said Holly, 'I've found something.' She retrieved a blackened object. 'I think it used to be a mobile phone. But I don't reckon it'll be making any more calls.'

She passed the remains of the phone to Becca, who examined it carefully. The device was clearly damaged way beyond repair. Its surface was blistered and blackened, its screen warped, and the plastic parts melted and fused together. 'The forensics guys might be able to tell us the make and model, but I bet the SIM card will be toast.'

'And any data too,' said Jess.

They waited while Holly continued her search of the body and the surrounding area, photographing the site from all angles, but it seemed that no other personal possessions had survived the fire. As she had said, there would be very little to identify the victim.

Once Holly's work was done, Becca trudged back down the mound to tell Pete and Jim that they could take a stretcher up to remove the body. Or what was left of it. It wasn't an enviable task.

Jess came over to her. 'I've had a chat with Ronald, and we've decided to call off the walk. It's too late to continue on to Ravenscar tonight.'

Becca was astonished they'd even contemplated carrying on under the circumstances and especially so late in the day. They had been out for almost eighteen hours already. Becca had only been on the moors for an hour or so, and that was one hour too long. She just wanted to get back in the Land Rover and out of the wind. Then home.

But Jess's disappointment was tangible. 'I've been wanting to do this walk for such a long time,' she told Becca. 'I feel like a failure.'

Becca took hold of her hand. 'It wasn't your fault. It's just one of those things.'

'Well, at least I'll be able to return to work tomorrow,' said Jess.

'I'm glad to hear it,' said Raven, hobbling down the mound behind Holly and the mountain rescue guys as they carried the stretcher bearing its gruesome load. 'Team meeting at nine o'clock sharp.'

CHAPTER 5

*T*he Hercules transport plane bumps through cloud cover and banks sharply before beginning its rapid descent towards the airstrip.

The sudden drop in altitude causes nineteen-year-old Lance Corporal Thomas Raven's stomach to turn over and his eardrums to feel as if they are about to burst. Yet even as the engines roar furiously to bring the plane in to land, a surge of adrenaline makes his heart beat faster at the thought of what he is about to encounter on the ground.

The atmosphere inside the aircraft is charged with a mix of fear, anticipation and excitement. Young men from the Duke of Wellington's Regiment, edgy and tense yet eager to be tested after months of training. Now they are being sent into the middle of a war zone.

The guy strapped into a seat near Raven is full of bravado, boasting to anyone who will listen of the battles he will win, of the enemies he will kill. Meanwhile, the lad facing him looks scared shitless. His eyes are closed, his lips moving voicelessly. He seems barely old enough to be out of school. Months of training and preparation, yet everything he's learned has been forced from his mind by the howl of the engines and the lurching of the plane.

Raven has never been abroad before. When the "Dukes" were told they were being deployed to Bosnia, he had to go and look it up. Bosnia and Herzegovina, capital city Sarajevo. But the atlas he found was old and showed only a long country called Yugoslavia, across the Adriatic from Italy. Now that country has fractured into half a dozen different states, scrawling bloody borders across the map and leaving thousands dead or displaced.

In any case, a map tells Raven little about a country. All he knows is that this is a place well beyond his limited experience of life. Some of his army mates have been on holiday to Spain or France. But none of them have visited Yugoslavia. Nor do they understand the first thing about the confusion of ethnic groups that are now fighting for independence or survival in a brutal war on Europe's southern fringe.

The plane drops another hundred feet, almost as if the pilot doesn't give a shit about his human cargo, and Private Sean Collins, who is sitting next to Raven, swears like the trooper he is. Collins is another recruit in Raven's platoon. They've forged something of a bond in training. Raven didn't join the army to make friends, but Collins is all right. He's never travelled either and knows just as little about what's in store for them as Raven does. Raven knows they'll look out for one another, whatever happens.

The plane's wheels hit the tarmac with a thud.

An alarm goes off.

Raven woke up, the alarm still beeping. Bathed in sweat, the duvet tangled around his legs.

It took him a moment to realise where he was. In his bed in Scarborough and not in a military aircraft about to land in the middle of a conflict zone. He was alive and safe, two things he hadn't been able to take for granted during his time in Bosnia.

But his heart was racing as if he was about to go into battle.

He silenced the alarm on his phone and staggered to the bathroom, hoping the power shower would wash away all traces of his dream. Or nightmare. Or memory.

Flashbacks. That's what the army psychiatrists called them. He'd thought he was long since done with those.

He stuck his head under the pounding water at the hottest setting he could stand. Images of war still clung to his mind like burnt-on residue. The destruction; the fear in people's eyes. Death.

You couldn't wash that away so easily.

He knew full well what had triggered these long-buried memories. The encounter with Sean Collins on the North Bay beach, and then, just a few days later, the bumpy ride in the Land Rover to view the burnt body on the moors. A discovery as gruesome as anything he had witnessed as a soldier.

Sean Collins he could do nothing about. The poor guy had clearly lost his mind. Or however the psychiatrists would insist on calling it. They did like to use the proper words, those psychiatrists.

Flashbacks, post-traumatic stress, acute psychotic disorder.

Talk, talk, talk. Their cure for everything.

No amount of talking would help Sean Collins.

But it was Raven's duty to find out who the burned victim had been in life and what had happened to them. Perhaps if he could solve this crime, he could take his own memories of the horrors of Bosnia and wrestle them back to the place they belonged.

Well and truly buried.

He turned off the water and prepared to face the day.

*

Everyone was keen to get started. By the time Raven arrived in the incident room, Becca had already laid out fresh pens by the whiteboard and was chatting to Jess, who had returned from her walking ordeal looking none the worse for wear. DC Tony Bairstow was bringing in a tray of teas and coffees.

Raven did a double take, then checked his watch to confirm he wasn't late. He was used to being the first at his desk in the mornings. In fact, he was earlier than usual since he hadn't needed to take Quincey to the dog minder's before coming into work. He had called Melanie the previous night on getting back from Lilla Cross but it had been late and she'd told him not to worry, Quincey was welcome to spend the night at her place – a *sleepover* she'd called it – and she would happily drop him off at Vicky's in the morning. Raven had been too exhausted to protest and had thanked her for her support. He would have to find a way to repay her kindness.

'Mug of coffee for you, sir,' said Tony, holding out the tray.

Raven was a coffee connoisseur. Instant coffee from the police station kitchen wasn't up to the standard he was used to at home, but he accepted the mug gratefully. He would need all the help he could get to bring him up to speed. 'Thank you, Tony. Will DI Dinsdale be joining us this morning?'

'He's on holiday again,' said Tony. 'Portugal, this time.'

'All right for some,' said Raven, somewhat relieved. 'I'm sure we'll manage without him.' Dinsdale wasn't exactly Raven's favourite colleague. Scrub that. He was Raven's least favourite, and he would happily do without Dinsdale's grumpy and argumentative presence on the team.

He called the room to attention. 'Okay, I'm sure you're all keen to get started.'

He was greeted by a general nodding of heads. The beginning of a new investigation was a heady time, everyone eager to get stuck in and find out all they could about the new case. It was a good feeling, almost as satisfying as when a perpetrator was eventually collared. At this point in the process, it was easy to forget the depressing statistics about how few crimes resulted in a suspect being charged, and to believe that the job was worth doing. It was almost like being young again.

He stuck a photograph of the victim on the whiteboard.

The image didn't make for pretty viewing. The crime scene photo showed a blackened shape that was barely recognisable as human. Male or female, young or old, it was impossible to tell. The fire had left little behind but bones and ashes.

'Our first challenge,' said Raven, 'will be identification. Whoever this person was when they were alive, they are now burnt beyond recognition. The only personal item recovered from the crime scene was the victim's phone, which is now charcoal. All we know is that the victim's remains were found at Lilla Cross in the middle of Fylingdales Moor. We believe that the body was most likely burned there on Monday night, but we should keep an open mind about timescales. As for how the victim and the killer got to Lilla Cross, that's very much an open question. There aren't any inhabited places for miles around, and I can vouch from personal experience that it's not an easy place to reach.' He looked to Jess. 'I think you're our local expert, Jess. Would you like to tell us what you know about the area?'

'Sure. I'll tell you what I know. Lilla Cross marks the spot of a Bronze-Age burial mound. It's a landmark on the Lyke Wake Walk, which is a route that crosses the moor. I was part of a group doing the walk when we found the body. The nearest settlement is the village of Goathland, which is tiny, and the RAF base at Fylingdales, which is a couple of miles away. People travel to work there from towns like Whitby and Pickering. Otherwise, there's not much else around. Walkers cross the moor regularly, and a group passed that way on Monday evening and didn't notice anything unusual, so as DCI Raven says, the body was probably placed there on Monday night.'

Raven nodded. 'Tony, can I ask you to comb through missing persons reports for the past fortnight? Put together a list of anyone who might be our victim.'

'Will do, sir.' Tony made a note.

'At present, the sex of the victim is indeterminate, the cause of death is unknown, and no identifying items have been recovered from the crime scene. We'll need to wait for the post-mortem to see what that can tell us. Meanwhile, what else do we have to work with?' Raven had his own thoughts, but he liked to hear what his team had to say. It fostered a more cooperative approach if everyone chipped in, and he liked his juniors to learn to think for themselves.

'I've been thinking about the logistics of burning a body out there, miles from anywhere,' said Becca. 'It must have involved a high degree of premeditation. You'd need a can of petrol or some other kind of accelerant. Why go to all that trouble?'

'To cover your tracks?' suggested Tony. 'To destroy evidence?'

'Sure,' said Becca. 'But what I mean is, there are easier places to commit a murder. Assuming that this was murder. And if not, why destroy the evidence?'

'True,' said Raven. 'So is there any significance in the location?'

'This is just an idea,' said Jess, 'but the site is an ancient burial mound. Could that be the reason it was chosen as the place to dispose of a body?'

Raven chewed the idea over in his mind. At this point, he was willing to pursue any lead, no matter how tenuous. 'So, where do we go with that?'

Jess seemed pleased he was willing to entertain her idea. 'Ronald, the leader of our walking group, is an expert on the history and folklore of the moors. We could try talking to him for starters.'

'That's not a bad idea,' said Raven. 'At least while we wait for the post-mortem results. How well do you know Ronald?'

'Really well. He's a retired vicar from Rosedale Abbey and a friend of the family.'

'All right, then,' said Raven. 'You can take me to see him and introduce us properly.'

'I'd be happy to,' said Jess, beaming.

'Good, and Becca, can I ask you to make the most of

your "special relationship" with Dr Felicity Wainwright, and see if you can persuade her to carry out the autopsy right away?'

The senior pathologist at Scarborough Hospital had been engaged in a battle of wills with Raven ever since he had come to Scarborough. Quite what he had done to upset her still eluded him, but he had observed that while Felicity seemed determined to maintain frosty relations with him, she was always perfectly friendly with his sergeant.

Becca grimaced. 'I don't really have any kind of special relationship with Felicity.'

'Well, she seems to like you a lot better than she cares for me. Give her a call and see what you can do. And then perhaps you could attend the post-mortem and report back?'

Becca glowered at the suggestion but didn't argue. She knew Raven was right.

CHAPTER 6

Ronald Fairchild lived in a terraced cottage overlooking a triangular green in the heart of Rosedale Abbey. His house had gothic upstairs windows and a gothic-arched front door, lending it a distinctly ecclesiastical appearance, well suited for a retired vicar. He welcomed Raven and Jess into his home and told them to make themselves comfortable in the sitting room while he put the kettle on.

It was a pleasant room, small but cosy. The alcoves on either side of the fireplace were lined with a wide assortment of books. Raven wasn't surprised to see various editions of the Bible on the shelves, but also Bertrand Russell's *A History of Western Philosophy*, T. E. Lawrence's *Seven Pillars of Wisdom*, several political biographies, books on history and folklore, and what looked like a complete collection of vintage Agatha Christies. Ronald was clearly an intellectual, yet one who liked to relax with a good, old-fashioned murder mystery.

The rest of the room suggested a man of simple but tidy habits – a sofa with cushions neatly arranged, a picture above the mantelpiece of the sun rising over the moor, a pair of reading glasses folded neatly on the table beside the armchair. The only personal photograph in the room stood in a silver frame on the bookshelves. It showed a much younger Ronald and, presumably, his wife, standing either side of a young man in a graduate gown. The photograph had been taken outside Durham Cathedral. Jess had told Raven on the drive over that Ronald had been widowed many years earlier. He had one son who'd moved down south for work. He was a recognised and popular member of the community and kept himself fit by walking up Chimney Bank, just outside Rosedale Abbey, two or three times a week.

'It's the steepest road in England,' Jess had explained. 'Along with Hardknott Pass in Cumbria. Its maximum gradient is one in three.'

'I'll take your word for it.' The time when Raven had been capable of walking up ridiculously steep hills was long gone. He'd been fit and active in his army days, but now it seemed he was no match for a retired vicar. Raven much preferred the flat streets of London where he'd lived for much of his adult life. So why he'd decided to move back to Scarborough, with its famously hilly streets, was rather mystifying.

Ronald entered the room bearing a pot of tea and a plate of biscuits. He deposited it on the coffee table, clearing a pile of walking maps out of the way, and fetched some cups and saucers from a side dresser. 'I forgot to ask. Is tea all right for you?'

'Fine, thank you,' said Raven, regarding the teapot with suspicion. He knew that he would never be accepted as a true Yorkshireman until he started drinking tea, and yet he couldn't stand the stuff. He waited politely as Jess poured mahogany-coloured liquid into a cup, topped it up with milk and handed it to him with a knowing smirk.

'Perhaps a digestive to go with it?' suggested Ronald, offering him a biscuit.

Raven accepted it and settled back on the sofa.

'Any news about the investigation?' quizzed Ronald,

sitting down on the armchair and leaning forward eagerly. His gaze flitted to the collection of Hercule Poirots and Miss Marples that lined his reading shelves, then back to Raven. 'I'm sorry, how silly of me to ask you. I know you can't discuss police matters with a member of the public. Tell me, how can I help you?'

Raven gave him a reassuring smile. 'At this stage in the investigation we really don't know very much at all. We wanted to talk to you because we're interested in the location where the body was discovered. Jess thought you'd be a good person to fill us in on some background information.'

'Well,' said Ronald. 'I'll certainly tell you as much as I can. What is it you'd like to know exactly?'

'Perhaps we could begin with the walk you were doing. Jess tells me you're a member of the Lyke Wake Club. What exactly is that?'

Ronald leaned back in his armchair, a look of delight appearing on his face at being asked. He began to speak in an authoritative voice sharpened by years of delivering sermons from the pulpit, articulating his thoughts clearly and confidently. 'Back in 1955, a Yorkshireman called Bill Cowley conceived the idea of walking across the moors from Osmotherley in the west to Ravenscar in the east. Forty-two miles across rough terrain and not for the faint-hearted. The route traverses deep heather moorland and peat bogs and involves over 5,000 feet of climbing. The highest point on the walk is Botton Head at 1,489 feet. In bad weather it can be impossible to complete.' He tilted his head as if weighing up Raven's suitability for undertaking such an endeavour and finding him wanting.

An accurate assessment, by Raven's reckoning.

Ronald continued with his story. 'Bill thought it would be fun to set people the challenge of completing the crossing in twenty-four hours. So he got a group of friends together and they set off. That was the beginning of the Lyke Wake Club. Anyone who makes it from start to finish in the required time is eligible to become a member. Here, let me show you my badge.'

He sprang to his feet with an agility Raven envied and took a wooden box down from one of the shelves. He opened it and retrieved a small object that he passed to Raven. It was a black, enamel badge, about an inch in length, shaped like a coffin lid and engraved with a silver candle and two stars. It seemed a rather macabre prize for having walked forty miles across inhospitable terrain. Raven returned the badge to its owner and Ronald put it back in the box.

'Why a coffin?'

'The moors have long been associated with death,' said Ronald darkly. 'The Bronze Age people who lived in these parts thousands of years ago cremated their dead before burial and placed their ashes in urns. They believed that burning the dead prevented their ghosts from returning to haunt the living. Chiefs and leaders were often buried with grave goods for them to use in the afterlife. Lilla Howe is just one example of these burial mounds. There are round barrows or howes all across the moors – Simon Howe, Jugger Howe, Ana Cross, to name a few.' He ticked them off on his fingers as he named them. 'Some estimates suggest there could be thousands of barrows in north-east Yorkshire.'

'So the moorland is the burial ground of ancient people,' mused Raven.

'Indeed,' said Ronald, 'and several of the barrows serve as marker points for the Lyke Wake Walk. But the walk takes its name from slightly more recent history. In the Middle Ages, Yorkshire folk used to sing the Lyke Wake Dirge at funerals. The verses are written in an archaic form of Yorkshire dialect so they're a little tricky to understand, but the basic idea of the dirge is that after death everyone has to make a journey across a wide and difficult moor. It's a bit like Purgatory, I suppose. If you've been a good person – given away socks and shoes, money, food and so on – then you'll make a safe crossing and reach Paradise. Otherwise, you'll sink into the flames of Hell.' He gave a little chuckle. 'Or perhaps into a peat bog if it's been raining hard.'

'What do the words *lyke wake* mean?'

'That's a good question,' said Ronald, giving Raven an approving nod. '*Lyke* means "corpse" and is derived from the Saxon word *lych*. Perhaps you've heard the entrance to a graveyard being referred to as a "lychgate". As for *wake*, nowadays people often use it to refer to the get-together after a funeral when everyone eats sausage rolls and enjoys a drink in honour of the deceased. But traditionally the wake is when you keep watch or vigil over the body *before* the funeral.'

'And this club, how many members does it have?'

'Oh, I can't give you an exact number. It's quite informal, really. There's no membership fee and people are entitled to call themselves members if they complete a crossing following all the rules. Female members are awarded the title of "Witch" and male members are called "Dirgers." The club encourages members to come and join in the annual wakes, which are really just social gatherings with some committee business and other activities thrown in, including a singing of the Dirge. Various honorary titles are conferred, such as "Past Master" for a member capable of finding their way across any moor by day or night, drunk or sober, without map or compass. It's all good fun.'

'One thing has been puzzling me,' said Jess, interjecting for the first time. 'If Lilla Howe dates from the Bronze Age, why is there a Christian cross there?'

'Ah, yes,' said Ronald, 'that's another good question. The story is that the cross was placed there by King Edwin of Northumbria in honour of Lilla, one of his thanes. Legend has it that Lilla bravely sacrificed himself to save his king from an attempt on his life, and was buried at the spot, with the cross marking his resting place. The original cross was placed there in the seventh century, but the current cross is a replacement, dating back to the tenth century. It's the oldest Christian marker on the moors.'

'I see,' said Raven. The information Ronald was telling him was interesting enough, but it didn't seem to relate directly to the discovery of the body. He leaned forward, returning the cup of tea to the table, undrunk. 'What I'd really like to know is why someone would choose to burn a body at an ancient burial mound.'

Ronald nodded thoughtfully. 'Lilla Cross isn't an easy place to reach, either on foot or by vehicle. It's several miles' walk across deep heather from the closest parking spot near the bridge at Eller Beck. Ancient tracks traverse the moors, but they're not good roads for a car to use, as you are no doubt aware from personal experience.'

Raven nodded, recalling the bumpy Land Rover ride of the previous day. There was no way a normal car would be able to make the journey. He imagined trying to drive his own car, his beloved BMW coupé across such a rough road, and shuddered at the thought.

Ronald pressed his palms together in an unconscious echo of prayer. 'The moors are an ancient land, one of the largest uncultivated tracts in England, and filled with superstitions and legends. It's said that a lifetime is insufficient to know the whole area, and I can vouch for that. There are traces of Stone Age settlements, as well as the later Bronze Age tumuli. The round-barrow people lived on the high moors, and then a succession of Britons, Danes and Norwegians came and settled there. Each wave of settlers left their mark. On the land, on the language, and on the mythology. The challenge for modern researchers is sifting truth from myth.'

It was a challenge Raven could identify with. He nodded encouragingly, hoping the vicar would quickly come to a point.

'You know,' continued Ronald, 'the idea of burning the dead to prevent their ghosts from returning is an ancient and pervasive one, and some echo of this superstition lingered on in the dales even until modern times with the tradition of throwing charcoal along with a dash of salt into graves to keep the dead in place. Even now, a belief in ghosts persists. If you asked my former parishioners, I expect you'd find a good proportion who believe in some kind of ghostly activity.'

'So what are you saying?' Raven asked.

Ronald gave a tentative smile, yet his eyes remained solemn and serious. 'Could it be that the body was burned there to stop the ghost of the dead person from rising?'

CHAPTER 7

It was perfectly understandable to Becca that Raven would want to take Jess with him to Rosedale Abbey to speak to Ronald Fairchild. Jess was a friend of the walking group's leader and had been with him when the body was discovered. She was absolutely the right person to introduce Raven to Ronald, and her local knowledge would no doubt prove invaluable. Yet Becca couldn't help feeling put out by the way Raven had sidelined her.

She would much rather be having tea and biscuits with a retired vicar than attending a post-mortem. And the idea that she enjoyed some kind of special relationship with Dr Felicity Wainwright was nonsense.

Wasn't it?

It was true that the somewhat prickly senior pathologist demonstrated something of a soft spot for Becca. While some of Becca's colleagues complained vociferously about Felicity, finding her cold and abrasive – even malicious – Becca always received a warm welcome from her. But Becca had done nothing to cultivate her relationship with Dr Wainwright, other than being generally civil in return. Perhaps that was Raven's problem. He was incapable of remaining on good terms with anyone.

She donned a spare set of scrubs and joined Felicity in the chilly mortuary. The body was already laid out on the gurney beneath a green sheet.

'Good to see you, Becca,' said Felicity from behind her mask. 'I see that DCI Raven has very sensibly got into the habit of sending his best women along to these events. Last time it was Jess, and now it's you.'

Becca wasn't certain whether this was intended entirely as a compliment towards herself and Jess, or whether it was a veiled criticism of Raven for not attending the post-mortems himself.

'He's good at delegating,' said Becca, deciding to offer a defence of her boss. Although even as she said it, she doubted it was true. On their last big case, Raven had promised to let her take more responsibility, but that had never really materialised. He was, now she thought about it, in the habit of keeping his cards close to his chest and not sharing all the relevant facts even with his closest colleagues.

'Well, I'm glad you're here,' said Felicity, carefully laying out the tools of her trade on a metal tray. Scalpel, scissors, forceps, rib shears and bone saw. 'I hope you're not going to faint on me, like young Jess did last time.'

'I'm sure I won't.' Becca eyed the contours of the corpse stretched out on the trolley beneath its green cover. She hadn't fainted yet during a post-mortem, although she supposed there was a first time for everything.

Felicity seemed in no particular hurry to begin working on the body. She picked up a scalpel and tapped it against the side of the trolley, making the stainless steel sing. 'I hear your boss has got himself a dog.' She sounded incredulous and more than a touch mocking. Becca wondered how the pathologist had learned about Raven's recent acquisition of a four-legged companion. Felicity obviously had sources within police gossip circles. And, despite her intense dislike of Raven, she did seem to take a very close interest in his activities.

'Yes,' said Becca. 'A Black Labrador called Quincey. I think the dog is good for him.' She'd noticed that Raven appeared happier and more relaxed recently, as if canine company agreed with him.

Felicity scoffed. 'Does that man know how to look after a dog?'

'Quincey goes to a dog minder during working hours.'

'Well, that rather proves my point. Being a detective isn't a nine to five job, is it?'

'True.' Becca had wondered herself how Raven was going to combine dog care with the unpredictable hours of his profession. But so far, he and Quincey seemed to be doing just fine. 'Do you have a dog?' she ventured. She realised that she knew next to nothing about Felicity's personal life. Despite the older woman's curiosity – you might say nosiness – about everyone else's domestic arrangements, she wasn't one for sharing information about herself.

Felicity's brow furrowed in consternation. 'An animal? Certainly not.' She replaced the scalpel on the tray and picked up the saw. 'Anyway, enough of Raven and his pet,' she said, dismissing the detective and his dog with a wave of her hand, 'how are you?' Her voice had changed and she sounded suddenly as if she genuinely cared. 'How is that flat share working out?'

It was now three months since Becca had moved in with Ellie, and Becca's social life had never been so hectic. After her boyfriend, Sam, went to Australia, it had been time for her to move out of her parents' Bed & Breakfast and find her own feet. Sharing with Ellie, who was Sam's cousin, had seemed like the perfect solution. Becca wouldn't have been able to afford such a nice apartment with a sea view on her own. And she enjoyed Ellie's company enormously.

And yet.

'Ellie's really good fun,' she found herself saying, trying to make it sound convincing. 'I'm having a great time.'

Felicity raised her eyebrows. 'Really?' She had clearly caught a hint of uncertainty in Becca's voice.

'Well,' said Becca, 'Ellie's a lot more sociable than me. I'm finding it hard to keep up the pace.'

'Hmm.' Felicity swapped the bone saw for a pair of wicked-looking scissors. She snipped the air thoughtfully. 'You know what the solution is, don't you?'

'What?'

'Live alone, like I do. It's the only way to find true happiness. Only when one is alone, can one be oneself. What did Schopenhauer say? "Great men are like eagles, and build their nest on some lofty solitude." Great women too, I'd say.' She dropped the scissors onto the tray with a clatter and whisked the sheet away from the body. 'So. Shall we make a start?'

The pathologist set to work, her interest in Becca's living arrangements seemingly over. She spoke into a microphone, recording her findings as she worked. Cool. Clinical. Precise.

Becca did her best to pay attention while avoiding lingering over the gruesome panorama before her. The corpse was blackened, the flesh charred and burnt away from the bones. Its arms and hands lay twisted, and all recognisable features had been obliterated by the heat. Only rags and scraps of clothing remained. Even now, in the sterile, air-conditioned space of the mortuary, the acrid smell of burning lingered on. The one saving grace was that the body was so badly burned, it was barely human anymore.

As Felicity sliced and diced, Becca took her mind off the horrible scene by thinking over the pathologist's advice. Could a solitary life really be the answer to her problems? She didn't think so. She would never be able to afford such a nice apartment on her own. She enjoyed Ellie's company, and missed her parents. Sometimes she still missed Sam. For so long she had believed that by now, in her late twenties, she'd have been married and sharing a house with him. Making a home together, maybe even starting a family. She didn't like to have regrets, but it was hard not to think about what might have been.

'Here we go,' said Felicity cheerfully, breaking into Becca's thoughts like a saw cutting through bone. 'Look at this.'

Becca leaned forward cautiously, shifting her gaze to where Felicity's gloved finger was pointing.

'The cause of death was blunt force trauma to the temporal bone of the skull. This poor chap received a nasty bash to the side of his head from a heavy object.'

'You're certain it's a man?' said Becca. All she could see was blackened bones.

Felicity sounded affronted. 'When have I ever been wrong?'

'Never,' said Becca quickly, not wanting to rouse the pathologist's temper. 'So you think he was dead before the body was burned?'

'Yes. The blow would have resulted in massive internal haemorrhaging.'

'Can you say anything about the time of death?'

'That's a tricky one,' admitted Felicity. 'Normally I would use body temperature to give you an estimate. However, after a body has been exposed to fire, temperature measurements are unreliable because of the extreme heat generated by the fire.'

'Yes, of course,' said Becca. She had known that a positive answer to her question was probably too much to hope for.

'However, I think we might be able to get something from his feet.'

'His feet?' echoed Becca, not sure if she was being teased.

'Certainly.' Felicity moved to the far end of the body. 'His feet escaped the worst of the flames, thanks in part to sturdy boots.' She indicated the strong leather boots that had largely survived the ravages of the fire. They were blackened, perhaps from smoke, but still intact. 'Let's remove them and take a look, shall we?'

Becca waited as Felicity made incisions into the thick leather with her scalpel, peeling the boots away to reveal skin beneath. The feet were in remarkably good shape. Felicity inserted a thermometer into the flesh and took a reading. 'This is far from ideal, you understand? We really want a core temperature, not one from the periphery, so I won't be able to give you an accurate time.'

'Anything you can tell us will be useful,' said Becca.

Felicity noted the temperature reading and consulted some charts. 'Like I say, the uncertainty is wider than usual, but I'm fairly confident that the time of death was no later than midday on Monday. It may have been earlier, but the fire makes it impossible to be sure.'

Becca was impressed. But Felicity's answer left her confused. 'That's hours before the body was burned. That means the victim must have been killed somewhere else and taken to Lilla Cross to be burned.'

'Well,' said Felicity, 'I have to leave some parts of the puzzle for you detectives to work out.'

'You've been really helpful,' said Becca. 'Now we just have the challenge of identifying him.' In cases like this, dental records could sometimes be the key to obtaining a positive ID, although the fact that some flesh had been preserved intact meant that DNA might also be used. But both methods could only confirm a provisional identification already made by other means. There would be a lot of police legwork to do, and Tony's missing persons records would probably be their best starting point.

'Perhaps this will help you,' said Felicity, bending over the blackened remains of the body. She used her scalpel to scrape away a layer of charred flesh that clung to the victim's lower leg, revealing a piece of metal about three inches in length, screwed into the bone. 'This bone plate has been inserted to repair a fracture. With any luck, there will be a serial number on it.' She carefully cleaned the metal surface, exposing a series of engraved numbers and letters. 'There you go. I'll get a photo taken and send it to you.'

'That's amazing,' Becca said, pleased to have

something tangible to take back to her boss. 'Raven will be pleased.'

'He ought to be.' Felicity fixed Becca with her penetrating stare. 'And remember what I said to you. Solitude is the key to contentment.'

'I'll think about it,' promised Becca.

CHAPTER 8

After being forced to abandon Quincey the previous day, Raven was determined to get to Vicky's on time to collect his dog that evening. With any luck he'd bump into Melanie and be able to thank her for having Quincey to stay overnight. As he pulled up outside the house on Barmoor Lane, he recognised Melanie's car – a red Volkswagen Golf – and knew she was inside. He walked briskly up the drive, hoping that Quincey would have forgiven him and be pleased to see him.

He wouldn't have blamed the dog for deciding that Raven was a lost cause and he'd much rather go home with Melanie instead. Raven's ex-wife, Lisa, had come to much the same conclusion a couple of years back, and had found another man to go home with.

But he needn't have worried. As soon as he entered the building, Quincey bounded over to him, barking in delight, his tail wagging furiously. It seemed that dogs were more forgiving than wives.

Melanie was holding Lulu in her arms and chatting to Vicky. When she saw Raven, she came over.

'Thank you so much for keeping Quincey last night,'

said Raven. 'I hope he was no trouble.'

Melanie smiled. 'It was a pleasure. He's a lovely dog.'

'I owe you one,' said Raven, preparing to leave.

But before he could go, Melanie stepped closer and stretched out a hand to stop him. 'I hope you don't think this is too forthright,' she said, 'but perhaps you'd like to take me out for a meal? If you're serious about saying thank you.'

Raven stopped in his tracks, taken aback by her suggestion. 'Well, sure, I'd love to take you out.' He could hardly refuse after all she'd done for him. 'We'll definitely do that sometime soon.'

'How about tomorrow night?'

'Tomorrow?'

'There's a pub not far from here that serves the nicest food. Dogs are welcome too.' Her smile widened, lips parted in anticipation.

Quincey barked, as if in full agreement with Melanie's proposal. He looked from her to Raven.

Raven couldn't say no. And why would he want to? Melanie was a lovely person. Kind, attractive and warm, despite being ever so slightly desperate. Besides, the thought crossed his mind that he might need her help looking after Quincey in the future. Cynical, you might call it. Or practical. Raven much preferred the latter.

'All right,' he said. 'It's a deal.'

'No,' said Melanie, her fingers brushing his collar. 'It's a date.'

★

Despite a positive outcome, the post-mortem had left Becca feeling disturbed. Hardly surprising after spending so long staring at the burned remains of a corpse, struggling not to think too hard about the fact that this was once a living person with friends, relatives, perhaps a wife and children. She didn't know how Felicity could stand to spend all her time cutting open and dissecting dead bodies.

Then again, Felicity Wainwright wasn't like anyone else Becca knew. Despite her chatty manner and her apparent interest in Becca's personal life, Felicity always left Becca with a vague feeling of unease, as if the pathologist was getting all her questions out of an instruction manual about how to make friends, or was secretly cataloguing her answers for some sinister purpose. She tried to imagine Felicity at home alone, contented in her solitude, and shuddered.

However exhausting it might be to share a flat with Ellie, Becca knew with certainty that she didn't want to spend the rest of her life alone.

'Hiya,' called Ellie's cheerful voice from the kitchen. 'How was your day?'

Becca slipped off her jacket and walked through to the open-plan kitchen diner, glad to find that Ellie was home. It would have been hard to return to an empty flat after an afternoon in the mortuary. 'Good, thanks. How was yours?'

One of the difficulties of being a police officer was that she could never discuss an ongoing case with friends and family, although that never stopped her mum from fishing for information. And she could hardly tell Ellie about her gruesome session in the company of Felicity. The best thing was to change the subject and get Ellie to do the talking instead.

Her flatmate didn't need any encouragement. 'I've had a great day,' said Ellie. 'I've been to visit one of our suppliers on a local farm. It's going to be a really good year for barley, and they're hoping for a record crop. We're thinking of launching a new range of beers to celebrate the occasion.' Ellie was the managing director of a brewery, and her favourite topic was beer, and alcoholic drinks in general. Whenever she spoke about the business, Becca had to try to forget how close she had come to marrying into the family business and becoming an Earnshaw herself.

But Sam was gone and she had to put all of that behind

her.

Ellie fished a bottle of white wine from the fridge and unscrewed the lid. 'Want some?'

'Not for me, thanks.'

Becca enjoyed a glass of wine as much as the next person but tried to avoid drinking every night of the week. It would be so easy in Ellie's company to slip into an unhealthy pattern.

Ellie opened the cupboard and pulled out two glasses. 'Are you sure? You look like you could use some.'

Becca shrugged. 'Oh, go on then.' If she couldn't allow herself a glass of wine after an afternoon spent watching a particularly grim post-mortem, then when could she?

Ellie filled two large glasses and didn't bother to screw the lid back on the bottle. Becca knew from experience that it would be in the recycling bin by the end of the evening.

Well, it was a bit late to worry about that now. Horses and stables and all that. She accepted the drink and took a sip. 'Cheers!'

'Cheers!' Ellie drifted over to the sofa and sat down, looking out across the North Bay. The apartment enjoyed amazing views of the beach and the sea beyond. Today was the summer solstice, the longest day of the year, and the blue sea sparkled invitingly beneath the light of the late evening sun.

Becca went to sit next to her and kicked off her shoes.

'I hope you're not busy on Friday night,' said Ellie.

'Why? What's happening?' Becca had nothing planned, but things could change quickly when she was working on a murder investigation. Overtime was pretty much to be expected.

'I have arranged,' said Ellie, taking a sip of her wine, 'for us to go out to dinner with a couple of friends.'

'Oh, who?'

Ellie seemed to know half the people in Scarborough. Becca had thought her mum knew everyone, but Ellie's social network was even more extensive.

'You'll like them,' said Ellie, avoiding answering

Becca's question.

Becca frowned, her detective brain coming back onto duty. 'Hold on, are these guys?'

'Might be,' said Ellie teasingly. 'Could be fun to meet them.'

'Hang on a minute, are you trying to fix me up with a date? Don't tell me this is a double date or something.'

'I'm not telling you anything, but this could be just what you need,' said Ellie, reaching out and touching Becca's arm. 'After everything that happened with Sam, well… when did you last go out with a guy?'

Becca said nothing. They both knew she'd seen no one since Sam had gone to Australia.

'Exactly,' said Ellie.

'I don't know,' said Becca. 'I've just started working on a new murder investigation. I'm almost certainly going to have to work late.'

'Stop trying to wriggle out of it,' said Ellie with a smile.

'I'm not.'

'Yes, you are! You're so transparent, Becca Shawcross.'

Becca sighed. 'Look, I'm just not ready for a relationship yet.'

It was six months since Sam had disappeared from her life. After the years they'd spent together and the year she'd spent sitting by the side of his hospital bed willing him to wake up from a coma, six months felt more like six weeks.

'Whoa, who said anything about a relationship?' said Ellie. 'This is a dinner date. It doesn't have to lead to marriage and two-point-five kids. If you don't like the guy, you won't have to see him ever again. Promise. And you won't be on your own. I'll be there with… with *my* date. So if you two have got nothing to say to each other, you can just listen to us.'

Put that way, Becca had to admit it didn't sound like such a big deal. Plus, she didn't really have the energy to argue with Ellie. Sometimes it was easier just to go with the flow. 'All right,' she said. 'I'll come along.'

'Super,' said Ellie, retrieving her phone from her back

pocket. 'I'll let the guys know.'

As Ellie typed out a message, Becca wondered what she'd just let herself be talked into. She'd received a lot of unsolicited advice from people today about how to live her life. Be a hermit, Felicity had told her. And now Ellie was fixing her up with a romantic dinner with some guy she'd never met. She didn't even know his name. Becca really needed to decide what she wanted for herself.

But right now, she was too tired to care.

*

Jess's plans for the week had taken a battering. She had failed to complete the walk she'd spent so long preparing for, and instead had been plunged straight into a murder inquiry. But at least that was helping to take her mind off the fact that her ankle joints were killing her. And as for her poor feet...

Even though they hadn't reached the end of the Lyke Wake Walk, fourteen hours of trekking through knee-deep heather, trudging across peat bogs and climbing rocky trails had left her whole body sore and aching. It was a relief at the end of the day to put her feet up, and she wished she could take a hot bath. But the house she shared with three other tenants on Prospect Road, a long, straight street of Victorian terraces, didn't have a bath, only a shower.

It didn't have a sea view like Becca's snazzy apartment either, but Jess didn't mind. Having grown up inland, she wasn't as attached to the water as her colleague. Instead, she missed the views from the high ground above Rosedale Abbey across miles of open moorland. Right now, though, the idea of climbing up that high ground held little appeal, and all she longed for was to sit back on her bed and binge-watch Netflix on her laptop.

She had just started the next episode of her favourite crime drama when her phone buzzed with an incoming call. She checked the screen. Caller unknown.

With a sigh she paused the show and took the call. 'Hello?'

'Jess?' She vaguely recognised the voice. 'It's me, Matthew. From the walk.'

'Oh, Matthew!' She hadn't expected to hear from him. How had he got hold of her number? From Ronald? 'Uh, how are you?'

'My legs are aching all over. And my arms too. The bits in between aren't feeling so good either.'

She laughed. 'Tell me about it.'

'But I was really phoning to see how you are, you know, after finding the body and all that.' Matthew spoke in a hushed, reverential tone, as if fearing she might be about to break down. It occurred to her that maybe this was the first dead body he had seen. For Jess, who had investigated several murders since becoming a police detective and had witnessed more than one post-mortem, dead bodies were, sadly, quite routine. She should be the one concerned about his wellbeing, not the other way around.

'That's kind of you to think of me,' said Jess. 'But I'm perfectly all right. In fact, I'm part of the team investigating the death.'

'Seriously? That's like, wow.' Matthew's voice perked up and he sounded keen to talk. 'Do you know who did it yet? Or whose body it was?'

Jess immediately regretted mentioning it. 'We've barely got started. I can't really talk to you about it. Sorry.'

'No, of course not. I shouldn't have asked.'

'No worries,' said Jess, unable to stop herself from yawning. 'Sorry. I'm exhausted.'

'I should let you go,' said Matthew. 'I'm tired too. That was such a hard walk. It's a pity we weren't able to complete it.'

'Maybe some other time.'

'Yeah,' he said eagerly. 'Definitely.'

'Well, thanks for calling,' she said.

'No problem. Bye now.'

Jess slipped the phone back onto her bedside locker,

but she was too tired now to watch the rest of the episode. The on-screen detectives were always pumped with energy and ready for the next challenge, whether that was chasing after a suspect or examining a crime scene for the vital clue that everyone else had missed, but Jess could hardly keep her eyes open. Outside it was still daylight, but she closed her laptop and got ready for bed.

CHAPTER 9

*T*he army convoy rumbles into Goražde, south-east Bosnia, close to the Serbian border. *The town, or what remains of it, lies on the River Drina, a broad expanse of water that meanders slowly through the valley. Densely wooded hills surround the town on all sides, creating a picturesque backdrop, and providing the perfect hiding places for the Bosnian Serb forces who have shelled this idyllic spot since May 1992.*

No building has escaped the rockets and artillery fire. Blackened, bombed-out blocks of flats that used to be people's homes teeter like monuments to the dead. Rubble, shrapnel and spent bullets litter the streets. The town's one and only hospital, where operations are now carried out without anaesthetic, has not been spared, and shows structural damage from a recent bombardment by Serb tanks. And no family has escaped the touch of war.

Thousands killed or wounded. Over five hundred of them children.

Women, children and old men cower in basements, short of food, fear in their eyes. The influx of refugees from neighbouring towns in the region has exacerbated the food shortage. The majority Muslim population no longer trusts the local Bosnian Serbs, their friends and neighbours, who they have lived and worked alongside for years. Bosnian Serb families are suspected of collaboration with the Bosnian Serb forces besieging the town. The human cost is incalculable.

This is Lance Corporal Thomas Raven's first experience of war and its effect on civilian populations. It bruises his heart to see underfed, dirty children roaming the streets. He guesses their mothers are dead. He knows how that feels.

The UN has established a so-called "safe zone" around the town. But it doesn't feel very safe to Raven. Sporadic shelling continues to bombard the town and its inhabitants. Snipers are active in the nearby hillsides. And just the previous day, one of their own company lost a leg to an anti-personnel mine.

'It's all so bloody senseless,' says Private Sean Collins one evening as their unit is patrolling the streets on foot. 'Why can't they just live together and get on with their lives? I don't get it.'

'Well…' Raven doesn't fully understand the situation either but he suspects it's more complex than Collins would like to believe. Ethnic tensions run deep. Identity and allegiance are matters of life and death. Goražde is proof of that.

Since coming to Bosnia, Raven has learned a lot of new vocabulary. Safe haven. Enclave. Ethnic cleansing. Equipped with his new phrases, he struggles to articulate what's happening and why. 'I suppose the thing you've got to understand is–'

But Raven's attempt to explain the ins and outs of the Bosnian conflict never comes to fruition.

A shot from a sniper rifle goes off like a firecracker.

Raven whips around, his weapon at the ready.

He took Quincey to the North Bay early, hoping that a bracing walk along the beach would shake off the unsettling flashback of his second Bosnian dream in as many nights.

This time it had been the once beautiful town of Goražde. Memories of its ruined buildings and traumatised people would never leave him. And nor should they. But he could only function in the present if those memories stayed buried far beneath the surface. Raven couldn't afford to let the past intrude into his new life here in Scarborough. And definitely not when he was in the middle of a murder inquiry. If he wasn't firing on all cylinders, the investigation would sink.

Sean Collins had made his unwelcome appearance less than a week ago, drunk and clearly deranged. As Raven paced the sands, Quincey trotting beside him, he kept a wary eye out for his old army pal. But Collins was nowhere to be seen. Perhaps he had left Scarborough and moved on in search of pastures new.

I've been looking for you everywhere. I need your help.

Raven shrugged off Sean's insistent voice. What had he meant?

But Raven knew the answer. The man had meant nothing. His plea for help had been the ravings of a madman. If Collins had really needed his help, he would have returned to ask for it again. Wouldn't he?

After half an hour of pacing the sand, Raven decided it was time to drop Quincey at the dog minder's. The early-morning walk had cleared his head and blown away the memories of war for the time being. But the only real antidote Raven knew for dealing with trauma was work.

After he'd returned from Bosnia, the army psychiatrists had wanted him to open up to them and talk about his experiences. Talk about his thoughts. Talk about his feelings. But Raven hadn't wanted to talk. He had wanted to forget.

He called to the dog and they headed back to Royal Albert Drive where Raven had parked his BMW. An M6 sports coupé wasn't an obvious choice for transporting a large dog, but Quincey hopped obediently into the back of the car and settled down on the rear seats, his head on his paws, his eyes glued to Raven as he manoeuvred himself carefully into the driving position. At least the dog didn't complain about lack of rear passenger space the way Lisa had done.

As Raven buckled up and pulled out onto the road, he

mused once again how having a dog was so much easier than having a wife.

⋆

'Sir, we have a name for the victim.'

'That was quick work, Tony. Well done.' It seemed that while Raven had been trying to shake off his unwanted recollections of his army days, DC Tony Bairstow had been diligently getting on with the job of identifying the burnt body from Lilla Howe. This was the kind of focus and discipline that Raven admired. Becca and Jess looked equally impressed.

'Fortunately for us,' said Tony, 'the victim had been fitted with a metal plate due to a fractured fibula. The plate has a manufacturer and serial number. By contacting the manufacturer I was able to obtain details of the hospital where he was treated. It was the military hospital at Catterick Garrison, two and a half years ago. They were able to provide the name of the patient and the date of the operation.'

'Don't keep us in suspense,' said Becca. 'Who is he?'

'Sorry, I was just getting to that. His name is Dean Gibson. He is, or was, a constable with the Military of Defence Police, based at RAF Fylingdales. Thirty-five years old.'

Raven allowed himself to breathe a sigh of relief. For a moment, he'd been certain the name on Tony's lips would turn out to be Sean Collins, his old army mate. But whatever had happened to Sean, whether he had taken Raven's advice and gone to stay at the homeless shelter or had moved on, he was still alive.

Tony continued to read from his notes. 'The victim lived in Goathland, on Beck Hole Road. There's a wife, a Mrs Laura Gibson, who teaches at the primary school there.'

'Did she report her husband as missing?' Raven asked.

'No, I double-checked that,' said Tony.

'Curious.'

'Actually,' said Becca, 'I have some news related to that. According to Felicity, the time of death was no later than midday on the day the victim went missing.'

'Is she certain about that?' queried Raven. 'According to Ronald Fairchild's walker friends, the body couldn't have been burned any earlier than Monday night.'

'Felicity conceded that it was difficult to be accurate, but she was adamant that midday was the latest possible time.'

'So the body must have been transported to Lilla Cross after the murder.'

The door to the incident room opened and Detective Superintendent Gillian Ellis barged into the room. Gillian was a large woman, heavyset, with a solid chest, and arms that would flatten a wrestler. She lumbered to the front of the room, making Jess draw back and Tony rise to his feet as if about to salute his commanding officer. She came to a halt a short distance away from Raven, about a foot or so closer than he would have liked.

'Well?' she demanded. 'What do we have so far?'

Raven wasn't sure whether he disliked his commanding officer's impromptu interruptions to his team meetings more or less than being summoned to her office to provide feedback or to receive rebukes. It wasn't as if she provided much assistance. She simply liked to poke her substantial nose in. Didn't she trust him?

His boss at the Met had tended to hide himself away in his office, emerging only to chair meetings or when someone needed a good bollocking. That hands-off style had been more to Raven's taste. Gillian's unannounced interventions smacked of micro-management, which tended to bring out his natural defensive instincts. It wasn't a good combination.

Thanks to Tony, however, he was able to ward her off this time with a positive progress report. 'The victim was MOD Police, ma'am. Constable Dean Gibson. He worked at RAF Fylingdales.'

'MOD police,' muttered Gillian, her eyes narrowing. 'That complicates matters. Don't tread on anyone's toes, Tom. I don't want the Ministry of Defence banging on my door.'

'No, ma'am. Me neither.' Raven hadn't been planning on treading on anyone's toes. Or at least, no more than usual.

'Handle it carefully, Tom. Go through the appropriate channels.'

Raven gritted his teeth. He was a senior police officer with more than twenty-five years in the force. He hardly needed Gillian to tell him how to do his job. 'Of course, ma'am.'

'On the other hand,' she said, 'a military connection should be just up your street.'

Raven didn't like to be reminded of his military past, especially in the presence of his police colleagues. He preferred his life to be neatly compartmentalised. Military in one box, civilian in another. A clear line between past and present, professional and personal. Mixing it up always led to complications. He merely nodded in response.

Gillian seemed to have heard enough for now. 'Well, I won't keep you from your work. But be sure to keep me informed at all times.'

'Of course, ma'am.'

He watched as the detective superintendent marched out as quickly as she'd appeared.

'Okay then, let's get cracking,' he said, once she had gone and closed the door behind her. 'Jess, Tony, could I ask you to find out everything you can about the victim? Bank statements, phone records, all the usual stuff.'

'We're on it,' said Tony.

'And Becca, you and I will drive over to Goathland.'

'Being careful to go through all the appropriate channels?'

'Naturally.' He gave her a wink. 'You know me.'

CHAPTER 10

There was no easy way to get from Scarborough to Goathland. Despite being just fifteen miles as the crow flew, the distance was twenty-five along the road that circled the edge of the moors. First, Raven's satnav took him north along the Whitby road to a place called Sleights.

'Do you think they feel slighted here?' he quipped, to be met by a half-hearted shrug of indifference from Becca. There was something on her mind perhaps, or else his pun was a particularly weak effort.

The road turned south again and began to rise steeply and remorselessly as it left the village, taking them up Blue Bank. Up and up it went, then up again. The car settled into a low gear, whining its way relentlessly up to higher ground. Soon they were driving across some of the most desolate landscape Raven had ever seen. There were no hedgerows or dry stone walls to line the roadside, and the high, featureless moors stretched out for miles to either side. Sheep roamed freely amid the heather and wandered into the road whenever they felt like it, forcing Raven to slow to a crawl.

'Bit bleak up here,' he remarked.

'It'll be nice when the heather is in flower,' said Becca. 'It all turns purple then. If you want to see it, you can take a ride on a steam train from Pickering to Whitby right across the moors.'

Raven grunted a non-committal reply. Never mind the steam age, this place was so untouched by man, you could imagine yourself back in the time of the round-barrow people that Ronald had referred to.

'I wouldn't want to live up here in winter though,' continued Becca. 'It gets cut off in heavy snowfall. You'd need a reliable vehicle out here.'

'Just as well we've got the BMW then,' said Raven, giving the steering wheel a gentle pat. Not that the M6 would be much use in these parts during the winter. Rear-wheel drive and wide sports tyres were a good combination for track racing, not so much for driving in snow. He gently pressed the accelerator and the engine purred in response.

After a while, the road descended steeply down Cow Wath Bank and crossed a railway bridge before arriving in the village of Goathland, which, just like the surrounding moor, was flat and open and seemed to have more sheep wandering around than people.

They soon located the primary school, a small stone building with a couple of dozen children running around the playground. It reminded Raven of his own school in Friargate, just a four-minute walk from Quay Street. He'd left at the age of eleven to attend the big comprehensive school and had fallen under the wing of Darren Jubb and his retinue of rogues and undesirables. It had all been downhill from there.

Hannah, under Lisa's insistence, had lived a more sheltered life, attending a posh private day school. It hadn't been the most expensive independent school in London, but it had stretched them financially and provided Raven with a convenient excuse for working long hours of overtime. Looking back, he wished they'd sent her to the local state school and he'd spent more time with her instead.

Looking back was a fine way to view the world.

The headmistress at Goathland, a motherly woman in her forties who introduced herself as Mrs Buckfast, met them at reception. If she was hoping to find prospective parents looking for a small village school for their offspring, Raven soon disabused her of that idea. 'We're here to see Mrs Laura Gibson,' he explained, showing his warrant card and adding that it was a personal matter to ward off any nosiness on the part of the headmistress.

She frowned with apprehension but asked no questions. 'Of course. If you'll come with me, I'll go and fetch her.' She led them to a room marked *Head's Office* and indicated a small sofa and comfy chair set around a low table. 'Please, do take a seat. I won't be long.'

The room was half a working office, with desk, computer and pupil record files lining one wall, and half a child-friendly space where pupils would not be intimidated. Bright artwork adorned the walls and various soft toys were arranged on the sofa. A wooden abacus sat on the table. Raven reached out, unable to resist playing with the rainbow-coloured beads.

'That will help you with your numbers,' remarked Becca. 'If you're good, you can go out and play later.'

The door opened suddenly and Raven jerked his hand away from the toy as if he'd been caught handling something he was forbidden to touch. It was like being at his old school again, always finding his way into trouble. The last time he'd sat in a headteacher's office, he had surely been there for detention.

'You wanted to see me?' The woman who stood hesitantly in the doorway was in her mid-thirties with shoulder-length light brown hair tied back in a ponytail. She was dressed in dark trousers and a loose-fitting daisy-print shirt with the sleeves rolled up.

'Mrs Laura Gibson?'

'Yes.' She looked enquiringly from Raven to Becca.

'Please, would you come and sit down?'

She closed the door and perched on the edge of the comfy chair, her hands clasped in her lap. Her forehead creased in a puzzled frown. 'Mrs Buckfast said it was a personal matter?'

'Mrs Gibson,' began Raven. 'I'm afraid we have some bad news regarding your husband.'

'Dean? Why? What's happened?'

This was the worst part of Raven's job. Breaking the news of a death to a family member. No matter how many times he did it, it never got easier. If it ever did, perhaps that would be the time to quit, knowing he no longer had the capacity to feel another's pain.

When he hesitated, Becca leaned forward and spoke in her most sympathetic voice. 'We're very sorry to have to tell you that his body was discovered on Fylingdales Moor, on top of Lilla Howe, on Tuesday afternoon.'

'What?' Laura Gibson's face registered disbelief. 'But that's not possible. Dean's away this week on a training course.'

'Is that why you didn't report him missing?'

Laura's hands remained resolutely clasped together, her knuckles white. 'But he's not missing. He's...' Her voice petered out and she looked from Becca to Raven, as if willing him to contradict what Becca had just told her. She was in a state of denial, a common enough reaction to shocking and unexpected news.

'I'm afraid his body is badly burnt,' Raven said, 'but the post-mortem revealed a metal bone plate in his left leg. We traced it to an operation performed at Catterick Garrison military hospital in 2018. The patient was Dean Gibson, a constable with the MOD police based at RAF Fylingdales.'

'Oh my God.' Laura's hand flew to her mouth and her eyes welled with tears.

'I really am very sorry,' he concluded feebly, knowing that no words were adequate to convey his feelings.

Laura Gibson dissolved into convulsive tears and Raven sat grim-faced as Becca reached into her bag for her ever-ready supply of tissues and began passing them across. No matter how hard it was to convey tragic news, he knew it was necessary to do it in person whenever possible. How else to make the human connection with a victim and their family and truly appreciate the magnitude of their suffering?

With a stab of guilt he recalled the relief he'd felt at learning the dead man wasn't Sean Collins, but some stranger. That the murder was nothing to do with him. That it wasn't his fault.

When Becca was done handing out tissues and Laura's crying had subsided to a sniffle, he asked, 'When was the last time you saw your husband?'

Laura gave her nose a blow and dabbed at her eyes. 'He left early on Monday morning. I saw him drive off myself.'

'At what time?'

'Before seven. I think it was about a quarter to seven. He had to leave early to get to his training course.'

'What course was this?'

'Public Order Management. It was basically a refresher in crowd control techniques.'

'And where was it being held?'

'Somewhere down south. Dean did tell me, but I can't think clearly right now. I've got it written down at home.'

'Did you have any communication with him after you saw him leave?' Raven asked.

Laura shook her head sadly. 'I tried calling him on Monday evening and again on Tuesday, but I assumed he was busy. He was due back this evening.' Her eyes shone once again with tears.

'What car was he driving?' asked Becca.

'We have an old Ford Kuga.' She gave them the numberplate. 'It's my car too. But I don't need it to get to work. Dean and I live here in the village.'

She didn't appear to notice she was talking about her husband as if he were still alive. Raven knew it would take time for her to fully accept the fact that he had gone. Under normal circumstances, a visit to the mortuary to make a formal identification of the body could help to cement the reality of a loved one's passing. In this case, the only proof the dead man was Dean Gibson was the metal plate recovered from his leg. That would certainly be sufficient to satisfy the coroner. Raven hoped it would be enough for Laura.

'Did your husband mention anything that might have been concerning him during the last few days or weeks?' he asked.

'No.'

'Any financial problems?'

Laura shook her head. 'We're not rolling in money, but we get by just fine. We don't have children, and we both work full-time, so we have enough.'

'Can you think of any reason somebody may have wanted to harm him?'

'None whatsoever.'

There was a tap at the door and the headmistress poked her head in. 'Sorry to disturb. I was just going to offer tea or coffee.' She stood in the doorway, taking in the emotional state of the teacher. 'Laura, dear, whatever is the matter?' She glanced accusingly at Raven as if this was all his fault.

'Mrs Gibson has just received some distressing news,' said Raven. Sometimes he hated being a police officer. Whenever he came to call, the news was always distressing. Then again, he could hardly picture himself in a more cheerful occupation. Customer service, perhaps, or a motivational speaker, always with a winning smile and some ready words of encouragement. No, that would never work. It was better for him to stay in the outcast corner and be forever the bearer of bad news, the person no one wanted to meet. He had the face for it.

The headmistress rushed to put her arm around the younger woman who collapsed onto her shoulder and began to sob once more.

Raven knew when he had outstayed his welcome. He rose to his feet. 'We'll send a Family Liaison Officer around to take care of you, Mrs Gibson. Becca, can you arrange for PC Sharon Jarvis to attend?' Sharon was the best in the business as far as Raven was concerned, and he knew his business inside out. 'We'll see ourselves out.'

CHAPTER 11

'**R**ight,' said Raven when they were back in the car. 'Next stop, RAF Fylingdales.'

'Do you think we ought to have contacted them in advance?' asked Becca. 'I imagine you can't just turn up at a place like that and expect to be let inside, can you?'

The voice of Detective Superintendent Gillian Ellis rang in Raven's head. *Handle it carefully, Tom. Go through the appropriate channels.* Well, it was a bit late for that now.

'They can't turn us away. We're the police,' he told Becca with slightly more confidence than he felt. 'Anyway, it's just down the road so I'm not driving all the way back to Scarborough to make an appointment before showing up.'

'Fine by me,' said Becca, who clearly understood the perks of not being the senior officer in charge of the operation.

It was a ten-minute drive over the moors to RAF Fylingdales, and for the last half of that journey, the concrete pyramid of the radar dominated the skyline. The military base where Constable Dean Gibson had worked may have been top secret in nature, but there was no hiding its location from the public. In this wild and empty landscape, there was nothing to be seen for miles around apart from the huge structure towering above the flat moor.

Becca checked her phone. 'No reception. It was the same at Lilla Cross. There's no signal for miles around the radar station.'

'Then let's hope we don't have to call for backup,' said Raven.

The base was set back from the main road and surrounded by a wire fence. Scarcely four feet high, the fence didn't seem like much of a deterrent – certainly the sheep on the other side had paid scant attention to the signs declaring it to be a *Prohibited Place: No Unauthorised Access* – but Raven knew this was only the outer perimeter marker. Gaining access to the radar station itself would involve breaching multiple defensive barriers.

He paused briefly at another sign informing him that this was a *Prohibited place within the meaning of the Official Secrets Act* before driving slowly up to the checkpoint. There, a metal barrier blocked the access road, and a small brick hut stood off to one side.

Two burly MOD police officers emerged from the hut and approached the car. In their arms they cradled Heckler & Koch MP7 submachine guns, and Raven knew that beneath their dark waterproof jackets they would be wearing full body armour. The MP7 was a more modern weapon than the rifle Raven had used in Bosnia. Compact and lightweight, it was capable of firing armour-piercing high-velocity steel rounds.

He wound down the driver's side window, warrant card at the ready, and waited for the first officer to arrive. Then, putting on his best army voice, he said, 'DCI Tom Raven, Scarborough CID. And this is Detective Sergeant Becca Shawcross. We're investigating the murder of a person connected with this facility and we need to speak to the station commander.' He had no intention of being turned away.

His words must have had the desired effect because the MOD officer directed Raven to move the M6 into a parking area, then asked them to step out of the car while the second officer carried out a thorough search of the vehicle, even scanning its underside for bombs. Raven and Becca were escorted inside the hut where they submitted to a body scan by a third officer using a handheld metal detector.

A sign on the wall informed them that the current threat level to the United Kingdom from terrorism was *Substantial,* which Raven knew meant an attack was considered likely. The threat was a lot more serious than *Low* or *Moderate* but wasn't as high as *Severe* or *Critical.* When he'd been in Goražde, threat to life had been an everyday reality.

When the search was done, the officer in charge regarded Raven with a stern face. 'You say you want to speak to the station commander, sir?'

'That's right.'

A shrug of the shoulders conveyed the man's assessment of Raven's chance of success. 'I'll see what I can do.'

Yet despite the apparent unreasonableness of Raven's request, after a great deal of toing and froing and making calls to those higher up the food chain, the officer in charge informed him that a military escort would come to meet them.

'Thank you,' said Raven. 'We appreciate it.'

Ten minutes later a military-spec Land Rover Wolf pulled up on the other side of the checkpoint and a man in blue RAF uniform jumped out. He strode briskly over to meet them.

'Flight Lieutenant Mark Jones.' The new arrival was early forties, with a fresh, boyish face and thick wavy blond hair. His cobalt blue eyes sparkled, keen to impress. He grasped Raven's hand and shook it with a strong grip, then did the same with Becca. 'I'll be your escort at all times on the base. Security is our top priority.'

'Of course,' said Raven.

The flight lieutenant's accent wasn't local like that of the MOD police at the checkpoint, but instead had the refined cut of the home counties. *Dead posh*, a Yorkshireman might call it.

'Right then,' said Jones. 'Hop in and I'll drive you to where you need to be.' It seemed the BMW was to remain outside the checkpoint. Raven reluctantly handed over his car keys and climbed into the front of the Land Rover while Becca got into the back.

Jones swung the vehicle around in a tight arc with the confidence of a driver who likes to show off and they headed into the heart of the site. 'I suppose you know what we do here?'

'You watch out for a nuclear attack,' said Raven.

'In essence, yes. Back in the days of the Cold War, we formed part of the Ballistic Missile Early Warning System. Our job was to keep an eye out for an incoming Soviet intercontinental ballistic missile strike. The system was upgraded in 2001 to a solid state phased array radar. That's the kit we have over there.' He pointed proudly to the gigantic pyramid that loomed ever closer. 'Each face of the radar consists of thousands of individual aerials that can change beam direction almost instantaneously. That gives the radar 360-degree visibility and allows it to track objects with a range of 3,000 nautical miles, including space surveillance. The system consumes as much power as the town of Whitby, so we have our own power station here on the base.'

'Impressive,' said Raven. It seemed to be what was expected.

The flight lieutenant smiled in acknowledgement. 'We're part of a network of five stations, three in the US, one in Greenland, and one here in good old Blighty. We work closely together with our American allies to provide a round-the-clock ballistic missile warning service. We also track foreign spy satellites and give the all-clear when it's safe for the UK to carry out secret activities.'

'Such as?' asked Becca.

'Ah, you won't catch me out that easily,' said Jones good-naturedly. 'But believe me, if it's up there, we know about it.' He chuckled. 'Nothing gets past us. Our motto is *Vigilamus*. That's Latin for *We Are Watching*.'

Raven knew nothing about Latin but he detected in Jones the self-confidence that came from a private school education. It was the same confidence he saw in his own wife and daughter. He got the impression that the flight lieutenant was giving them the prepared spiel he gave to all visitors. His speech was fluent, his delivery polished.

Jones stopped his vehicle at a second checkpoint. The fence here was taller and fixed to concrete posts. There was a more formal reception area than at the outer perimeter.

'I'm afraid I'll have to ask you to hand over your mobile phones,' said Jones. 'You've probably noticed there's no phone signal out here anyway.'

'No problem,' said Raven, handing over his phone to the MOD police officer at the gate.

Once past this second hurdle, Jones drove them into the main part of the base. Here the road divided, one branch heading for the radar itself, which was surrounded by yet another fence and checkpoint. Jones headed straight on and stopped in front of a long rectangular building. 'This is HQ,' he said. 'Come on. I'll introduce you to the station commander.'

*

Wing Commander Fitzwilliam-Brown – early fifties, salt-and-pepper hair, imposing stature – had clearly been apprised of Raven and Becca's imminent arrival well in advance of their reaching the meeting room where he greeted them.

'DCI Raven and DS Shawcross.' He shook both of their hands in turn. 'Please, take a seat.'

The station commander spoke with the voice of

authority in a clipped, upper-class accent that made even Flight Lieutenant Jones sound common. In the presence of his superior, the voluble flight lieutenant had become noticeably more subdued.

The meeting room was nondescript. Functional rather than comfortable. Raven and Becca sat on one side of a highly polished wooden table, Jones and Fitzwilliam-Brown on the other, a row of windows looking out across the flat moor. Sunlight filtered through the blinds, reflecting off the surface of the table.

'I understand you're investigating the death of a member of RAF Fylingdales personnel,' said Fitzwilliam-Brown, getting straight to the point of their visit. He was clearly not a man to waste time.

'Yes,' said Raven. 'The body of PC Dean Gibson was discovered on Tuesday afternoon by a group of walkers doing the Lyke Wake Walk crossing. Gibson worked for the MOD Police here. His body was burnt beyond recognition but we were able to identify him from a metal bone plate in his leg. We've already informed his wife.'

The station commander listened intently to what Raven was telling him, nodding his head to show he understood the gravity of the situation. 'You're treating this as a murder inquiry?'

'That's right,' confirmed Raven. 'The cause of death was blunt force trauma to the skull, and the body was deliberately taken to Lilla Cross and burned there, presumably to destroy evidence.'

That was the rational explanation, at any rate, although Raven couldn't quite dismiss the notion that Ronald Fairchild had suggested – that the body had been burned to prevent the victim's ghost from returning.

'Do you have any suspects for the killing?'

'Not as yet,' admitted Raven. 'It's still early days.'

The station commander thought for a moment. 'Fylingdales is an RAF base, but our security is in the hands of the Ministry of Defence. We have a total of twenty MOD Guard Service personnel stationed here, and something like a hundred MOD Police. They're the chaps you met at the checkpoints.'

Raven nodded, recalling the Heckler & Koch submachine guns which were clearly not just for show.

'Dean Gibson was a member of that team,' continued Fitzwilliam-Brown. 'I expect Flight Lieutenant Jones has already explained what we do here.'

'Yes,' said Raven.

'So I don't need to tell you that anything that affects the operational capabilities of this station is a matter of national security. We are on the frontline of our nation's defences. Without this radar system we would be at the mercy of hostile foreign powers. So when you tell me that an MOD police officer based at this site has been found dead in suspicious circumstances, I take that very seriously indeed.'

'Good,' said Raven. 'I'm pleased to hear it.' The military top brass were, in his experience, generally keen to do the right thing, and Fitzwilliam-Brown was clearly no exception.

'I will grant you and your colleague' – he nodded towards Becca – 'the access you need to carry out your duties, but due to the sensitive nature of our work I will require you to be accompanied at all times. Flight Lieutenant Jones will escort you while on site and will be your first port of call for any enquiries you have once you have left.'

'Understood,' said Raven.

Jones handed Raven a card with his telephone number on it. A landline, Raven noted.

'You'll want to speak to the sergeant in charge of the MOD personnel on site,' continued Fitzwilliam-Brown. 'Flight Lieutenant Jones will take you to see him now.'

The wing commander rose to his feet, indicating that the meeting was at an end. Jones, Raven and Becca stood too.

'You will receive full cooperation from the military side,' concluded Fitzwilliam-Brown, 'and in return I expect you to keep me fully informed via Flight Lieutenant Jones. Just remember that this is going to be a two-way process and I'm sure we'll get along fine.'

He smiled for the first time in the meeting and reached across once again to shake Raven's hand.

CHAPTER 12

Social media could be depressing at the best of times.
Finding out that your old school friends lived more
exciting lives than you did. Or claimed to, at least.
Watching videos of influencers telling you about the latest
must-have lifestyles and mustn't-miss trends. Getting
sucked into toxic arguments that were bound to end badly.
Jess always tried to limit her exposure to online channels.
But in the modern world it was impossible to avoid them
altogether.

But looking at a murder victim's social media footprint
was different. Here, you could maintain a sense of
detachment. Dean Gibson's friends weren't her friends.
Dean's life wasn't hers.

The problem was, Dean didn't have many online
friends. Nor did he display any interest in comparing his
life with others. From the evidence Jess had amassed so far,
he didn't seem to have much to say about anything.

The only online photos of him had been placed there
by his wife, and they didn't reveal a lot. The couple
enjoyed annual beach holidays in sunspots like the Greek
islands, the Turkish Riviera and Sharm El Sheikh. Back

home in Yorkshire, they sometimes went for walks across the moor or visited local beauty spots like Whitby and York. Dean's hobbies, if you could call them that, consisted of drinking beer, listening to rock music and eating steak and chips.

There was nothing to indicate why he might have ended up with his head caved in and his body set alight on a burial mound in the middle of a moor.

Jess printed off a photo showing a well-tanned Dean posing in front of the sea at Crete, a picture of health and vigour, with no obvious trace of the injury that had required a bone plate to be inserted into his leg. She pinned it to the whiteboard and went to see how Tony was faring.

'Any luck?'

Tony looked up from his desk. The older constable seemed to be in his element in front of a computer. Whereas Jess would have preferred to be out and about – perhaps accompanying Raven to Goathland – Tony clearly relished his desk duties, sifting through archives and databases, searching for facts and leads in the world of paper records and digital files. It was important work, and Tony was the best. Jess knew she could learn a lot from him.

'I ran a routine check to see if Dean Gibson had any criminal convictions, but as you'd expect for a serving MOD police officer, he was perfectly clean. Then I submitted a request for disclosure of his bank records. I'm still waiting for a response.'

'Okay,' said Jess. Bureaucratic hurdles always made her eyes glaze over, and she wondered, not for the first time, if she was really cut out to be a police detective. If only there could be more action, and less sitting about. Her mind drifted to those TV detectives she had watched, always dashing from one compelling lead to another.

Tony was only just building up to the main event, however. 'So then I started working with the mobile phone companies to see if he had an account with them. I managed to identify his phone network, and they sent me a list of calls and texts from the last three months. Look at this.' There was a tangible edge of excitement to Tony's voice now. A quavering lilt that hinted at something big.

Jess peered over his shoulder at the printed list. He had highlighted every occurrence of one particular number with a fluorescent marker.

'Notice anything about that number?' he asked.

Jess studied the string of digits, trying to work out what had aroused his interest. It was an international number, with a country code of "1". 'It's American, isn't it? Why was Dean calling a US number so often?'

'Good question,' said Tony. 'I think this is worth looking into.'

*

Sergeant Gary Murphy of the MOD Police was a fifty-something giant with the build of a heavyweight boxer and a buzz cut that reminded Raven of his army days. He regarded Flight Lieutenant Mark Jones with a sneer of ill-disguised contempt, then turned his attention to Raven. 'Who's this, then?' His accent was pure Geordie.

The flight lieutenant responded with evident irritation at Murphy's offhand manner. 'DCI Raven and DS Shawcross are here to investigate a suspicious death. A murder, in fact. The wing commander has asked me to accompany them while they are on site.'

'So you're a babysitter, eh?' Murphy leaned back in his chair and gave Jones a mocking grin before addressing Raven directly. 'Well, DCI Raven, you'd better tell me what you need from me. But I'll warn you, I'm a busy man.' He indicated the desk in front of him, which was empty apart from a computer screen and keyboard. There was scant evidence of any work being done.

'Then I'll try not to waste your time,' said Raven. He had already taken a strong dislike to the MOD police sergeant. Whereas Fitzwilliam-Brown had commanded respect, and the flight lieutenant was going out of his way to be helpful, antagonistic vibes were coming off Murphy in waves. 'We're investigating the murder of one of your colleagues, Constable Dean Gibson. He was found dead on Tuesday afternoon.'

The effect on the police sergeant was instant and dramatic. 'Bloody hell,' he said, sitting bolt upright in his chair. 'How did it happen?'

The news seemed to have knocked Murphy for six. But Raven still didn't trust him. 'When did you last see PC Gibson?' he asked, choosing to play his cards close to his chest.

'Hang on a minute.' Murphy consulted his computer. 'Dean worked the late shift on Saturday night. I didn't see him then, but he would have knocked off around midnight.'

'Tell me about the training course he was due to attend this week.'

Murphy's forehead wrinkled in confusion. 'Training course? What course would that be?'

Raven returned his gaze with equal puzzlement. 'Dean Gibson told his wife he was going on a Public Order Management course this week. He left his house first thing on Monday morning and was due back today.'

'First I've heard of it,' said the sergeant. 'Dean booked this week off as annual leave. He may have told his wife he was going on a course, but there was no such course.'

'So where did he go?' asked the flight lieutenant.

Murphy jerked his head in the direction of Raven and Becca. 'These two are supposed to be the detectives. I think that's for them to work out.'

Raven shook his head. The MOD police officer had some enormous chip on his shoulder, that was for sure. 'Perhaps you could let me have a printout of all the leave Dean took during the past year? Plus any training courses he actually did attend. If it's not too much trouble for you.'

'Hey,' said Murphy. 'Dean was a good bloke. I want to find out what happened to him as much as you do.'

'Well, then perhaps you could start by showing a bit

more professionalism,' said Raven.

'Yeah, all right.' Murphy clicked a few keys, and a printer in the corner of the room sprang into life. Becca retrieved a sheet of paper.

'How long had PC Gibson worked here?' asked Raven.

'About five years,' said Murphy.

'And what job did he do, specifically?'

'Manning the checkpoints, patrolling the perimeter. Taking care of these fine people.' He nodded to Jones, once again unable to disguise his hostility.

'A few years ago,' said Becca, 'he was treated at the military hospital at Catterick Garrison for a fractured bone. How did he receive that injury?'

'Playing squash. Nothing to do with his job.' Murphy shrugged. 'These things happen.'

'Did he have any issues at work?'

'Such as?' Murphy was back on his guard.

'Anything,' said Raven. 'Money? Alcohol? Had he fallen out with any of his colleagues? Did he have any special friends at work?'

Murphy looked uncomfortable, as if debating with himself whether to say anything.

'I'm sure I don't need to remind you that this is an active police investigation,' said Raven. 'Obstructing a police officer is–'

'Yeah, yeah, I get that,' Murphy interrupted. 'I'm police too, remember. But I'm also responsible for security at a site on the frontline of defence for the Western world, as I'm sure the flight lieutenant here will be quick to remind you.' He rapped his fingers against his desk before seeming to come to a decision. 'One thing I can tell you, which may or may not be relevant, is that Dean reported an incident a short while ago.'

'When?'

'A couple of weeks. I'd have to check the date.'

'What sort of incident?'

'He was patrolling the inner perimeter fence when he experienced an altercation with an intruder.'

'An altercation?' queried Raven.

'A non-physical confrontation,' said Murphy.

'Could you be a bit more specific? Did he file a report?'

'Of course he filed a report.'

'Can I see it?' Dragging information out of Sergeant Murphy made Raven think of blood and stones.

'It's classified.'

'I need to see that report.'

Murphy's fingers drummed against the desktop again. 'I can't give it to you here and now. I'll need to go through the appropriate channels.'

Raven knew this was the best he was going to get for now. 'You do that then,' he told Murphy. 'You can send it to me at Scarborough. But please make it your highest priority.'

*

By the time the financial records Jess had requested came through, she had lost count of how many mugs of tea she had consumed. Good police work needed lots of tea. And biscuits too. Everyone knew that.

She printed the documents and showed them to Tony who selected the bank statements for himself. 'I'll do these while you work through the credit card statements,' he told her. 'Do you know what to look for?'

Jess nodded. 'Any large or unusual purchases, balance transfers or anything that seems unusual or out of character, especially in the days preceding the murder.'

'Good,' said Tony. 'The credit card statements ought to be straightforward. If there's anything illicit going on, it's more likely to show up in the bank statements. That's where we'd expect to find any large cash withdrawals, payments or receipts from other accounts, and so on. But you never know – you might find something in the card transactions.'

Jess took the wad of papers back to her desk and started to work through them. The credit card was a personal one issued to Dean. Presumably his wife had a card in her own name. Jess decided to start at the beginning and tackle the statements chronologically in order to build up a picture of what was "normal". Taking a leaf out of Tony's notebook, she armed herself with a set of coloured highlighters and began to mark the entries according to type.

The work was dull and monotonous, and she needed a fresh brew and a top-up of biscuits at the halfway point to keep going. Dean's spending habits were as boring and predictable as his social media presence. Weekly trips to the supermarket, petrol from the garage, regular takeaways on weeknights and visits to nearby pubs at the weekend. He was a man of simple tastes and reliable habits. So far, Jess had only used four colours of highlighter.

And then she spotted something new. She marked it in red and took it to show Tony.

'This is interesting,' she said. 'He booked a hotel in Scarborough for three nights this week. Monday, Tuesday and Wednesday.'

'Why would he want to stay at a hotel in Scarborough?' asked Tony. 'It's not so far from his home.'

'I know the hotel,' said Jess. 'It's a smart place on the Esplanade. Boutique. Pricey. Well beyond what he normally spent on himself.'

'I'll give the boss a call.' Tony dialled and waited, then shook his head. 'Not available.'

'If he's still out on the moors,' said Jess, 'he won't have a signal. But he'd want us to use our initiative, wouldn't he? I'll go round to the hotel now. See what they can tell me.'

She felt a sudden rush at the prospect of escaping outside into the fresh air. It was surely her reward for finding the lead. She grabbed her jacket and headed for the door before Tony could disagree.

★

'I'm sorry about Sergeant Murphy's behaviour,'

apologised Flight Lieutenant Jones. 'He doesn't really hit it off with the RAF personnel here. Now, is there anything else I can help you with?'

'Yes, as a matter of fact.' Raven wasn't ready to leave RAF Fylingdales just yet. After all the rigmarole of getting inside, he wanted to get as much done as possible before being banished beyond the perimeter fence. 'I'd like to take a look in the victim's locker.'

'I'm sure that can be arranged,' said Jones. 'I'll see if I can obtain a master key from human resources.'

Raven was rather enjoying having the flight lieutenant at his beck and call. The man was always keen to assist and was proving useful. Raven knew he would be reporting everything back to the station commander, but he didn't mind that.

It didn't take Jones long to secure a master key from the head of HR. He led Raven and Becca to the MOD locker room. 'Is it all right if I open it?' he asked.

'Go ahead,' said Raven as Becca snapped on a pair of forensic gloves. 'Just leave it to us to look inside.'

The locker contained clean uniform, a pair of sports shoes, a motoring magazine, and a small white paper gift bag. Becca fished it out and held it up for Raven to see. The paper was of fine quality and the bag exuded an air of luxury. At least, as far as any paper bag could. It was emblazoned with the words *Bergdorf Goodman, established 1901*. It looked decidedly out of place in this otherwise functional locker.

'Bergdorf Goodman,' gasped Jones in surprise.

'You're familiar with the name?' asked Raven.

'It's an upmarket department store in New York. My wife bought a pair of shoes there when we visited last year. They weren't cheap, I can tell you.'

'Very nice,' said Raven, who did most of his clothes shopping at Marks and Spencer on Newborough. 'What's inside?'

Becca withdrew a small gift box and opened the lid. Nestled in a bed of red silk sat a pair of jewel-encrusted black and gold cufflinks in the shape of skulls. They wouldn't have been Raven's first choice of cufflink – what was wrong with plain chrome? – but even he recognised a luxury fashion statement when it was that in-your-face.

'A gift, presumably,' said Becca. 'One he wanted to keep hidden from his wife?'

'Most likely,' said Raven. He turned to Jones. 'We'll take these as evidence.'

'Of course. Is there anything else I can help you with?'

'No, I think we're done for today, thanks.'

'Right you are, then. I'll drive you back to the checkpoint.'

For the first time in his life, Raven could see the attraction of having a personal assistant.

*

Jess trotted up the steps of the hotel on the Esplanade and presented her warrant card to the receptionist on the desk. Just as she'd told Tony, the hotel was small but luxurious. The décor was minimalist and stylish in muted greys with mahogany accents. A vase of cream orchids adorned the highly polished counter. It didn't look like the kind of place where a bloke who listened to Britpop bands and whose favourite meal was steak and kidney pie would choose to stay. Especially when he lived not many miles away.

On discovering why Jess was there, the man at the reception desk lowered his voice so that other guests wouldn't overhear their conversation. A visit from the police clearly wouldn't do the hotel's reputation any good. 'Mr Dean Gibson, you say,' he murmured, checking the reservation system.

'He had a booking for Monday through Wednesday,' explained Jess, 'paid for in advance.'

'Just one moment,' said the receptionist in a hush-hush voice. He tapped at his keyboard and frowned. 'Mr Gibson booked a double room for the three nights you mentioned. But he didn't check in.'

'Did he call or email to cancel?'

'No, he simply didn't show up. We kept the room available for him, obviously, as it had been fully paid-for. But it was never occupied.'

Jess sighed in frustration. She had hoped that by using her initiative she might learn something that would explain why Dean Gibson had booked this room. But if he had never even been here…

'There was a second guest listed for the room,' said the receptionist.

'A second guest?'

'A Ms Nicole Anderson.'

Jess noted down the name. 'Do you have any contact details for Ms Anderson?'

'I'm sorry, no.'

'Well, thank you for your help,' said Jess, pleased to have extracted some useful information at last.

'You're welcome,' said the receptionist, looking relieved she was leaving.

On the steps outside, Jess called Tony.

'Found anything?' he asked her.

'Yes,' said Jess. 'Dean booked a room with a woman as the second guest. And it wasn't his wife.'

CHAPTER 13

The savoury smell of roasted chicken was making Becca's mouth water. After a long and tiring day in Goathland and at RAF Fylingdales with nothing more for lunch than a chilled sandwich and a packet of crisps, it was comforting to be sitting at the wooden kitchen table in the guest house while her mum, Sue, put the finishing touches to the evening meal and her dad, David, opened a bottle of Sauvignon Blanc. This was where Becca had grown up and it would always be home for her. She even found herself wishing that her brother, Liam, could be there too, to complete the family.

'Who wants a leg?' asked Sue, as she carved the perfectly browned bird. 'Becca? You look as if you need feeding up.'

'Go on then,' said Becca, who had certainly lost weight now that she wasn't eating her mum's full English breakfasts every morning. She had dropped a dress size, which was good, but she knew Sue worried about what she was eating. She'd be horrified if she knew the truth about how many takeaways Becca and Ellie consumed. And how much alcohol.

As if Sue had read her mind, she asked, 'How are you getting on with Ellie?' She put a plump chicken leg on a plate and passed it to Becca. 'Help yourself to vegetables.'

'Good,' said Becca, spooning broccoli, carrots and buttered new potatoes onto her plate. It was real, home cooking, which meant she could eat as much of it as she fancied. There were no calories in vegetables, were there? Or only good ones. She added a Yorkshire pudding and poured thick gravy on top, drowning the meal in brown liquid.

'I expect you're having a lot of fun,' said Sue. 'Two single girls living in a flat together. Do you go out with friends much?'

Becca sighed. Sue was entirely transparent in her desire to see Becca fixed up with a boyfriend at the earliest possible opportunity. She'd been devastated when Becca and Sam had split up.

She forked a morsel of chicken and popped it into her mouth. It was melt-in-the-mouth perfect. How did her mum manage that? When Becca had tried to cook chicken, it had ended up with the consistency of rubber. 'If you must know, Ellie's fixed me up with a date for tomorrow night. It's a double date with her and some new guy she's met.'

'Well, that sounds fun, doesn't it, David?' said Sue, passing a plate with the other chicken leg to her husband. She carved a few slices of breast meat for herself. 'It's time you met someone new.'

'I don't know,' said Becca. 'It all seems a bit soon.' She looked to her father for support.

'You take your time, Becca love,' he said, pouring her a generous glass of wine. 'If you're not ready, you're not ready.'

Becca gave him a grateful smile. She could always rely on her father to take a more measured approach. And to take her side.

'Taking your time is all well and good,' said Sue, 'as long as you don't leave it too long.'

'Mum, I'm only twenty-seven,' said Becca. 'Anyway, I've agreed to go, but I'm not expecting much.'

'Well, you never know,' said Sue, hopeful as always.

Becca was keen to change the subject. 'Have you seen much of Liam recently?' She hadn't seen her brother for a while and was surprised to discover that she might actually be missing him.

'Well, yes,' said Sue. 'He popped in for breakfast only this morning. He's busy renovating a Victorian house at the moment, turning it into holiday lets. He's had to wait ages for that builder, Barry, to get started on the work. Apparently he was tied up for months doing a job for your boss. How are you getting on with him, by the way?'

'Who, Raven?' Becca never knew quite what to say when her mother probed her about her boss. That he was grumpy, moody and uncommunicative, not to mention terrifying whenever he got behind the wheel of his car? Sue didn't need to know any of that. 'He seems happier since he got his dog,' said Becca. 'More relaxed.'

'Still living on his own?'

'Apart from Quincey.'

'Mmm,' said Sue. 'A man needs more than a dog for companionship. You know, by the time I was your age I'd already met your father and he'd proposed to me.' She beamed at David who smiled back wistfully.

Becca grimaced. 'Yes, I know that, Mum.'

'Well,' said Sue, 'just something to think about, Becca, dear. Let's hope that date of yours goes well tomorrow night, eh?'

*

Raven and Quincey arrived at the pub shortly after seven thirty. It was a traditional sort of place with dark wooden beams overhead, wood panelling on the walls, brass fixtures around the open fireplace, and a large selection of ales at the bar. As a teetotaller, Raven was indifferent to the range of beers on tap, but he appreciated the fact that the pub wasn't too fancy and welcomed dogs.

He looked around and saw Melanie waving to him from a corner bench by the window. Lulu, her King Charles Spaniel, was sitting next to her. The dog yapped in response to Quincey's appearance.

Raven crossed the room to join them, Quincey pulling him forward. The Labrador was large for his breed and quite capable of dragging his owner around on the end of his lead, making Raven wonder whether man or dog was in charge. But the fact that Quincey was so obviously keen to greet Melanie and Lulu boded well.

Melanie rose to greet them, brushing Raven's right cheek with hers before reaching down to pat Quincey. Her perfume was strong and floral, and Raven thought he detected a hint of rose. She smelled different to Lisa, whose perfumes, in their elaborate packaging, had claimed all manner of rare and exotic ingredients.

She had obviously made a big effort with her appearance. Instead of her usual work attire, she was wearing a summer dress, and her hair was down and softly waved. Her face was more made-up than usual too. Raven was conscious that he had made zero effort over his appearance and had simply rushed straight from work. But at least that meant he was wearing a suit.

He sat down, gently nudging Quincey under the table so he wouldn't get in the way of anyone walking past. 'I hope I'm not late.'

Melanie shook her head, making her long hair glimmer as it swayed. She had chosen a table next to the window, and the evening sun shone bright against her bare arms. 'Not at all. Lulu and I arrived just before you.' She passed him a menu. 'But we've already chosen food, haven't we, Lulu?'

The menu consisted of hearty pub grub, and Raven decided on bangers and mash. It wasn't exactly midsummer fare, but daily dog walking was giving him more of an appetite than usual.

'I thought I'd have the fish and chips,' said Melanie.

'I'll go and order,' said Raven, noting their table number. 'What would you like to drink?'

'Do you want to share a bottle of white?'

'I'll stick with water,' said Raven. 'But I'll fetch you a glass.'

He placed their food order and returned to the table with a glass of wine for Melanie and a sparkling mineral water for himself. In Raven's brief absence, Quincey had placed his head on Melanie's lap and was gazing up at her as she stroked him. The dog's loyalty was easily won.

'Cheers,' said Melanie, tapping his glass with hers. 'How was your day?'

Raven's mind ran back over his working day, beginning with the team meeting and Tony's identification of the murdered man, the visit to notify the victim's widow at the school in Goathland and the subsequent encounters at RAF Fylingdales with the flight lieutenant, the wing commander and the MOD police sergeant, culminating with the discovery of the cufflinks hidden in the locker. A busy day for sure, and one that had brought him significantly forward in the investigation. But he couldn't go into any of that with Melanie.

'Just a routine day for an overworked police detective.' He took a sip of his drink, seeking to close off discussion of his work. 'You're a nurse, aren't you?'

If Melanie minded his clumsy switching of the subject of conversation, she gave no indication of it. 'Occupational therapist, actually. I work mainly with people recovering from accidents. Teaching them to walk again, that sort of thing.' She smiled at him and faint laughter lines crinkled around her eyes and mouth. She was really very pretty and quite a few years younger than him, something he hadn't appreciated before, always being in such a hurry to drop off and pick up Quincey at Vicky's.

'I had some occupational therapy once,' he said, then wondered why he had said it. He didn't usually reveal so much about himself, certainly not to someone he barely knew. And never on a first date. If this even was a date. He dismissed the notion as soon as it came to mind. This was simply a way of thanking her for looking after Quincey the other night.

Melanie gave him an encouraging smile. 'What was your therapy for, if you don't mind me asking?'

'Oh, just a leg injury. Nothing serious.' He had deflected the truth so many times now, it no longer felt like a lie. It was just a story he told people to stop them asking questions about his past. He certainly wasn't going to start talking about his time in Bosnia this evening. His nighttime visits there were already too much. Not to mention the encounter with Sean Collins on the beach that had brought it all so starkly back and had triggered the nightmares.

Melanie gave him a querying look, but much to Raven's relief, a member of the kitchen staff arrived with their food. Quincey's interest switched immediately from Melanie to the plate of sausages. His black head popped up from beneath the table, his long tongue drooling.

'You've already had dinner,' Raven told him. 'You're a greedy guzzler.' But the dog was shameless and didn't care. Raven slipped him a portion of sausage and pushed him back under the table.

Melanie took a doggy treat from her bag and gave it to Lulu. 'So what do you do when you're not working?'

'When I'm not working?' The question was a tricky one. When was Raven ever not working? Even when out walking with Quincey, his mind returned inevitably to whatever investigation he was currently involved with. He didn't have time to read books or go to the cinema or even to watch TV, and he didn't think Melanie would share his musical taste for goth rock. It suddenly occurred to him, was he boring? 'Quincey takes up a lot of my time.'

'Of course,' said Melanie. 'It's the same for me with Lulu. She keeps me company now that I'm divorced.' She gave him a shy smile. 'It's been three years,' she volunteered, in answer to a question Raven hadn't asked. 'I see you're not wearing a wedding ring, Tom. Sorry, I hope you don't think I'm being nosy, only–'

'No, not at all,' Raven reassured her. It was a fair question. 'There was a Mrs Raven once.'

Melanie laid a sympathetic hand on his arm. 'You don't have to tell me about it if you don't want to.'

He hadn't planned to say anything, but he found himself talking nonetheless. There was something about Melanie that made it easy for him to open up. 'Lisa and I married young and grew apart. Or, to be more accurate, the demands of my career drove us apart.' Lisa's career had been demanding too, of course, and the strain of bringing up a child with two working parents had stretched the marriage further. In the end, it had been Lisa's choice to leave him for another man. But the story was much simpler if he heaped all the blame on himself. 'We got divorced at the beginning of this year.'

'I'm sorry,' said Melanie.

'Don't be.' The truth was, he had never really loved Lisa. His first, and perhaps his only true love, had been Donna Craven, the girl he'd known at school. But he'd walked out on Donna when he left Scarborough at the age of sixteen, so he was the villain of that story too. Perhaps that was how he liked his stories.

'The best thing to come out of the marriage was my daughter, Hannah. She's in her final year at Exeter, studying Law.'

'Clever girl,' said Melanie. 'You must be very proud of her.'

'I am,' said Raven. 'She's planning to come to stay with me in Scarborough when she finishes at uni.'

'Good for her,' said Melanie. 'And good for you. I'm glad that's worked out well. You have to make the most of life and take the opportunities that come your way. I mean, it's not as if we're getting any younger, is it?'

She reached across the table and took him by the hand.

*

Jess had just settled down to finish watching the episode

she'd started the day before when her phone rang. It was Matthew. Again.

'Hello,' she said warily, hoping he wasn't going to ask more questions about the police investigation. She wondered why she hadn't simply let the call go to voicemail.

'Hi. How are you?' Matthew sounded as keen as ever.

'My legs have just about stopped aching. How about you?'

His words gushed out as if he couldn't say them quick enough. 'Good. Listen, I've been thinking about you ever since we did the walk and we found that body. That was such a weird experience.'

'It was,' agreed Jess. Even as a police detective, she wasn't in the habit of stumbling upon dead bodies. Usually it was members of the public who found them and called them in. This time, she was a member of the public. It did feel weird.

'I was wondering if we could meet up?' said Matthew. 'You know, to hang out together, talk over what happened.'

'To hang out?' Jess considered the suggestion. Maybe Matthew was keener on her than she'd realised. Or perhaps he just needed to talk to someone about what had happened, to process his feelings. 'What did you have in mind?'

'I could come over to Scarborough to see you anytime. Tomorrow, maybe.'

'Er, well I'm working all day tomorrow.'

'Oh, yeah, of course. What about after work?'

'I'm not sure.'

If Matthew needed to speak to someone about his experience of discovering a body he would be far better off meeting a professional. Jess could put him in touch with someone suitable. But perhaps that wasn't what he wanted.

She had an idea. 'I tell you what, why don't you come over to Rosedale Abbey on Saturday? It's our family's traditional midsummer barbecue. Dad doing the cooking, you know the sort of thing. Sausages and burgers. Ronald will be there. In fact, I wouldn't be surprised if Janice was coming with him. She could give you a lift.'

Matthew sounded pleased with the suggestion. 'Sounds awesome. It would be really good to catch up with everyone from the walk.'

'Okay, then,' said Jess. 'I'll see you there.'

'Cool, catch you later.'

Jess ended the call, glad to have found a way to keep Matthew happy without encouraging him too strongly. Now all she needed was some time to watch that TV show without being interrupted.

CHAPTER 14

*T*he shot from the sniper rifle goes off like a firecracker.

Raven whips around, his weapon at the ready.

The three privates under his command also ready their weapons. As a lance corporal, Raven has been put in charge of a sub-team of four: Private Sean Collins and two others by the names of Smith and Ayres.

'What was that?' says Collins.

'It came from over there,' says Smith, pointing down a side street.

More shots are heard in the distance. They're coming from a wooded area overlooking the town. The UN has pushed the Bosnian Serb army out of the Safe Area and back to the surrounding hillside, but enemy incursions are still a regular event.

Then more shots ring out, at closer range.

The handful of civilians in the town square scatter, running for cover. In seconds, the place is like a ghost town.

The team led by Raven's commanding officer, Corporal Havers, runs up the deserted street.

'We're under attack,' shouts Havers. 'Close range fire. Raven, take your men and cover the area south of here. We'll *cover the front of the hospital.'*

Raven obeys without another thought. This is what he's been trained to do. His men follow him, taking up positions behind the burned-out wreck of a T34 tank.

And then he sees the enemy. A rag-tag bunch of Bosnian Serbs, seven in total. They've entered the town using the sniper fire as cover and are looking for trouble. As soon as they spot Raven's unit, they open fire at the British soldiers. Bullets fly past Raven's head, striking sparks from the armour of the tank.

'Return fire!' orders Raven and his men do as they are told. A firefight erupts at close quarters with automatic weapons.

Two of the attackers are killed within seconds. It's impossible to know if they were hit by one of Raven's bullets or shot by one of his men.

He expects the enemy soldiers to withdraw now that two of their number are down, but the remaining five leave their fallen comrades and continue advancing up the street.

Corporal Havers and his men reappear and engage the enemy in a blaze of gunfire, downing two more in quick succession. But the open square makes them vulnerable to attack from all sides. A shot from the sniper on the hillside catches Havers from behind. The corporal crumples and falls to the ground.

Shit! Now Raven's the commanding officer. Think!

Heavy small arms fire opens up as the surviving Bosnian Serbs continue to advance. One of Havers's men is hit and falls to the ground. Beside him, Collins roars in pain as a shot hits his shoulder. He drops his rifle, his arm useless. They have to get out of here.

'Move him!' Raven shouts to Smith and Ayres.

'But, sir–' begins Smith.

'Just do it!'

As they escort the wounded Collins from the field of battle, Raven turns his attention to the three remaining invaders. He advances towards them, opening fire with his rifle, providing cover for his men to get to safety. The leader of the Bosnian Serb group tumbles to the ground. The others flee, but not before one of them fires a parting shot.

The bullet strikes Raven in the right thigh and he stumbles forward, screaming in agony.

He crawled from his bed, memories of that pain as fresh and raw as the instant he'd been shot. A savage jolt, followed by a growing pain as the blood left his leg. He had passed out after the firefight, awakening to find himself being loaded onto a stretcher ready for emergency evacuation. His army career ended in an instant. By year end, he'd been discharged from a military hospital and had signed up with the Met, reinventing himself as a police officer, nothing more than a limp and a medal to remind him of his time with the "Dukes".

The flashbacks had continued for some while after leaving the army. But he'd dealt with them in his own way, by refusing to talk about them. That tactic had worked well enough until Sean Collins had reappeared in his life, raving about conspiracies and treason before vanishing again without a trace.

Bloody hell.

Raven's whole body was bathed in sweat. He stripped the sheets from the bed, showered, dressed, and took a somewhat surprised Quincey down to the North Bay for an early morning session before dropping him off at Vicky's.

'You're early,' said Vicky. 'First one in this morning.'

'Lots to do,' said Raven.

He was quite relieved not to bump into Melanie and Lulu. He'd driven her home from the pub the previous night, politely declining her invitation to go inside for a coffee, giving the excuse that he needed to be up early for work the next day. But as he'd driven home, he'd asked himself why he was so afraid of committing to a relationship. It was obvious that Melanie's invitation to go into her house meant more than a late-night coffee. She was offering herself to him. And why shouldn't he take her up on that? They were a good fit. Both dog owners, both divorced, both with demanding careers. He enjoyed her company, and as she'd said in the pub, neither of them was getting any younger.

But he had too much on his mind at the moment. Aside from his nocturnal returns to a war zone, the investigation into the body on the moors was absorbing too much of his focus for him to have any spare capacity for a romantic entanglement.

He drove to the station, keen as always to lose himself in work.

*

'The victim, as we now know, was Constable Dean Gibson, thirty-five years old. He worked for the MOD Police at RAF Fylingdales, providing security and surveillance of the base's perimeter and checkpoints. His commanding officer, Sergeant Gary Murphy, confirmed that Gibson worked the late shift on Saturday night and had booked this week off work. However, Gibson told his wife he was going on a training course. That was a lie. He had actually booked himself and a woman by the name of Nicole Anderson into a hotel in Scarborough. Becca, would you like to show everyone the items we found hidden in his locker?'

Raven stood back and watched as Becca passed around two evidence bags, one containing the Bergdorf Goodman gift bag and cufflink box, the other containing the cufflinks themselves. 'I looked them up online,' she said. 'They cost nearly a thousand dollars.'

'Wow,' said Jess, examining the jewel-encrusted skulls. 'These are... different.'

'Certainly not to everyone's taste,' agreed Raven. 'But very expensive. They were purchased from a store in New York.'

'Laura Gibson works as a teacher at the primary school in Goathland,' remarked Tony, 'so her salary isn't really high enough to splash out on expensive items of jewellery. And there's nothing in the couple's bank records to indicate that they travelled to the United States during the past year.'

'Nothing on social media either,' chipped in Jess. 'Laura always posts photos when they travel abroad, and there's been nothing from America.'

'So the cufflinks were almost certainly a gift,' said Raven. 'And not from his wife. Which presumably explains the need for him to conceal them at work. Tony, you identified a United States telephone number the murdered man called on a regular basis. Any further news on that?'

'Sorry, sir. It's a US cell phone number. Unfortunately I can't compel a US company to disclose subscriber information. I could submit a request to Interpol, but we'd need to obtain high-level authorisation first.'

It was much as Raven had expected. 'So one scenario is that the mystery number belongs to this Nicole Anderson, and that she's the dead man's American lover. We need to find out all we can about her as a top priority. Tony, can I assign you to that?'

'Sure thing, sir.'

'And Jess, I'd like you to try to trace the victim's car. Dean left his house early on Monday morning, telling his wife he was going on a training course, but in reality heading for a possible romantic liaison in Scarborough. He never made it there. Instead, he was dead by midday, and his body was taken to Lilla Cross later that night. We still haven't found his car. Work with Traffic to see if you can find out where it went on the day of his murder and where it is now. Look at speed cameras, ANPR records and parking tickets. Ask Tony, if you need any help.'

Jess nodded. 'I'll do my best, boss.'

Becca cocked her head to one side. 'What about you and me?'

'I think we'll take another trip to Goathland. Laura Gibson isn't going to like what we have to tell her, but there are questions that need answering.'

CHAPTER 15

As soon as she climbed into the passenger seat of Raven's car, Becca's nostrils detected a floral perfume overlaying the smell of wet dog that was now a permanent feature of the BMW. She wondered who had been in the car since the trip to RAF Fylingdales the previous day but didn't like to ask. Making enquiries into Raven's personal life was a guaranteed way of bringing his protective shutters clanging right down.

There was clearly something on his mind. His eyes were ringed with shadow, as if his sleep had been disturbed. He seemed even more taciturn than usual, driving north out of Scarborough without saying a word, just staring at the road ahead with a frown engraved on his forehead. Troubles on the romantic front, or was Becca reading too much into the scent of perfume? If she asked him straight out what was up, she'd only get a denial there was anything the matter.

To get him talking, it would be better to ask about something tangential. Slip under his radar, so to speak. 'How's Quincey doing?' she asked. 'It must be difficult looking after him now that you're busy on a case.'

'Quincey's no trouble. I walk him each morning, then Vicky looks after him all day.'

'I know that. But what about when you're working unpredictable hours?'

Raven deftly parried the question. 'Vicky's quite flexible. She doesn't mind if I'm a little bit late.'

'But what if you're really late,' persisted Becca, 'like on Tuesday night when we were out at Lilla Cross?'

'Tuesday?' Raven gave a shake of his head. 'That wasn't a problem. Quincey stayed with Melanie that night.'

Melanie? Aha. Was Melanie the source of the floral perfume?

Raven seemed to realise he'd allowed more information to slip out than he'd intended. 'Melanie's one of the other dog owners who goes to Vicky's,' he explained hastily.

'Right,' said Becca. 'What kind of dog does she have?'

'A King Charles Spaniel,' said Raven. 'Lulu.'

'Lulu.' Becca tried to keep her voice free of mirth, struggling to suppress a mental image of a woman in a frilly dress and a dog with a bow in its hair. Vicky's dog minding service was starting to sound more like a doggy dating agency. 'And how do Quincey and Lulu get along?'

'Just fine.' Raven was sounding weary of Becca's interrogation. Perhaps her sub-text had been too obvious. 'So,' he said, reclaiming control of the conversation, 'what are your plans for the weekend?'

Becca's mood took a sudden nosedive. She'd been trying to avoid thinking about the double date with Ellie, which was on for that evening. She knew she couldn't wriggle out of it. But she had decided she would go along to be polite and then leave early.

'Nothing much, really.' There was always the chance that the murder investigation would intervene and she'd have to work overtime. That would make the perfect excuse to cancel. 'How about you?'

She wondered if Raven would volunteer more info about Melanie and Lulu, but he merely grunted and fell silent. Becca gave up trying to make conversation and instead just stared out of the window at the rolling miles of heather. The moors were huge but were not a place that Becca often visited. Living in Scarborough, it was easy to forget about the miles of untamed wilderness on the doorstep.

Forty minutes after setting off they were back in Goathland. Raven slowed to a crawl as a lone sheep by the roadside nibbled grass and watched them through one eye. Before leaving Scarborough, Becca had checked with the family liaison officer that Laura Gibson wouldn't be at school that day. She had been given a week's bereavement leave from work. Raven pulled up outside her home on Beck Hole Road. The house was a modest, semi-detached bungalow, very plain and simple. In Becca's mind, it reinforced the impression that Laura Gibson hadn't bought the skull cufflinks for her husband.

A red Ford Galaxy – a licensed taxi-cab – was parked on the grass verge in front of the house. Becca followed Raven up the short drive to the front door. He rang the bell.

A group of sheep ambled past the front of the property, more interested in the roadside grass than in the arrival of the detectives. Could you call them a group? They were hardly a flock.

The door was opened by a man of tall, stocky build in his late thirties or early forties. His prematurely balding head had been shaved, leaving a minimum of hair growth. The rolled-up sleeves of his shirt revealed heavily tattooed forearms. 'Yeah?' The man's tone wasn't welcoming.

'Is PC Sharon Jarvis here?' asked Raven. 'I assigned her as the Family Liaison Officer.'

'I sent her packing. Laura doesn't need a busybody fussing about. I'm looking after her now. I'm her brother, Gavin Wilcox.'

'May we come in and speak to your sister, Mr Wilcox?'

Wilcox looked Raven up and down. 'If you must,' he said reluctantly. He stood to one side while Raven and

Becca made their way into the house, then shut the door behind them. 'Go through to the sitting room,' he told them gruffly.

Laura Gibson was sitting on a plain grey sofa, a half-drunk mug of coffee on the table beside her, the TV switched on with the volume turned down. Daytime telly – some kind of antiques show by the look of it, but Laura wasn't watching. She stared vacantly into space, giving no indication she was aware of Raven and Becca's arrival.

The lounge was neutral and tastefully decorated – unlike the cufflinks concealed in Dean's locker. A silver-framed wedding photo of Laura and Dean occupied a prominent position on the mantelpiece. The happy couple stood arm-in-arm outside a small country church with a square tower – presumably St Mary's Goathland – and looked very happy. The bride was in traditional white with a trailing bouquet of cream flowers. The groom looked very handsome in a grey morning suit with a white rose in his buttonhole. More photographs of the couple adorned the walls. They made a very photogenic pair.

Laura gazed blankly at the images.

'We're sorry to disturb you, Mrs Gibson,' said Raven, 'but I was wondering if I could show you something?'

She nodded. She seemed calm. Way too calm. A sedative, Becca suspected.

Meanwhile, her brother stood in the doorway, bouncing on the balls of his feet, fists clenching and unclenching. He was like a caged animal waiting to pounce.

'Would you like to sit down, Mr Wilcox?' Becca asked him.

'No, ta. I'll stand.'

Becca moved away from him, taking up position on the other side of the room with her back to the window. Behind her, sheep munched merrily away.

Raven produced the bag containing the outlandish cufflinks and showed them to Laura. 'Have you seen these before?'

She turned the evidence bag over in her hands, a puzzled look in her eyes. 'No, I've never seen them before. Where did you find them?'

'They were in your husband's locker at work,' said Raven.

'But how did they get there?'

'That's what we were hoping you might tell us,' said Becca. 'They were bought from Bergdorf Goodman, a New York department store.'

'We've never been to America,' said Laura. She stared at the black-and-gold cufflinks. 'These look expensive. How did Dean have them?'

'We don't know, Mrs Gibson,' said Becca.

Laura's grip tightened around the bag, her fingers trembling. 'Is Dean... do you think he...?' Her voice quavered. 'Was he having an affair?' Tears sprang to her eyes as she gripped the bag.

'We don't know,' said Becca kindly, holding out her hand for the cufflinks.

Laura passed them back absent-mindedly.

'What do you think you're playing at?' Gavin Wilcox pushed his way into the room, confronting Raven face-to-face. The two men were the same height and Gavin was broader. He stood in front of Raven, their noses almost touching. 'You can't just barge in here and show my sister shit like that. Can't you see the state she's in? Someone just murdered her husband for fuck's sake!'

Raven narrowed his eyes. 'I think you need to calm down. You won't help your sister by getting mad at me.'

Wilcox balled his hands into fists. 'Like fuck I need to calm down.' He raised his right fist and threw a punch in Raven's direction.

Raven dodged the blow and seized the aggressor's wrist before he could take another swing. He manoeuvred Wilcox's arm behind his back and pinned it there.

'Right,' he said. 'Outside now!'

He marched Wilcox through the kitchen and out the back door. Becca checked that Laura was okay, then followed the two men outside.

Raven had his attacker up against the back wall, his face pushed against the brickwork of the bungalow. 'Fuckin' 'ell,' muttered the brother. 'You're breaking my arm!'

'If I'd wanted to break it,' said Raven, 'it would already be broken. Now, if I let you go are you going to keep your head?'

'Yeah,' gasped Wilcox. 'Just let go of me.'

Raven released him. 'I could arrest you for assaulting a police officer.'

Wilcox rubbed his arm, subdued. His appetite for a fight seemed to have drained away. 'I'm sorry,' he said. 'It's been a stressful few days.'

'I think we can overlook that little outburst,' said Becca, 'if you tell us what you know about the cufflinks.'

'I've never seen them before,' said Wilcox.

'Maybe not,' said Becca. 'But you know who gave them to your brother-in-law. You knew he was having an affair, didn't you?' She could tell that Wilcox hadn't been surprised by the cufflinks, just angered by the fact that Raven had shown them to his sister.

Wilcox's shoulders slumped in defeat. 'All right,' he admitted. 'I knew Dean was having an affair, the stupid prick.'

'How did you find out?' asked Raven. 'Did he tell you?'

'No. I'm a taxi driver, working out of Pickering. About a month ago, I was dropping off a fare in Scarborough when I saw him coming out of some posh hotel with a woman. It was obvious what they were up to. They were holding hands and kissing. I didn't want to tell Laura about it. It would have broken her heart. I hoped the whole thing would blow over.'

'Did you talk to Dean about it?'

'No. But maybe I should have. I could have fixed things there and then.' Once again his fingers were tightening into fists. It looked like Gavin Wilcox knew only one way of talking.

'Do you know who the woman was?' asked Becca.

Wilcox shrugged. 'I don't know her name, but I know who she is. I saw her again at RAF Fylingdales when I was dropping a visitor there. She was in US military uniform, so she's American.'

'Does the name Nicole Anderson mean anything to you?'

'Is that what she's called?' Wilcox shook his head. 'Never heard the name before. Like I said, I should have confronted Dean. The arsehole was cheating on my sister. But I figured this woman was going to return to America and dump him sooner or later, so there was no point stirring up trouble. It would have killed Laura to know Dean was cheating on her.' He threw a resentful look in Raven's direction. 'Well, now she knows anyway, thanks to you.'

'What were you doing on Monday between 7am and noon?' asked Raven.

Wilcox dragged thick fingers through his almost non-existent hair. 'What do you wanna know that for? You don't think I did it? Dean was my brother-in-law. He was family.'

'Just answer the question.'

Wilcox thought for a second. 'If you must know, I was working that day. I took a passenger to Leeds Bradford airport in the morning. All the pick-ups and drop-offs are logged electronically. You can check with the taxi firm if you don't believe me.'

'Trust me,' said Raven, 'we will.'

CHAPTER 16

'How does anyone manage to live in this place?' said Raven in frustration. He stared at the screen of his phone. Zero bars of signal. Emergency calls only.

Becca's phone was the same. 'There's a phone box outside the village shop. You could try calling from there.'

'I'll have to,' said Raven in disgust. When had he last used a public telephone box?

He drove to the centre of Goathland and parked outside a shop that sold gifts and souvenirs.

'This is like being back in the 1950s,' he told Becca as he got out of the car and made his way to the old-fashioned red telephone box on the village green. All he needed was a raincoat and a trilby to complete the picture.

Fortunately the telephone was in working order. It even accepted credit cards. Raven dialled Tony's number and waited.

'DC Tony Bairstow speaking.'

'Tony, it's me, Raven. I'm calling from a public phone box in Goathland. Listen, could you do something for me? It's possible that Nicole Anderson is with the US military working at RAF Fylingdales. Could you check her out for me?'

'Just give me ten minutes.'

Raven gave him the number of the public telephone and told him to call back as soon as he had something. 'There's no bloody mobile signal out here,' he explained.

'I guessed that, sir.'

Raven hung up and stepped outside the phone box. The shops along the edge of the village green were like something from another age. A village store, a post office, an ice cream parlour, a newsagent's and even a grocer's. When Raven had been a little boy, he had trailed around with his mother, buying provisions at shops much like these. There had been few supermarkets in those days. Looking back, it was hard to believe how much the world had changed since his childhood. He must be even more ancient than he realised.

Becca was just emerging from the nearby tearoom. She came over to join him and handed him a paper bag. 'I thought we could use some flapjacks.'

'Oh, cheers,' said Raven. He hadn't stopped for a proper breakfast that morning before taking Quincey out and was glad of an energy booster.

They sat together on a wooden bench, munching their flapjacks which were perfectly sweet and buttery. Although the day was warm, the wind blowing off the moors was fresh and invigorating. More sheep stood nearby nibbling the grass, their black-and-white faces intent on their task. The council probably didn't need to use lawnmowers in Goathland.

'Gavin Wilcox already knew about the affair,' said Becca. 'You could see how angry he was about it, and how protective he was towards his sister.'

'Protective?' said Raven. 'Controlling might be a better word. Did you notice how calm she was. I think he must have given her a sedative of some kind. I'd feel a lot more comfortable if Sharon Jarvis was still there, keeping an eye on Laura.'

'True. He's a piece of work all round. And if he knew about Dean's affair, that's got to make him our number-one suspect.'

Raven recalled how quick the taxi driver had been to throw a punch in his face. Gavin Wilcox was a brute, and Raven didn't think he was any stranger to brawls. 'He's certainly reckless enough to kill a man if he lost his temper. Even his own brother-in-law.'

'It would be interesting to send CSI to give his taxi a once-over.'

'We'd need a good reason to do that,' said Raven. 'Right now, all we have is an angry man with a grudge.'

The public telephone suddenly started ringing.

'That'll be Tony.' Raven gave his hands a quick wipe and dashed back inside the red box. He picked up the receiver. 'Hello?'

'Sir, you were right about Nicole Anderson. She's a major with the US Air Force, currently seconded to RAF Fylingdales.'

'Excellent work, Tony.'

'No problem, sir. Is there anything else you'd like me to do?'

'Yes, could you check out the victim's brother-in-law, Gavin Wilcox. He's a taxi driver based in Pickering. He says he was taking a passenger out to Leeds Bradford airport on Monday morning. Can you see if his alibi stands up?'

'Will do, sir.'

'Oh, and check if he has a criminal record too.'

'I'll get onto it,' said Tony. 'How should I contact you when I find out? Should I call this number again?'

Raven looked out through the small panes of glass of the kiosk. 'Not unless you want a sheep to answer.'

'Sir?'

'Don't worry, Tony. I'll talk to you again when I get back to civilisation.'

★

Even though it was Raven and Becca's second visit to RAF Fylingdales, they still had to endure the lengthy rigmarole of security checks at the outer gate and await the arrival of Flight Lieutenant Mark Jones to escort them onto the base.

'I wasn't expecting you back so soon,' said Jones, cheerful as ever. 'Do you have news?'

'We're making progress,' said Raven cautiously. Jones was clearly eager to hear more, but Raven preferred to keep the few facts he had learned to himself for now.

'Well,' said the flight lieutenant, 'how can I help you this time?'

'We'd like to speak to one of the military personnel on the base. Major Nicole Anderson of the US Air Force.'

The flight lieutenant's face fell. 'All US personnel here are operating under the Status of Forces Agreement. Do you know what that is?'

'Yes.' Raven did, but he explained it for Becca's benefit. 'It sets out the terms under which the armed forces of a NATO member state are allowed to live and operate within another NATO member state.'

'Precisely,' said Jones. 'US military personnel are not obliged to answer your questions.'

'I'd still like to speak to her,' said Raven.

'Understood. Then come with me.'

Raven and Becca joined Jones in his Land Rover and were driven back to the inner checkpoint where they handed over their phones.

'Hardly worth us hanging onto these,' remarked Becca. 'Out here, they're just dead pieces of plastic.'

Jones gave her a wry grin. 'We don't exactly get value for money from our phone providers if we live and work around here. The cellular networks operate at a similar frequency to the phased array radar, so it's no surprise which one takes priority.' He glanced meaningfully in the direction of the pyramidal radar facility. It was strange to think of that giant block of concrete continuously transmitting signals into the sky and receiving and analysing their reflections from a distance of thousands of miles.

Jones took them to the same building as before and asked them to wait while he made the necessary overtures through appropriate channels that would enable them to be admitted into the presence of Major Nicole Anderson.

Raven drummed his fingers impatiently on the desktop but knew he could do nothing to speed the process along. He was stepping into a diplomatic minefield by involving a foreign national, especially one with special privileges and an exemption to the normal rules of the UK criminal justice system. No doubt he ought to have informed Gillian about what he intended to do, but there was enough red tape to cut through already. No point bringing in more.

Eventually, Jones gave them a thumbs-up. 'Okay, I've made the arrangements. But I warn you, she's under no obligation to cooperate with a civilian police investigation.'

'Let's just find out what she has to say,' said Raven.

'Go carefully,' cautioned Jones. 'Major Anderson has a reputation for being feisty. She's a highflyer, groomed for the top. She's been stationed at all the bases making up the radar network: Beale Air Force Base, Cape Cod, Alaska, and Pituffik Space Base in Greenland. Rumour has it that her next posting will be to the Ballistic Missile Defense System Command Center at Peterson Space Force Base in Colorado Springs.'

'Thanks for the heads-up,' said Raven, 'but I'm quite used to dealing with difficult people.'

Major Anderson was sitting in her office, working on a shiny laptop at a big desk. She was younger than Raven had expected, perhaps late-thirties. She was dressed in military uniform of dark blue jacket and trousers with silver rank insignia on her epaulets. Her blonde hair was uncovered, but drawn sharply back from her forehead. Her features were regular, and with her hair long and loose she would be a very attractive woman. An impressive array of silver ribbons decorated her jacket above her left breast pocket. She immediately closed her computer as Raven and Becca entered the room, Flight Lieutenant Jones leading the way.

'Major Anderson.'

'Flight Lieutenant Jones.'

It was hard to judge from the brief exchange whether the pair were on good terms. The formality of military hierarchy rendered all such encounters starchy, especially when the two officers represented different countries.

Even though they were supposed to be on the same side.

The major rose from her seat and Jones ushered his guests inside. Raven had already resigned himself to the fact that the flight lieutenant would be present throughout the interview. It was obvious that Wing Commander Fitzwilliam-Brown hadn't appointed his deputy merely to assist Raven. He was also here to keep tabs on him. Raven didn't doubt that the RAF officer would report their every move to Fitzwilliam-Brown as soon as they'd left.

Jones attempted to justify his presence by making the introductions. 'DCI Raven and DS Shawcross from North Yorkshire Police here to speak to you, ma'am.'

The major gave them a tempered smile. 'Well, good day to you both. How can I be of service?'

Her speech was laid-back and relaxed, but without the drawl that often characterised the southern parts of the United States. West coast, possibly Californian, was Raven's best guess, although he was by no means an expert. Her manner was confident. She was the kind of woman who knew what she wanted and wasn't afraid to take it.

'We're investigating the murder of an MOD police officer who worked at this base,' said Raven.

The major raised her eyebrows high. 'I see. How terrible.'

'The name of the murdered man was Constable Dean Gibson.' Raven watched her closely, looking for any reaction that might betray the fact that she and Dean had been sleeping together.

But the major was unflappable. 'And how may I help with your investigation?' she asked politely.

'Did you know him?'

'Well,' said Major Anderson, 'you know I'm not obliged to answer your questions.'

It was just as the flight lieutenant had warned. She was taking refuge behind the Status of Forces Agreement.

'It's a perfectly simple question,' persisted Raven.

Anderson drew her shoulders back and raised her chin. 'According to the terms by which US military personnel operate in this country, I am subject to the jurisdiction of the United States military court, not the UK criminal justice system.

'I'm only asking if you knew him.'

'You said this was a murder enquiry?'

'Yes.'

'Then I refer you to my previous answer. Will that be all?'

Raven reached into his jacket pocket and pulled out the cufflinks that had caused so much trouble when he'd showed them to Laura Gibson and her brother. 'Have you seen these before?'

A brief flicker of recognition crossed Anderson's face before she had chance to compose herself. 'They appear to be a pair of cufflinks.'

'They were purchased at a New York department store. Bergdorf Goodman. Did you buy them as a gift for your lover?'

'DCI Raven,' said Nicole Anderson, sounding thoroughly vexed. 'Was I unclear in some way about why I'm not obliged to answer your questions?'

Raven had heard quite enough about the Status of Forces Agreement and the immunity it conferred to the air force major. But she wasn't the only one who understood the terms of the NATO agreement. 'If a US officer commits a crime outside the scope of their official duties,' he informed her, 'they can still be prosecuted by the British authorities.'

She shook her head in disbelief at his sassy persistence. 'And do you intend to take me into custody on a murder charge, Detective Inspector?'

They both knew he didn't. But he had one last card to play. 'On the day Dean Gibson died, he was booked into a hotel in Scarborough. You were named as his room guest.'

He could tell by her raised eyebrows she hadn't seen that coming. No doubt she had expected Dean to use a fake name for his lover. It was becoming clear that the murdered man hadn't been the brains behind the affair. Nicole had selected him for his looks, not his intelligence.

But before she could respond, the flight lieutenant cleared his throat and interrupted. 'Um, maybe this sort of questioning should proceed under the appropriate official channels.'

Raven ignored him. He was as close as he'd ever been to getting a reaction from the reticent major.

Nicole crossed her arms with a loud sigh. 'Listen, all I can tell you is that Dean didn't show up at the hotel that day, so I didn't see him. I know nothing about what happened to him, and I have no idea why anyone would want to harm him.' Her expression hardened. 'And I don't expect you to come back and ask me any more questions. Is that understood?'

Raven nodded, knowing his time was up. At least he'd managed to provoke a reaction and get an answer to one of his questions. 'That will be all for now,' he said. 'And by the way, your poker face could use some work. It's your eyebrows that give you away.'

CHAPTER 17

'Found it!' said Jess to no one in particular. Raven and Becca were still out, and Tony was so engrossed in his computer he didn't hear.

No matter. She was pleased she'd managed to get the job done without having to ask Tony for help. First, she'd put the registration number and description of Dean Gibson's missing car out to Traffic. Having got no hits from cameras or road reports from across the whole of North Yorkshire, she'd begun to think she would need to widen her search.

But then a report had come in about a car that had been "dumped", according to the person who made the complaint. There was no description of the vehicle, but the registration matched the Ford Kuga belonging to Laura and Dean Gibson. The car he'd been driving when he left his house in Goathland on Monday morning.

By Jess's reckoning, the car hadn't exactly been dumped, merely parked in a quiet residential cul-de-sac in Whitby. But she was grateful to the busybody who had noticed it and made the effort to notify the police. Most people wouldn't have given a strange car parked on their street a second glance, let alone felt the need to report it to the authorities.

It was also a potential crime scene. Jess called Raven, eager to share her news. If he and Becca were still out and about then it wouldn't be far for them to nip across to Whitby.

'Come on,' she muttered to herself, but the call to Raven's number just wouldn't connect. She tried Becca's mobile and got the same result. She knew why. She'd had the exact same problem when the body was discovered at Lilla Cross. She'd had to send Ronald and Janice trekking all the way over to the Flask Inn on the main road to raise the alarm.

She tried a different number. The other person picked up immediately. 'Jess, what can I do for you?'

'Holly, hi, it's Jess here.' She'd always got on well with Holly Chang, the CSI team leader. She explained what she'd discovered. 'The car belonging to Dean Gibson has been found in Whitby. I've tried calling Raven and Becca but they're out of range.'

'Well, that doesn't stop us from driving over there and having a nose about, does it?' said Holly.

'I was hoping you were going to say something like that. Are you free now?'

'Give me five.'

It was just like being one of those Netflix cops.

Jess put the phone down and told Tony what was happening. 'You don't think Raven will mind, do you?' she asked, suddenly unsure if she was doing the right thing.

'Of course not. CSI need to give that car a good once-over. You did well, Jess.'

Reassured, she met Holly outside the station, where she was just disembarking from the CSI van. Jess spotted Erin in the driver's seat.

'I'll ride with you,' said Holly. 'Erin can follow us with all the gear.'

'Okay.' They were soon heading north towards Whitby, Jess at the wheel of her Land Rover, Holly riding in the passenger seat and Erin following in the CSI van. The seat groaned and squeaked loudly as they drove. Screws loose again, probably. Jess really needed to take the battered old vehicle for a service one of these days. Maybe her dad could take a look at it at the weekend.

'So, have you recovered from your walk?' asked Holly as they drove. 'Bloody mad thing to do, if you ask me.'

Jess laughed. 'My hamstrings are feeling a lot better, thanks. And my blisters, too.'

'And what about you, Jess?'

Jess knew what the older woman was getting at. The shock of finding a dead body where you least expected it. And especially one in such a terrible state.

'I'm all right,' said Jess. 'It... it wasn't like when Scott was found.' A silent understanding passed between them. Jess had been the detective called out when a body had been found in Scarborough harbour. At the time, neither woman had been prepared for the shock of discovering that the victim was a member of Holly's team, someone very close to Jess. Holly had been very supportive, and a bond had formed between the two women. Despite her gruff exterior, Holly Chang could be very sensitive when the occasion demanded. Jess strongly suspected her grumpy banter was simply a ruse to stop people getting too close to her. Perhaps she'd lost someone too, and didn't want to be hurt again.

'Still,' said Holly, 'not the sort of thing you want to find on your day off.'

'True. But it hasn't put me off walking. I'm planning to try the route again, once this case is over.'

Holly gave an exaggerated roll of her eyes. 'Some folk never learn. You mean you're going to pick up from where you left off at Lilla Cross and walk to the finish?'

'Oh no,' said Jess. 'You can't do the walk in stages. I'll have to start from the beginning again and walk all forty miles in under twenty-four hours, otherwise I won't qualify for membership of the Lyke Wake Club.'

'Bloody Nora!' said Holly. 'You must be stark-raving

bonkers!'

*

Raven left the meeting with Major Nicole Anderson of the US Air Force thoroughly disgruntled with the protection conferred on her by international treaty. So much for being on the same side. It would have been far easier to deal with a British citizen, whether civilian or military. Even one as cagey and guarded as the major.

Nevertheless, Raven reckoned he'd got as much out of her as he could have hoped.

She had admitted to having an affair with Dean Gibson and confirmed she was planning to stay with him at the hotel in Scarborough. She had also revealed by her reaction on seeing the cufflinks that she had indeed bought them as a gift for her lover.

No surprises there.

But the interview appeared to have left Raven at a dead end. If Nicole was telling the truth and had no idea what had happened to Dean or why he had been killed, then the investigation had moved no further forward.

Raven was determined not to leave the RAF base empty-handed. 'I'd like another word with Sergeant Gary Murphy,' he told Flight Lieutenant Jones.

The MOD police sergeant was another difficult character to handle. Despite promising to send the report describing Dean Gibson's encounter with an intruder at the perimeter fence, so far nothing had been delivered. Raven was in the mood for a bit of chasing.

'Sergeant Murphy,' said the flight lieutenant, looking as if Raven had just named the person he least wanted to see again. 'You want to speak to him now?'

'Now,' confirmed Raven.

They returned to the sergeant's office, Jones once again rapping on the door and being greeted by a gruff invitation to enter. He pushed the door open and ushered Raven and Becca inside, as if unwilling to be the first to enter.

The sergeant looked up from his screen and fixed a scowl to his ugly face. 'I'm busy.'

Raven shrugged. 'Then don't let us disturb you. We'll just stand here and wait until you've printed off that report you promised us.' He took up position in the middle of the room where he would be in the way of anyone coming in or going out. Becca leaned against the wall, running a finger across the grey box files lined up on a shelving unit. Jones loitered by the door, keeping his distance. Raven knew he would get little help from that quarter.

Murphy ignored Raven for a full minute before giving in. 'All right, I'll do it now,' he grumbled. 'Anything to get you out of my way so I can get on with some work.'

Raven kept his face neutral while Becca suppressed a smile. He knew how to handle these military types. You just had to show them who was top dog.

Murphy hit some keys on his computer, and the printer on his desk whirred into action. The report ran to a couple of pages.

'There,' said Raven. 'That wasn't so hard, was it?'

Murphy snatched the report from the printer and handed it to Raven with a look of undisguised loathing. 'Anything else I can do for you while you're here? I'd hate for you to have to come back.'

'No, that's everything, thank you,' said Raven with exaggerated politeness. He slipped the document into a black folder. 'Have a good day.'

He was glad to leave the MOD sergeant's office behind him. Two hostile encounters in one day. It was almost like being back on the battlefield. Why couldn't people just be nice?

'Where to now?' asked Jones, also visibly relieved to be out of Gary Murphy's presence.

'I think we're done here for today,' said Raven. 'We'll get out of your hair.'

He waited until they were back in the BMW and some distance away from the RAF base before pulling over by a five-bar gate and reaching for the folder on the back seat.

'Let's see what this says,' he said to Becca.

He held the report out so they could read it together.

The report was dated some two weeks previously. It had been written and filed by Constable Dean Gibson following a night patrol at the radar station. An intruder had been intercepted at the inner fence.

'White male, late forties or early fifties,' Becca read aloud. 'Medium height, medium build, grey hair, unshaven. Wearing an old army jacket and combat trousers.'

But Raven had already skipped ahead to the main substance of the report. 'When challenged, the intruder approached the fence and began to speak. His words were unclear, but he referred repeatedly to "the enemy" and to "traitors". "They're going to destroy everything. Boom!" he shouted, before fleeing.'

The hairs on the back of Raven's neck were standing on end. He'd heard those very same words only a few days ago from a man matching the intruder's description. 'I know who this is,' he told Becca.

'You do? Who?'

'An old army vet called Sean Collins. He was a private in my unit in Bosnia.'

'How do you know it was him?'

'I saw him recently. He looked like he was sleeping rough and he was spouting those exact words. He asked for my help.' Raven felt sick in the pit of his stomach.

'If you know who he is, we should go and find him,' said Becca.

Raven gave her a look of despair. 'That's the problem. I only saw him once, and I dismissed what he was saying as the rantings of a lunatic. Now I wish I'd listened.'

'Where did you see him?'

'At the beach on the North Bay. I was out walking Quincey. But I've been back there at the same time every day since, and Sean hasn't reappeared. Now I've no idea where he is.'

★

On arriving in Whitby, it didn't take long for Jess to locate the missing Ford Kuga. It was parked, just as the report described, in a street of 1950s semis. An average car, parked neatly in an unremarkable residential street. No wonder it had escaped detection for so many days. If it hadn't been for the vigilance of the eagle-eyed resident, its whereabouts might still be unknown.

Jess pulled to a halt behind it and was just starting to inspect the car when the CSI van drew up behind. Erin jumped out, whistling cheerily, as Holly made heavy weather of clambering out of the Land Rover. 'Friendly tip for you, Jess,' grumbled Holly as she struggled down from the passenger seat. 'Get yourself a proper car.'

Jess peered through the side windows of the Ford. There was nothing of interest visible inside. She snapped on a pair of forensic gloves and tried the driver's door.

'Locked?' asked Holly.

'Yes. We'll have to ask the victim's wife to supply a spare set of keys.'

'I think we can do better than that.' Holly turned to her assistant. 'Erin, do us a favour and break into it, will you?'

The junior CSI operative grinned and set about gaining entry into the Ford Kuga with the skill of a highly trained carjacker. It didn't take long.

Once the doors and boot were open, she and Holly set to work, dusting the steering wheel and gearstick for prints, examining the seat and carpets for fibres. 'Shocking, the state of most folk's cars,' muttered Holly. 'You wouldn't believe the rubbish we find in some of them.'

Jess said nothing, knowing that a forensic search of the Land Rover would no doubt uncover all kinds of horrors. She really must take it to be vacuumed one of these days. She continued her own examination of the victim's car, but couldn't see anything out of the ordinary.

'Time for the magic spray,' said Holly, looking in the boot of the car. 'Luminol,' she explained to Jess's questioning frown. 'Could you two stand behind me and block the light?'

They willingly obliged while Holly sprayed the boot and peered into the darkened interior. 'Just as I thought.'

As Erin took photographs, Jess peered over Holly's shoulder and saw the blue fluorescent stains on the black fabric of the car's interior.

Blood. Soaked into the lining of the boot and splashed over the underside of the parcel shelf. The car had been used either to store or transport Dean's body.

With gloved hands, Holly gently lifted the floor carpet to reveal the spare tyre compartment below. Next to a jack and wrench, a hammer had been wedged into the space above the tyre.

'I doubt you need one of those to fit a spare, boss,' remarked Erin.

'Ha!' said Holly. 'You should see the way I change a tyre.' But when she sprayed the luminol over the tools no one was surprised to see the head of the hammer glowing brightly.

'I think we've found our murder weapon, Jess,' said Holly.

After Erin had taken photographs of the hammer *in situ*, Holly bagged it up ready to go to the lab for further tests.

'I wonder why they left the car here,' said Erin. 'Why not simply torch it with the body inside? Get rid of all the evidence at once?'

'My guess,' said Holly, 'is that they used the car to take the body to Lilla Cross, but needed it to get back to civilisation.'

'They could have walked back,' said Jess. 'It's only a few miles from Lilla Cross to the main road.'

Holly laughed as if Jess had just cracked the funniest joke ever. 'Jess Barraclough, *you* might enjoy trudging for miles across a barren moorland, but most people would rather get home for their tea. And that includes murderers.'

CHAPTER 18

By the time Becca got home, it was already gone six and she and Ellie were supposed to be meeting their respective dates at seven. Drinks in a bar to get started, then dinner at the restaurant owned by Ellie's dad, Keith. Knowing Ellie, they might hit a club later if things got serious and Becca was still standing.

The chances of that were looking decidedly slim.

After her morning at Goathland in the company of the victim's half-tranquilised wife and angry brother-in-law, followed by an afternoon at RAF Fylingdales battling with international bureaucracy and petty uncooperativeness on the part of two key witnesses, Becca really just wanted to curl up on the sofa and binge on something mindless on the telly. Half a bottle of Chardonnay and a tub of Ben & Jerry's would see her good.

The last thing she wanted was the hassle of glamming up for a date and then forcing her best smile all evening.

When she entered the shared kitchen-lounge of the flat and dumped her bag on the floor, she found Ellie busy tapping on her phone, already dressed and made up. She looked amazing in a clingy, sparkly top and dangly earrings. Her hair, which tended to change colour every six weeks, was currently dyed turquoise at the ends to match her eyeshadow and nails.

She glanced up as Becca crashed on the sofa. 'Don't make yourself comfortable. You'll have to be quick. I just checked with the guys and they promised not to be late.'

'Give me half an hour,' said Becca.

With a supreme effort she dragged herself from the sofa and into her room. There, she stripped off her work clothes and jumped in the shower, careful not to get her hair wet because there wouldn't be time to dry it before going out. She applied some hurried makeup then padded back to her bedroom wrapped in a towel. What was she going to wear?

She hadn't given the slightest thought to it. Partly, she realised, because she'd been secretly counting on having to work late and miss the whole gig. But Raven had thoughtfully dropped her off outside her flat and wished her a pleasant evening before driving off.

She knew exactly how he would be spending his evening. He'd be out searching for Sean Collins, consumed with guilt for not having listened more seriously to his battle buddy when he'd encountered him earlier.

She wished Raven had asked her to go with him. She would much rather be out roaming the streets of Scarborough with her boss, hunting for a homeless person spouting mad conspiracy theories than getting ready to re-enter the dating arena after a break of two years.

Yet here she was.

She pulled open the wardrobe doors and contemplated her choice of outfits. Smart black trousers and plain white work shirts filled at least three-quarters of the available space. The rest was taken up with her winter coat, not needed at this time of the year, a summer skirt that only came out of hibernation on the very hottest days of the year, and a dress she'd bought a couple of years ago for a cousin's wedding. When had she turned into such a frump?

'Are you nearly ready?' called Ellie from the other side of the door. 'Do you need to borrow something?'

'No, I'm fine, thanks,' called Becca.

She pulled open a chest of drawers and rummaged inside until she found a pair of skinny jeans and a tunic top with blue embroidery around the neckline. She liked the Bohemian feel of the top which was feminine while still being comfortable. She brushed her hair, chose a pair of plain silver earrings and touched up her lipstick. She couldn't remember the last time she'd put so much effort into her appearance. She checked her watch. It was twenty-seven minutes precisely since she'd arrived home.

'Ready,' she called.

Ellie was waiting for her in the hallway. 'You look lovely,' she said, sounding like she genuinely meant it. 'It's so nice to see you out of your work clothes. Come on, let's get going.' She grabbed hold of Becca's hand and dragged her out of the apartment as if afraid she would change her mind at the last moment.

The seafront bar was crowded and noisy. Upbeat music pounded through speakers, and people spilled onto the pavement outside, drinks in hand. Becca followed Ellie inside to look for their dates. 'They're over there,' mouthed Ellie, turning to Becca and pointing towards the bar.

Becca squeezed her way through the throng, close on Ellie's heels. She couldn't see who they were meeting, but emerging from the crush she was surprised to find her brother, Liam, sitting at a bar stool.

'Hi,' she said, 'what are you doing here? I was only just talking to Mum and Dad about you last night.'

'Yeah, they told me you'd been over for dinner. What are you drinking?' Liam was already halfway through a pint.

'No, I'm good,' she told him. 'I'm here with Ellie.' She wondered whether she should tell him why she was there. After all, Liam had also been dropping hints for some while that it was time for her to meet someone new. But she didn't feel obliged to give her brother a progress report on her relationship status. On the other hand, if he'd spoken to Sue, then chances were he already knew, so there was no point hiding it. 'We're going on a double date,' she said, pulling a face.

'Me too,' said Liam with a grin.

'Really? What a coincidence.' And then the penny dropped. So did Becca's mouth. 'Wait, you're Ellie's date?'

'Too right he is.' Ellie emerged from the heaving crowd and Liam put his arm around her. Soon the pair of them were grinning like Cheshire cats. 'Sorry,' said Ellie. 'I should have told you, but I was worried you'd drop out if you knew. I had to twist your arm even as it was.'

Becca couldn't get her brain in gear fast enough to process the tumble of thoughts that were coming her way. *Ellie and Liam cooked this up between them? Her flatmate and her brother were an item?*

The questions were racing around Becca's head like greyhounds on a track.

How could Ellie not have told her she was dating Liam?

How could Liam not have told her he was dating Ellie?

And what on earth did Ellie see in him anyway?

Shock was quickly replaced with fury. How dare they trick her like this! She felt used and cheated. She would leave immediately and tell them both to sod off. She turned to leave but there were too many people for her to make a quick getaway. And then a tall, blond man appeared at her side.

'Becca, this is Daniel,' said Liam. 'Daniel, meet my sister, Becca. I think she's cross with me, but that's nothing unusual. Handle her carefully, she can be fierce.'

Becca glared up at the new arrival but her anger dissolved when he looked down at her and said, 'Well, this is awkward isn't it. I didn't want to come either, but your brother insisted on dragging me along.'

'What, you didn't want to come either?' said Becca indignantly, putting her hands on her hips. 'You mean you didn't want to go on a date with me?'

'Well,' said Daniel, 'that was only because Liam didn't tell me much about you. But now I've met you...' He cocked his head to one side.

'Come on, Becs,' said Liam. 'Live a little.'

She still couldn't believe that Liam and Ellie had arranged this without telling her what they were up to. But she could understand why they had kept it a secret. No way would she have agreed to come if she'd known what was in store.

The expression on her face must have given away her feelings because Daniel looked crestfallen. 'I feel really bad now. I shouldn't have agreed to come.' But then a shy smile spread across his face, lighting up his eyes. 'But now that we're both here, I think it would be nice if you stayed.'

It was impossible to say no to such a chivalrous plea. Becca felt her resolve crumble. She burst out laughing. 'All right,' she agreed, 'but I'll tell you who's buying the drinks all night.'

'Me?' said Daniel.

'No. Liam!'

'Get that down you,' shouted Ellie over the din. She thrust a glass of vodka into Becca's hand. 'Drink up, and then we'll get out of here and move on to somewhere quieter.'

*

'What did I tell you, Tom? Appropriate channels. Proper protocols. No treading on toes.'

Raven winced under Gillian's rebuke. He had popped back into the police station, hoping for a quiet moment to himself. But he had been ambushed by the detective superintendent almost as soon as he'd entered his office. He had the distinct feeling she'd been lying in wait for him to show his face. Now he wished he'd gone straight to the dog minder's to pick up Quincey. Vicky never gave him a hard time and neither did his dog.

'With all due respect, ma'am, I did follow protocols.'

'Then why,' demanded Gillian, slapping a sheet of paper on his desk, 'did I receive this sternly worded email from the Home Office?'

Raven glanced at the printed sheet. It was upside down, so he was unable to read any of the words. But he could clearly recognise the government logo of a crown perched above a quartered shield.

'This,' said Gillian, snatching the sheet away again, 'was sent to me by a senior official reporting directly to the Minister of State for Crime & Policing. He was responding to a question raised by the Legal Attaché at the United States Embassy in London. And when he says "question", that is diplomatic language for "complaint". It would seem that you have been harassing an officer in the US Air Force.' She clasped her hands behind her back, the paper crackling under the pressure of her grip.

Raven was surprised less by the nature of the complaint and more by its speedy arrival. He'd been under the impression that the cogs of diplomacy, like all bureaucracy, turned at a glacial pace. Governments and embassies weren't renowned for their rapid responses. Major Nicole Anderson must have known exactly which levers to pull.

'Ma'am, I know what this is about, but I can assure you that I did go through the appropriate channels. The station commander at RAF Fylingdales gave me permission to conduct inquiries at the base and appointed one of his officers to escort me at all times. Everything I did was under his direct supervision.'

Raven recalled the reluctance of the flight lieutenant to admit him into Major Anderson's office, and the lecture he had given him about the Status of Forces Agreement. He hoped that no detailed inquiry would ever be conducted into exactly how he had gone about interviewing the US major. Official inquiries had a nasty tendency to show everything in the worst possible light.

Gillian's nostrils flared. 'You say all that, Tom. And yet this lands on my desk. I told you I didn't want the Ministry of Defence banging on my door. Instead, I find myself being harassed by the Home Office.'

And now she was harassing Raven. Major Anderson

certainly knew her rights and had wasted no time in setting the diplomatic machinery into motion. A complicated chain of reporting which had led ultimately to him.

But who was Raven supposed to complain to?

'Ma'am, what else can I say? I went out of my way to follow the correct protocols. The US officer I interviewed is a suspect in a murder inquiry, and she was fully appraised of her legal rights. I needed to speak to her.' He had started out strong, with a vigorous defence of his actions, but somehow a note of pleading had crept into his voice near the end. He knew he depended on Gillian's support if he was going to have any hope of making progress in the investigation.

And now that Sean Collins, formerly Private Collins of the Duke of Wellington's Regiment, was entangled in the murder, Raven needed to get to the bottom of it for his own sanity.

Her cold eyes rested on him a while longer, as if seeking to extract the maximum amount of suffering before making any kind of concession. He did his best to appear contrite and eventually she seemed satisfied. But when she planted her fists on his desk and leaned over it, her final words weren't exactly what he'd been hoping to hear.

'Tom, I cannot state this more plainly. Do not speak to that woman again.'

*

Raven descended the steps to the North Bay in the shadow of the headland. The sun was low in the sky but wouldn't dip beneath the mound of Oliver's Mount for another hour yet. It would stay light enough to walk the beach until ten or eleven o'clock at night. In the distance, the sea murmured gently, the quiet evening punctuated by the cries of gulls.

He threw the tennis ball and watched as Quincey bounded after it in delight. The dog had so much energy, Raven found it exhausting just watching him. When he'd agreed to adopt the Black Labrador he hadn't realised quite how vigorous the breed could be.

But Raven wasn't there simply to exercise his dog. He was hoping that Sean Collins might make another appearance.

The details in PC Dean Gibson's report left little room for doubt. The MOD police officer had given a clear and meticulous description of the intruder he'd encountered at the fence, and the words the man had uttered established the facts conclusively.

They're going to destroy everything. Boom!

Raven had a bad feeling, and it was growing worse the more he thought about it. If Sean Collins had been out at RAF Fylingdales, then were the "traitors" he'd talked about somehow connected with the radar station?

Quincey returned, tennis ball soggy and sandy in his jaws. He dropped it at his master's feet and dashed off again as Raven threw it into the sky.

Collins had come to this very spot, seeking Raven out, spouting what sounded like a crazy conspiracy theory. Shortly afterwards, Constable Dean Gibson of the MOD Police had been killed and his body burned at an isolated spot on the moors. It couldn't be a coincidence.

If there was one person Raven wanted to speak to right now more than any other, it was Sean Collins. He regretted now that he hadn't taken the man for a coffee, sobered him up, and listened properly to what he had to say. The ex-soldier had clearly been in desperate need, and Raven had let him down.

I've been looking for you everywhere. You've got to listen to me.

If he had taken the time to listen, might Dean Gibson still be alive?

Raven's mind was a maelstrom of questions and regrets. It wasn't good enough that he had saved the life of his old friend a long time ago in the heat of battle. Somehow, Sean had got himself into trouble once again. Deep trouble. Raven couldn't even begin to guess how deep.

They'll kill us all, Raven! There's not much time!

One thing he knew. He had to do everything he could to help.

Quincey returned with the ball, dropped it at Raven's feet, and waited expectantly. Raven was happy to oblige. The dog bounded off once more, kicking sand as he raced across the shore.

They kept the game going until nearly midnight and dog and ball were black shadows beneath a diamond-studded sky, but Sean Collins didn't appear.

CHAPTER 19

For the first night since the discovery of the body on the moor, Raven didn't dream of being a soldier. He slept the grateful sleep of the dead. He was awoken early on Saturday morning by the ringing of his phone and answered it still groggy. The voice of the duty sergeant quickly brought him to full alert.

He sat up in bed with a start. 'What? Where?'

'At the old World War Two radar station in Ravenscar, sir. It's on the coast, just south of the town.'

'What's the description of the victim?'

'A bit sketchy on details. White. Male. Middle-aged.'

Shit. Raven prayed it wasn't who he feared. 'I'll be there as soon as I can.'

He ended the call and dialled Becca's number. The phone rang and rang before she eventually answered. 'Raven?'

'Did I wake you?'

There was a sound of fumbling at her end of the line, followed by a groan. 'It's only just after seven o'clock. On a weekend.'

'Sorry. Can't be helped. A body's been found. Can you

be ready in half an hour?'

She groaned again. 'Come and pick me up.'

Quincey must have heard him speaking on the phone. He nudged the bedroom door open with his nose and cocked his head enquiringly.

'Sorry, mate,' said Raven, climbing out of bed. 'No time for your morning walk. I've got to work. But don't worry, I'll sort you out first.'

He showered and dressed at lightning speed and then took Quincey for a short walk around the block while he debated what to do. Should he phone Vicky and see if she'd be willing to take Quincey for the day? She would probably agree, but he preferred to keep formal dog minding arrangements for weekdays. What about Melanie? She'd be only too delighted to have Quincey, but he didn't want to take advantage. The third option was to take the dog with him. That was the simplest solution, but he knew Quincey would end up cooped in the car for far too long. In the end, he dialled Melanie's number before he could change his mind.

Her voice sounded bright and sparkly despite the early hour. 'Hello, Tom, how lovely to hear from you.' She probably thought he was phoning to arrange some fun activity. A day out together, or an invitation to dinner.

Raven hated to let her down, but after he'd outlined his predicament she didn't sound the least bit disappointed.

'Bring him over,' said Melanie. 'I'd love to have him.'

'Are you sure? I feel as if I'm imposing.'

'Not at all. Don't be silly. I'll expect you here in ten minutes.'

'Well, that's that,' said Raven, looking down into Quincey's expectant face. 'Another day with Lulu.' He really was totally ill-suited to owning a dog. But Quincey didn't seem to mind. He thumped his tail enthusiastically against the ground. 'I don't deserve you,' said Raven. 'And you deserve better than me.'

He deposited Quincey at Melanie's house, apologising once again, then drove straight to Becca's apartment block on the beachfront. She was outside waiting for him, catching some early morning rays.

The expression on her face was hardly sunny, however. 'You told me half an hour,' she said accusingly, looking at her watch. 'I've been waiting outside for fifteen minutes.'

'Sorry,' he said. 'I had to make arrangements for Quincey.'

'I could have used another quarter of an hour in bed.' She climbed into the passenger seat and buckled her seatbelt. 'Ravenscar, you said. Any idea who the victim is?'

Raven had his suspicions, but still hoped he was wrong. 'No identification as yet.'

*

Becca could happily have spent a lot longer than a quarter of an hour in bed. More like all day. She hadn't got to sleep until the early hours of the morning, and her body was still working hard to process the vast amount of alcohol that had been consumed.

Once she'd got over the shock of realising that Ellie and Liam had tricked her into going on the double date from hell, she'd been pleasantly surprised to discover that her own date was quite charming and thoughtful. Not to mention a bit of a dish.

Liam had paid the price, literally, footing the bill for the entire evening. And Ellie had done her best to make up for her transgressions by being extra considerate and entertaining. She did most of the talking throughout dinner so that Becca and Daniel hardly spoke a word to each other. But Daniel had a good sense of humour, and when he contributed to the conversation his remarks were intelligent and well-considered. All in all, Becca thought she might like to get to know him better, but for that to happen she would have to meet him without the constraining presence of Ellie and Liam as third and fourth wheels.

By the end of the evening she was astonished to

discover that they had polished off four bottles of wine between them on top of the pre-dinner drinks at the seafront bar. She couldn't say how much she had personally consumed but had a nasty feeling it was more than her fair share. When she stood up to leave the restaurant, it took her a moment to get her balance.

'Steady as she goes!' Liam laughed, and Daniel reached out a helping hand to catch her.

They walked back through Peasholm Park, Ellie and Liam strolling ahead, their arms wrapped around each other like love-struck teenagers. Becca and Daniel ambled behind, side-by-side, but not touching. Daniel seemed to sense she wasn't ready to rush, and she was relieved that for this first meeting he was happy to walk with his hands in his jacket pockets and not try to take her hand.

'I hope that wasn't too awful,' he said as they skirted the edge of the boating lake.

'Not at all. I've had a great time. Although, I think I might have a hangover in the morning.'

When they reached the apartment block, Ellie announced that she and Liam were going for a paddle in the sea. Becca didn't think that was such a good idea in their inebriated state, but there was no point trying to stop them. They kicked off their shoes and chased each other across the sand.

'Don't worry,' said Daniel. 'They won't go in too far. The shock of the cold will sober them up.'

Becca glanced up at the sky. It was the deepest blue, scattered with jewels. A gorgeous summer night with scarcely a breath of wind to disturb the stillness. Far away across the beach, the sea murmured softly, glimmering in the darkness. She wondered if Daniel was expecting her to invite him in. Was that why Ellie and Liam had made themselves scarce? She opened her mouth to speak, but Daniel spoke first.

'You look tired,' he said. 'I'll let you get some rest.' He brushed her cheek with his hand and strode away with a friendly wave. 'Let's do dinner again sometime.'

'Yes, let's,' she called after him. 'Just the two of us next time.'

The BMW pulled onto a roundabout, throwing Becca to one side and bouncing her back to reality. She clutched at her stomach, hoping she wasn't going to be reacquainted with her meal of the previous evening.

'Heavy night?' asked Raven.

'Went out for a couple of drinks. But I'm fine now.'

'Good. Then you can tell me about this World War Two radar station we're going to.'

She turned an incredulous face in his direction. 'For someone who grew up in Scarborough, you really do know very little about the area.'

'It's been remarked upon before,' said Raven wearily as the car pulled north out of town, heading uphill. Ravenscar was on the coast, midway between Scarborough and Whitby. The satnav informed them they would be there in just over twenty minutes. 'So tell me what I missed.'

For once, Raven took the journey at a sensible speed, apparently not feeling the usual compulsion to put his foot to the floor and overtake every other vehicle on the road. The man they were going to see was dead already. Getting there in a hurry wasn't going to bring him back to life.

Becca and her half-digested dinner were grateful for the measured pace. 'Funny place, Ravenscar,' she began. 'It's known as the town that never was.'

Raven raised one querying eyebrow.

'It's not really a town at all,' she continued, 'just a tiny village on top of the cliffs, but there were grand plans in the late nineteenth century to build a seaside resort to rival Scarborough or Blackpool. There would have been houses, hotels, shops and even a railway station. There are maps showing what it would have looked like when it was completed. It was going to be a new town.'

'A bit like Milton Keynes?' said Raven.

Becca laughed. 'Think of it as Milton Keynes by Sea.'

'So what went wrong?'

'It started out well enough. Hundreds of plots were sold

and they got as far as digging sewers and laying new roads, but then the company went bust and the houses were never built. I think the problem was that Ravenscar has no sandy beach, just rocks at the bottom of the cliff. When investors found out the truth, they got cold feet.'

'A beach resort without a beach,' mused Raven. 'It sounds like a scam.'

He followed the instructions on the satnav and turned off the main road. Soon they were careering along a rollercoaster of a road with the name of Bloody Beck Hill. Becca thought the name exceedingly apt.

'Just take it a bit slower, please,' she begged.

They soon arrived in the village of Ravenscar, passing the church and a sign for Raven Hall Country House Hotel & Lodges. The road turned right and they followed it to its abrupt end. At Station Road, a small row of buildings, including a tearoom, overlooked a rectangular green. A number of marked police cars were parked around the edge of the green. A CSI van was there too. Holly Chang would definitely not be pleased to have been called out so early on a Saturday morning.

Raven parked the M6 behind the van and they got of the car. The sea at the foot of the cliffs was a shimmering blue beneath a cloudless sky. You could see for miles along the coast, right across the sweeping curve of Robin Hood's Bay to the north. Ravenscar may have lacked a beach, but it made up for it with breathtaking clifftop views.

Becca sighed. It was far too beautiful a day to be examining a dead body.

A uniformed officer approached.

'Which way to the crime scene?' asked Raven.

The PC tugged thoughtfully at his beard. 'You can follow the Cleveland Way down there,' he said, pointing to a footpath that ran along the cliff edge. 'That's the shortest route. Or you can take the Cinder Track over there.' He indicated a parallel path further inland. 'That follows the route of the old railway track.'

Becca saw that both paths had been closed off to the

public and were being guarded by a pair of officers.

'Which way is easier?' asked Raven.

'The Cinder Track is straight and smooth. The Cleveland Way can get a bit muddy in places.'

'Straight and smooth sounds good to me,' said Raven. He thanked the bobby for the advice and he and Becca set off inland.

There was no longer a station at Ravenscar, but the original platform was still in position. Beyond it lay the Cinder Track, which was, as promised, as straight as an arrow. The old railway tracks that had once passed this way were long gone but what remained was a broad, well-maintained path, perfect for walking or cycling. Hedgerows ran along the inland edge of the path. To the left, a dry stone wall separated the path from fields, beyond which lay the sea.

They walked for about half a mile before reaching a five-bar gate guarded by another uniformed officer. He seemed to be expecting them.

'Morning, sir, ma'am.' He nodded at Raven and Becca in turn. 'The body's over there inside the old radar station.' He pointed to a collection of low-lying buildings still some distance away on the other side of a farmer's field. The field was full of cows. They chewed the cud and regarded the detectives with mild curiosity.

'First sheep, now cows,' muttered Raven. 'What next?' But there was nothing for it – they would have to pass through the field in order to reach the crime scene.

Becca hoped the cows were docile creatures.

The PC opened the gate for them, then shut it quickly behind them to prevent any of the herd making a bolt for it.

That didn't bode well.

Becca began to make her way across the grass, mindful of the many cowpats that separated her from their final destination at the far end of the field. The cows mooed at the intrusion into their patch and one of the animals moved to block their path.

'Know anything about cows?' asked Raven.

'Stay calm,' advised Becca. 'And keep a wide berth. They're easily frightened by strangers.'

'They don't look frightened. They look… cross.'

More cows were approaching, plodding their way with determination across the muddy ground.

'Don't make any sudden movements,' warned Becca. 'If one panics, they'll all panic.'

'Great,' said Raven, making a wide detour around the oncoming herd. 'It's at times like this, I wish I was still back on the mean streets of London. At least then I had nothing more dangerous to deal with than armed gangs.'

The cows regarded them menacingly for a while, as if weighing up whether a frenzied mass charge was worth their while, but gradually lost interest in the newcomers as Raven and Becca trudged around the edge of the field and circled back towards the low-lying group of buildings where the white-clad CSI team was at work.

'And this was supposed to be the easy way,' moaned Raven, examining his muddy shoes.

At the edge of the site, they paused to study a tourist information sign informing them that the radar station had been built in 1940. A painting showed primitive radar equipment mounted over a long building that looked like a brick polytunnel with a corrugated asbestos roof. The semi-cylindrical structure was still there, now minus its radar equipment. A handful of nearby buildings resembling small concrete bunkers had been used as storehouses and an engine house.

If the radar station at RAF Fylingdales resembled the landing site of an alien super-race, the old World War Two station at Ravenscar looked more like a collection of derelict cowsheds. Radar technology had clearly advanced somewhat in the eighty years since the war. Nevertheless, this was where it had all started, back in the forties when the doughty men and women operating this equipment had helped Britain win the war by detecting low-flying enemy aircraft approaching the coastline. They had been pioneers of a sort. Could they have imagined something as high-tech as the – what had Flight Lieutenant Jones called it? – the Solid State Phased Array system?

Holly Chang, clad in her white coveralls, emerged from the radar building and approached them.

'Another inaccessible spot for a murder,' she complained. 'One of those bloody cows almost ran me into the ground.' She glared at the animals who were now quietly chewing grass and seemed resigned to having their home invaded by police and CSI teams alike.

Raven wisely made no comment.

'Where is the body?' asked Becca.

'Inside the Nissen hut.' Holly pointed to the brick and asbestos building. 'Follow me. I'll show you.'

Approaching the old building, Becca saw that although the entrance doorway was sealed with a padlocked metal gate, part of the corrugated roof was missing, leaving a gap wide enough for anyone to squeeze inside. No doubt the place attracted inquisitive tourists and bored teenagers alike. The rickety wooden fence placed around the building would do little to keep out anyone who wanted to get in. Even Raven was able to climb over the fence with ease, although Holly preferred to clamber underneath where one of the horizontal bars was missing.

Becca followed Raven over the top, her legs scarcely long enough to reach. She must look ridiculous, but that hardly mattered. She had left her dignity behind at the entrance to the cow field.

The rest of the CSI team were busy inside the hut. Peering in through the gap in the roof, Becca saw Erin and Jamie, Holly's latest recruits, taking photographs and dusting for prints.

And there, sprawled on the concrete floor of the building, lay the body of a man.

White, middle-aged, of scruffy appearance, his hair long and matted and his grey beard unkempt. A blood stain on his clothing showed where he had been stabbed multiple times in the chest and stomach. A brutal killing.

'Any sign of the murder weapon?' asked Becca.

'Not yet,' said Holly. 'But we'll keep looking. No ID for the victim either. We looked in his rucksack, but it contained nothing except a bottle of booze and some food and clothing. He didn't have a phone or a credit card on him.'

Becca glanced back to the body. The man was dressed in khaki combat gear and looked as if he'd been sleeping rough, perhaps here in this very hut. 'I suspect he didn't own anything like that.'

'Maybe not. We did find this on the body though. It was in an inside pocket of his cargo pants.' Holly held out an evidence bag containing a small brass key. 'Too small for a door key. We don't know what it's for.' The key was stained red with blood.

Raven turned away, his face pale. He said nothing, just clambered back over the fence and walked off a short distance.

Holly shot Becca a curious look. 'Not like your boss to be squeamish.'

'I think he may know the victim,' said Becca. Although she had never seen this man before, judging by what Raven had said, and from the description given by Constable Dean Gibson of the intruder at RAF Fylingdales, she guessed this was Raven's old army mate from the Duke of Wellington's Regiment, Private Sean Collins. She didn't need to see any more.

She climbed back over the fence and joined Raven. He had his back to the radar station and was staring out at the perfectly blue sea. A white sailing boat was just visible in the far distance.

'He survived the war in the Balkans, only to end up dead here,' Raven muttered. 'I should have listened to him. This is all my fault.'

Becca laid a hand on his arm. 'No, Raven, it's the fault of whoever killed him. And we're going to nail that bastard.'

Raven looked like he was choking back tears, but he

141

nodded, acknowledging the truth of her words.

CHAPTER 20

'So, you and Sean Collins knew each other from your army days?'

Becca was back in Raven's car, leaving the latest crime scene behind them. They had seen all there was and now it was up to Holly and her team to finish scouring the Nissen hut to see if any further evidence could be recovered.

They'd taken the longer route back from the old radar station, avoiding the cows this time and instead enjoying the scenic walk along the clifftop. Miles of rugged coastline stood above an aquamarine sea beneath a cobalt sky. The only cloud was the black one that seemed to follow Raven wherever he went. He lumbered silently along the narrow path, his collar up and his head down, as if the sunshine affronted him. Becca knew she would get nothing out of him when he was in that mood.

But in the car he had little choice but to answer her questions.

'We served together in the same regiment,' he confirmed, his focus on the road. His driving style had reverted to type, sprinting down the narrow straights and spinning hard around bends as if taking part in a time trial.

Becca waited until they were safely over the white-knuckle ride of Bloody Beck Hill and the contents of her stomach had resettled before resuming her interrogation 'And he was with you in Bosnia?'

'That's right.'

It seemed she was going to have to prise every last scrap of information out of him.

She knew there were things Raven wasn't telling her. She recognised this withdrawn, uncommunicative mode he adopted when he wasn't sharing information. It drove her mad, but she tried to keep her tone light and friendly.

'Where were you stationed?'

'In a town called Goražde. We were there as part of the UN protection force. Our mandate was to secure the so-called "safe area". But nowhere in that country was truly safe.'

Becca already knew that Raven had seen active combat during his deployment to Bosnia. During a routine patrol, his unit had come under fire from Bosnian Serb soldiers. Raven had left his position and engaged the enemy to provide cover for two injured members of his patrol, enabling them to escape with their lives. He had been shot in the leg, then later awarded a medal in acknowledgement of his bravery.

Becca hadn't even been born when the Bosnian War was fought. The whole thing was a mystery to her, as remote as World War Two. It felt weird to be sitting next to someone who not only remembered it but had been an active participant in its drama. Raven had opened fire on enemy soldiers, maybe even killing them. Perhaps that explained the darkness within his soul. And also his reluctance to talk about his experience.

But that was a lonely way to live your life.

Besides, if they were going to solve this double murder, Becca needed to know the truth.

'Was Sean with you when... when you were shot?'

Raven nodded grimly. 'He was injured too.'

'And you provided covering fire so that Sean could be taken to safety. You saved his life.'

The suggestion seemed to make him angry. 'I did what anyone would have done.'

Becca had little doubt he was downplaying his part in the skirmish that had finished his army career. She couldn't understand his unwillingness to take credit for his actions. His bravery was something to be proud of. But she knew she wouldn't get anything else out of him for the time being.

The car stopped at the junction with the A171 and Becca expected him to turn back towards Scarborough. But instead he swung the steering wheel to the right, taking them in the Whitby direction.

'Where are we going?'

'Back to RAF Fylingdales. I want to find out more about this encounter with Sean that Dean Gibson reported. I want to know why both men are dead.'

Becca nodded. The idea made sense. It was becoming clear that the RAF station was central to unravelling both murders. What once looked as if it might have been a simple case of an unfaithful husband and a knuckle-headed brother-in-law had taken on a darker and far more complex hue.

She knew it was pointless to probe Raven further about his time in Bosnia, but there was still more she wanted to know about the latest victim. 'Did Sean Collins have family?'

'His parents are dead,' said Raven. 'And he never married, at least as far as I know. But he did have a younger brother. He used to talk about him in Bosnia and write letters home.'

'They were close, then. Any idea where he lives?'

'None whatsoever. But if anyone can track him down, Tony can.'

'I'll get onto him on Monday,' said Becca.

'This is a murder inquiry,' Raven reminded her.

They both knew that fact trumped niceties like weekends and personal lives.

'I'll call him now,' said Becca. She dialled Tony's

number before they entered the no-signal zone that surrounded the radar station. The call was answered immediately. 'Oh, hi Tony. Listen, I know it's your day off, but if you wouldn't mind finding something out for me...'

★

Raven breathed a sigh of relief as the tip of the radar of RAF Fylingdales became visible above the flat horizon of the moors. For the entire car journey since they had left Ravenscar, Becca had been determined to squeeze every last drop of information out of him about his time in Bosnia with Sean Collins. But that was the last topic he wanted to discuss. He had survived the after-effects of war by resolutely not talking about it all these years to anyone and he had no intention of changing that habit now.

Besides, he was no hero. Just a wounded soldier. Yet another casualty of battle.

He knew that Becca's questions were perfectly reasonable. She was doing her job as a detective. Asking questions. Looking for patterns. But the solution to the murder investigation wasn't to be found in the past. The answer lay in the present.

A conspiracy. An unnamed enemy. An act of treason.

What secret had Sean Collins unearthed? And how had Dean Gibson become entangled in its sinister mesh?

The answer would be found at RAF Fylingdales.

He turned the car off the main road and approached the checkpoint. The MOD police officer on duty informed him that Flight Lieutenant Mark Jones wasn't available. It was his day off.

Raven gave the man a dismissive glare. Day off? It was Raven's day off too. And yet here he was. 'The person I really want to speak to is Sergeant Gary Murphy of the MOD Police,' he explained. 'Is he available?'

'Just one moment, sir.'

The officer made a phone call, asked to be put through

to someone, explained who was at the gate, said he didn't know what the matter was about, and eventually hung up, looking relieved.

'Sergeant Murphy will come to meet you himself.'

'Good,' said Raven. No doubt the sergeant would be in an even worse humour at being called away from his office than when they had interrupted him at his desk. Not that Raven cared what Gary Murphy felt. The man had been an impediment to the investigation from start to finish.

Becca was clearly of the same opinion. 'We'll just wait here for Sergeant Grumpy to show up,' she whispered.

But to Raven's surprise, after ten minutes a much more welcoming Gary Murphy appeared to meet them. 'Raven,' he said, reaching out jovially to shake his hand. 'Sorry to keep you waiting. Come with me. I'll drive you onto the base.'

The three of them climbed into Murphy's Land Rover and headed off towards the inner checkpoint.

'I'm sorry to drag you away from your desk,' said Raven, 'but apparently it's Flight Lieutenant Jones's day off.'

Murphy snorted dismissively. 'We don't need your minder to look after us.'

'Wing Commander Fitzwilliam-Brown assigned him to us,' said Raven. 'He's supposed to accompany us at all times.'

'To assist you?' Murphy gave Raven a sideways grin. 'Or to keep an eye on you?'

'Perhaps a bit of both.'

Murphy chuckled. 'The wing commander's a good bloke, even if he is Eton educated. That's what you expect of RAF top brass. Those right at the top of the social pecking order can often be quite down-to-earth, I find. They've got nothing to prove. Flight Lieutenant Jones on the other hand...'

'You don't like him,' said Becca. 'Is it personal?'

'Partly. He's the kind of bloke who sucks up to his superiors and lords it over everyone he thinks is below him.

People like me.'

Raven was surprised by the change in Murphy's demeanour and by his frank comments about his colleagues. He decided to capitalise on the sergeant's unexpected volubility. 'Does Flight Lieutenant Jones have something to prove?'

'Ha, you bet he does. In his case, it's more a matter of redeeming himself.'

Raven was all ears, and Murphy didn't need any encouragement. Now he'd got started, there was no stopping him.

'I know you've got a military background, DCI Raven,' he said. 'I've been reading up on you.'

Raven's heart sank. No matter how hard he tried to hide his past, the story of his army career was just a few clicks away on a search engine. News stories no longer faded into obscurity, they were preserved for eternity on the internet.

Murphy's voice was full of approval. 'I found a news article all about your exploits with the Dukes in Bosnia. Awarded the Conspicuous Gallantry Cross. Impressive.'

So this explained the turnaround in Murphy's attitude. In the sergeant's worldview, Raven had been transformed from just another superior officer "lording it over everyone below them" to someone worthy of respect. Raven grunted, wishing the sergeant would get on with his story. He avoided meeting Becca's eye.

Once they were through the inner checkpoint, Murphy slowed the vehicle to a crawl and leaned in towards Raven as if to impart a confidence. 'So you'll understand what I'm about to tell you. Mark Jones was a rising star in the RAF. He piloted Eurofighter Typhoons and was tipped to become a squadron leader. But then things went south. He gave an incorrect order to a junior pilot during an engagement with an unauthorised Russian Tupolev Tu-95 that had entered UK airspace. Could have been fatal. Nearly was. It could have kicked off World War Three. The incident almost ended his career, but he was given a second chance. He was grounded, taken off active duty and sent here to the radar base where he can't do any harm.' Murphy pulled up in front of his building and cut the engine. 'Here we are.'

Raven and Becca exchanged a glance as they followed Murphy inside. She'd clearly been as surprised as he was by Murphy's revelations regarding the flight lieutenant. Raven had quite liked Jones, finding him friendly and amenable. The RAF officer was clearly pulling out all the stops in his efforts to redeem himself and make up for past failings. But perhaps it was understandable that Murphy might harbour a grudge towards him.

'So, what can I do for you this time?' asked Murphy once they were inside his office.

Gary Murphy was going out of his way to be Raven's best buddy, but even though he was an MOD police officer, Raven felt no need to share the news of Sean Collins's murder with him. Nor did he want to reveal more about the direction of his thinking than was necessary. 'I'd like to know everything you can tell me about security incidents at the base. Intruders, protesters, that sort of thing. Any kind of subversive activity or threats.'

'How far back do you want to go?'

'A year or two?' said Raven.

'Hang on, let me see what I can dig out. Take a seat.'

Raven and Becca sat while Murphy tapped away on his computer keyboard. Soon the printer sprang to life, spilling out sheets of paper. Murphy scooped them up and handed them to Raven. 'That lot covers the past two years. You'll see that we've only had one incursion during that time – that's in the report that Dean Gibson filed. But we do have regular incidents with protesters at the gate.'

'What about threats?' asked Raven.

'Bomb threats, you mean?' Murphy frowned. 'Do you have some intel I should be aware of?'

'No,' said Raven. 'I'm just fishing.'

'We haven't had anything like that. Not specific to the base, at any rate. But you'll be aware of the general threat level.'

Raven nodded, recalling the sign at the checkpoint announcing the current threat from terrorism to the United Kingdom as a whole. *Substantial.* Not exactly a reassuring state of affairs, but not a cause for panic either. He slid the printouts into a folder.

'Was there anything else?' asked Murphy.

'Actually, just one thing,' said Raven. 'Do you mind if I use your landline for a moment?'

*

Did he mind being called into work on his day off? That was a question DC Tony Bairstow rarely asked himself. He'd known when he first joined the police force that irregular hours and overtime were part of the job, and he accepted that. The overtime pay sometimes came in handy, not that Tony had huge expenses. He didn't have an extravagant lifestyle, held little interest in flashy cars or travel to exotic places, and was happy with the small terraced house where he lived alone. His regular hobbies didn't cost much. Brewing his own beer was a good way to save money, and he didn't drink a lot, just a pint in the evenings after work.

However, there was one part of his life that did require time. And money too.

It wasn't a secret exactly, but he had never told anyone at work about it. The fact was that his colleagues rarely asked him how he liked to spend his weekends and days off. Raven tended to assume that his junior staff would always be available when he called them up with his requests, however late the hour or unreasonable the demand. That was probably how he had made it to the lofty heights of detective chief inspector. Tony knew he probably ought to be thinking about a promotion himself before he got too old. Being a detective constable at his age when Becca had already made it to sergeant probably pointed to a lack of ambition on his part. But Tony didn't really aspire to anything grander. Maybe detective sergeant one day, although he didn't really fancy the additional responsibility and management that would entail.

Anyway, about his secret. Which wasn't really a secret.

He wasn't ashamed of it, but perhaps he was a little embarrassed.

He liked dressing up. Not in anything kinky, nothing like that. But he had always had a strong interest in the English Civil War. People had sometimes asked him why, but he had never come up with a convincing answer. There was just something fascinating about it. Such a dramatic period of history. The execution of a king. The rise of Parliament and the New Model Army. Battles on a hitherto unprecedented scale. Muskets, pikes and cavalry.

The thought of it triggered images of polished metal armour, the beating of drums and the cries of men, the smell of gunpowder and the whinnying of horses.

If this weekend had been the occasion of one of Tony's battle re-enactment events, he would have dodged Raven's phone call, made himself scarce and shot off to war without a backward glance.

But fortunately his weekend was free.

And apart from being a foot soldier in Cromwell's New Model Army, the activity he most enjoyed was doing his job. He knew he had a special knack for ferreting out hard-to-find information. Financial transactions, property records, names, addresses and telephone numbers. No matter how well hidden they were, he could find them. And there were few things more satisfying than digging up a fact that would make a difference.

So, yeah, working on a weekend. It wasn't a problem. Not this time.

In this particular case, it hadn't been much of a challenge to track down the name and address of Sean Collins's brother. Tony had found the information he was looking for within half an hour of sitting down at his desk. Now all he needed was for Becca or Raven to call back. He'd tried to reach them but neither was answering their phone. Out on the moors, was Tony's guess. It was impossible to get a signal out there.

The phone on his desk burst into life and he picked up. 'DC Tony Bairstow speaking.'

'Tony, Raven here, just wondered if there was any news on the whereabouts of Sean Collins's brother?'

'Yes, sir. I tried to call you but couldn't get a reply.'

'We're at RAF Fylingdales. No signal here. In fact, no phones at all. We had to hand them in at the gate. I'm using the landline in Sergeant Murphy's office.'

'Thought that might be the case,' said Tony. 'Anyway, the brother's name is Brian Collins. Lives in Sleights, just south of Whitby.' Tony read out the address so Raven could write it down.

'Sleights, you say? That's on our way back to Scarborough. Good work, Tony. You can go home and relax now.'

'Thank you, sir. Just one other thing. I checked with the taxi firm regarding Gavin Wilcox's alibi. They confirmed that he started work early on Monday morning and was busy right through to mid-afternoon.'

'So he couldn't have murdered Dean Gibson.'

'No, sir. He was already on his way to the airport when Dean Gibson left home.'

'Well, thanks for doing that. Oh, by the way, there's something else you could do for me.' Raven had apparently forgotten that a moment earlier he'd told Tony to go home and relax. Tony listened patiently to what Raven had to say. 'Could you start looking into protests at RAF Fylingdales please?'

'Any particular protests?'

'Hang on, I've got some dates here.' There was a clunk as Raven put the receiver down. Tony heard paper rustling and indistinct voices in the background before the phone was picked up again. 'Start with these.' Raven read out a list of dates and Tony noted them down.

'Anything else?'

'That should keep you going for now. And thanks,

Tony, I do appreciate it.'

'No problem, sir.' Tony hung up. Raven wasn't a bad boss when all was said and done.

He made himself another mug of tea and opened a packet of digestive biscuits. A new challenge required fresh sustenance.

Raven's request was fairly vague, but Tony figured that news reports would probably help to explain what kind of protests might be taking place outside a radar station in the middle of the moors. It didn't take him long to dig out some articles that shed light on the matter.

A series of anti-nuclear demonstrations had been mounted outside the main entrance to RAF Fylingdales, aimed at drawing attention to the role the facility played in NATO's defences against long-range ballistic missile attack.

The leader of the protesters was named as a thirty-nine-year-old lecturer at Teesside University called Aaron Blake. Dr Blake taught sociology when he wasn't waving banners and causing trouble outside RAF bases. On one occasion he had been arrested and charged with causing criminal damage to the perimeter fence. It wasn't his first such offence, and he had been lucky to escape a custodial sentence.

Tony cross-checked the newspaper reports of incidents and the dates Raven had given him against the police database to see if anyone else had been arrested. Back in March, a number of protesters had been taken into custody during a big demonstration outside the main gate, including sixty-five-year-old Janice Sillitoe and twenty-five-year-old Matthew Whelan, who had both been given a warning for a first offence. Now where had Tony heard those names before?

He pulled out the notes from the current investigation and quickly found what he was looking for. Janice and Matthew had been doing the Lyke Wake Walk with Jess when they found the body of Constable Dean Gibson on top of Lilla Howe. Well, Raven would be very interested when he heard that.

Tony rewarded himself with another biscuit. It had been well worth giving up his day off after all.

CHAPTER 21

It seemed fair to say that Brian Collins was an average kind of guy. His home on Birch Crescent in Sleights was a typical semi-detached house dating from the sixties or seventies. Brick facade, brown front door, white PVC windows. A blue Ford Focus occupied the driveway in front of the house, and a man in his early forties, his sleeves rolled up, had his head stuck under the car's bonnet as he tinkered with the engine.

'Mr Collins?'

The man had his back to Raven, but when he straightened up and turned around, the resemblance to Raven's old army pal was unmistakable. The same deep-set eyes, broad forehead and prominent chin. Brian was the younger brother and looked like a softer-edged version of Sean. It was a vision of how Sean might have turned out if life had been kinder to him.

'Yes? Who are you?' He looked from Raven to Becca then back to Raven.

'DCI Tom Raven from Scarborough CID and this is my colleague DS Becca Shawcross. Could we come inside and have a word, please?'

Brian held an oil can in his right hand and an oily cloth in his left. 'I've got my hands a bit full. Can we do this outside?'

'It's about your brother, Sean.'

Brian's face fell. 'Oh, aye. You'd better come in then.' He wiped his hands on the cloth and closed the bonnet of the car.

He left them waiting by the back door while he put the engine oil away in the shed. Two children aged about ten were jumping on a trampoline in the back garden. 'Come through to the kitchen,' he said, inviting Raven and Becca into the house. They waited once more while he washed his hands at the kitchen sink. 'Wife's gone shopping,' he explained. 'She'll kill me if I get oil everywhere.'

They followed him into a beige-carpeted lounge containing a leather sofa suite and a TV. Children's toys were scattered over the floor and stacked in a box in one corner. It was a world away from the derelict shed where Sean had met his end.

Raven and Becca took the sofa while Brian sat down in one of the two armchairs. 'What's happened then?' he asked. 'Is Sean in trouble?'

'I'm sorry to tell you that we have bad news,' said Raven. 'Your brother's body was discovered this morning at Ravenscar. We're treating his death as murder.'

Brian bowed his head as he took in the news. 'Poor old Sean,' he muttered.

'You don't seem particularly surprised,' said Raven. Usually when he broke this sort of news to the relatives of victims he was met with shock, anger and grief, often all three.

Brian shook his head. 'Deeply saddened. But surprised? No, I can't say I am. Sean has suffered from mental illness for a long time. Ever since he left the army. I've worried for a long time that something bad would happen to him. He's been living rough on the moors and along the coast. I did what I could for him, but we didn't have room here to have him live with us.' He gestured with his arms, as if to indicate the lack of space. 'Sally, that's the wife, would never have stood for it. Anyroad, Sean was a proud man. He would never accept charity, even from his own kin.'

Raven nodded, remembering how angry Sean had become when Raven had offered him money to buy a hot meal.

'Any ideas who did it?' asked Brian.

'Not at this stage,' said Raven. 'We're keeping an open mind.'

Becca pulled out a photo of the small brass key that had been found on the body. 'Have you seen this key before, Mr Collins? Do you have any idea what it's for?'

'This belonged to Sean?' Brian looked surprised. 'He didn't own owt. Might just be something he picked up someplace. He did all kinds of strange things.'

'Can you tell us more about him?' said Raven. 'How did he end up living rough?'

Brian sighed. 'It's a long story. Do you have time for it?'

'Absolutely,' said Raven.

Brian's gaze drifted to his children's toys. 'He was my hero, when we were small. Two little boys, playing at soldiers. He was a few years older than me, and I always looked up to him. He liked that. But he didn't do very well at school, so when he was sixteen he joined the army. Duke of Wellington's Regiment. Our mum wasn't happy, but my dad was glad he'd found something to do. Jobs were hard to come by, in those days. Anyway, long story short, he got sent abroad. Dropped into the middle of the Bosnian War. Someplace I can never remember the name of.'

It was on the tip of Raven's tongue to say "Goražde" but he didn't want to interrupt the story. Nor to reveal his own part in it.

'Sean was dead excited to be going,' said Brian, now with a faraway look in his eyes as if seeing his brother as he was nearly thirty years ago. 'It was all he'd ever wanted, to be sent into battle. He wrote letters home to me, telling me all about it. I kept them, thinking I might follow him into the army. But I soon gave up on that idea.'

'Because of what happened to Sean in Bosnia?' prompted Becca.

'Aye. Soon enough, it all went tits up for him. His patrol was attacked by enemy soldiers. One dead, several injured, including Sean. He took a bullet, here in the shoulder.' Brian slapped his own shoulder with his hand. 'He would have died if it hadn't been for the lance corporal in his unit. That bloke saved his life. But Sean was never the same again. The doctors patched up his injury, but they couldn't do anything for his mind. He blamed himself for what had happened and convinced himself he'd let everyone down. But he wasn't the one to blame. He served his country as best he could. The British Army should have done a better job of rehabilitating him.'

'What happened after he left the army?' asked Raven, half-dreading to hear the story. For his own part, he'd done nothing to keep in touch with his former compatriots after leaving the military. He'd wanted to draw a line under that part of his life and move on. He couldn't have known what would happen to Sean. He'd been a young man himself, needing to stand on his own two feet and find a new career after the end of his soldiering. But perhaps he should have done more. Perhaps he should have done something.

Brian's voice grew bitter. 'Sean was never the same afterwards. He suffered from psychotic incidents, he couldn't get another job, at least nothing that lasted for long. He started drinking, and that was the beginning of the end for him. He went off the rails completely, started living rough, wandering about the countryside. He figured that if the world cared nothing for him, he would care nothing in return. I saw him less and less as time went by. To tell the truth, that was a relief.'

'Can you think of anyone who might have wanted to harm him?'

Brian shrugged. 'Dunno. There are people around who'll pick on someone like my brother 'cause they don't like the way he looks. They hate anyone who doesn't fit into society. And sure as hell, Sean didn't fit in. He could be a difficult man, starting arguments and so on, especially after he'd been drinking. Which was most of the time, in the end.'

The contrast between the paths the two brothers had followed through life could hardly have been starker. Yet Raven didn't think that Sean Collins had been the victim of a random hate crime. 'Shortly before he died, your brother told someone about a conspiracy. He talked of treason, about enemies who meant harm. Did he ever say anything to you about that?'

Brian looked shocked by the revelation. 'A conspiracy? Bloody hell! He really had taken leave of his senses, hadn't he?'

'So you don't know anything about it?'

'Of course not. What could he possibly have meant? Sean had some really crazy ideas. Some of what he talked about was just gibberish.'

'Like what?'

Brian shrugged. '9/11. The New World Order. The assassination of JFK. I'm an engineer, so I don't believe in complicated explanations for simple problems. I tried to explain to him why he was wrong. But he wouldn't listen.'

The children had now come inside. Raven could hear them in the kitchen, getting something to drink from the fridge.

'We'll need you to make a formal identification of the body later on,' said Raven, getting up to leave.

'Yeah, sure,' said Brian, also standing.

They started to make their way to the door.

'Hang on,' said Brian, as if he'd only just realised something. 'How did you know that the body was Sean's? As far as I know, he carried no ID. No passport, no driving licence, no credit card or anything like that. He lived completely off the grid.'

Raven nodded. 'I recognised him. Your brother and I served together in the army.'

'Raven.' Brian turned the name over, working through

the implications. Finally, he said, 'You're Lance Corporal Raven. You saved my brother's life.'

CHAPTER 22

The Barraclough family barbecue in Rosedale Abbey had become something of a local tradition. Taking place on the Saturday closest to midsummer, friends and neighbours were all invited, the idea being that the Barracloughs would provide the food and the guests would bring the drinks. Since the family knew everyone in the village and for miles around, the arrangement usually ensured they had enough bottles of beer and wine left over to keep them going until Halloween. As Jess's dad, Neil, joked every single year, the occasion was more Corkshire than Yorkshire.

Although Jess now lived in Scarborough, she was glad to be back for this particular family event. This year, the weather had exceeded all expectations, bringing a day of perfect sunshine with temperatures to match. The barbeque was set to be a good one.

Her brother, Jacob, and her sister, Nicola, were carrying sausages, burgers, ribs and kebabs outside to the purpose-built brick barbecue which was big enough to cater for dozens of people. Neil, appropriately dressed in his striped chef's apron, was tending to the burning charcoal with an extra-long pair of barbecue tongs. Meanwhile, Jess was helping her mother, Andrea, prepare bowls of salad in the kitchen.

'I'm so glad you could get away from work this weekend and join us,' said Andrea. 'We love having you around. You know that, don't you?'

'Of course I do and I wouldn't miss this for the world.' Jess knew her mother secretly wished she would resign from the police and find a "nicer" job nearer to home. Her sister taught in the local school and her brother ran a caravan site on the edge of the village. Her father was a vet working out of nearby Kirkbymoorside. Jess was the odd one out, the only member of the family to move away from Rosedale Abbey. Even though she had only moved down the road to Scarborough.

'Will Ronald be here this time?' she asked, changing the subject.

'Oh yes. He's bringing Janice with him from Goathland. And apparently her lodger will be coming too. You know – the one who went walking with you.'

'Matthew,' said Jess. 'Yes, I invited him. I hope you don't mind.'

Andrea smiled at the mention of Matthew's name. 'No, of course not. The more the merrier! It will be nice to catch up with your Lyke Wake Walk friends again. It was such a shame you couldn't finish it the other day. After all the training you did for it.'

'Yes, I'd like to try again sometime.'

'With Matthew?' It was impossible for Andrea to disguise her interest in the new man in Jess's life.

Her mother was showing rather too much interest in Matthew for Jess's liking. But she was saved from having to answer the question by the arrival of the first guests in the garden.

'I'd better take these outside,' said Jess, grabbing a dish of coleslaw and a bowl of cherry tomatoes and escaping with them into the garden.

It didn't take long for the barbecue to get going. The

air was soon filled with the enticing smell of sizzling sausages, glasses were filled and refilled, laughter and conversation were everywhere.

Neil was in his element, greeting everyone as they came to inspect the barbeque, drinks and bottles in hand. 'By heck,' he said to each new arrival, 'It's more Corkshire than Yorkshire!'

Janice and Matthew arrived in the company of Ronald, and Jess greeted them at the gate.

Janice enveloped her in a firm embrace and thrust a homemade cake into her hands. 'I baked it this morning,' she said. 'It's my speciality rum and banana bread.'

'It smells wonderful,' said Jess, clutching the still-warm cake and inhaling the alcoholic fumes. She wondered how much rum had gone into it. The smell was lethal. 'Thank you.'

Matthew presented Jess with an expensive-looking box of chocolates and gave her a slightly awkward peck on the cheek. She wasn't sure if the chocolates were intended just for her. It was a small box of ethically-sourced organic truffles and wouldn't go far among such a large crowd. She thanked him and turned to Ronald who was clutching a bottle of good-quality claret, his usual offering on these occasions.

'Hello Jess, love.' He gave her a quick hug. 'Where shall I put this?'

'Drinks are on that table over there.' She indicated a wooden trestle table groaning with wine, beer, juice, and fizzy pop. 'Just don't show it to Dad unless you want to be subjected to one of his terrible jokes!'

'I think I'll put it in the kitchen,' said Ronald, eyeing the drinks table. 'It's too good for drinking with burgers and sausages. You can share it with your family later.'

She knew he'd say that. He always did. 'Thank you. That's very kind. Come and get something to eat.'

Once Ronald, Janice and Matthew had helped themselves to food, Jess fetched herself a burger with onions and ketchup and went over to join them. The talk at first was about the wonderful weather and how long the sunny spell might last – not much longer was the general consensus – but it was inevitable that the conversation would soon turn to their failed attempt to complete the Lyke Wake Walk and, above all, the reason why they'd had to abandon it.

'Now,' said Janice, wiping barbecue sauce from the corner of her mouth with a paper napkin, 'you won't believe this, but I actually knew the victim, Dean Gibson. His wife, Laura, teaches at the primary school in Goathland where I do a bit of volunteer work. I met her husband at last year's Christmas carol concert. He worked for the MOD police up at the radar station. They seemed like a nice couple. She's devastated, of course. She's been signed off sick until the end of term.'

Jess was surprised to learn that Janice knew the murdered man and his wife. But perhaps that wasn't unexpected, Goathland being such a small village. She hadn't known that Janice helped out at the local school either, but again that wasn't so surprising, Janice being a retired PE teacher.

Janice turned to Jess. 'How is the police investigation coming along?'

Jess had known she'd be asked about the case. She could tell that Ronald and Matthew were all ears too. Despite the gruesome nature of their discovery, or perhaps because of it, they were all enjoying being caught up in a real-life murder mystery. All three of them leaned towards her, their shared experience of finding the body uniting them in their interest, like co-conspirators. They already knew more than most members of the public. Even so, Jess had to be discreet.

'We're making progress,' she said, 'but it's all confidential, I'm afraid.'

'Of course it is,' said Ronald, 'and you're far too professional to share the juicy details with us. I'm sure everything will come out sooner or later. Until then, we'll just have to wait in suspense.'

Jess thought it best to change the subject. 'Do you think we'll get another chance to do the Lyke Wake Walk this summer?' She directed the question to Ronald, who had organised and led the aborted crossing.

'I hope so,' he said. 'I'll see what I can arrange. We do need some fresh blood in the Lyke Wake Club,' he added, looking specifically at Jess and Matthew.

'I'm going to get some of those strawberries before they all go,' announced Janice in a booming voice. 'Why don't you come with me, Ronald?' She took his arm and they left together, heading in the direction of the dessert table.

Not exactly a subtle move. Ronald and Janice were as bad as Jess's mother.

She and Matthew were left alone together. For a moment neither of them spoke.

'So, how are you getting back to Goathland?' Jess asked eventually. She hoped that neither Janice nor Matthew was planning to drive anywhere after this. Ronald had already put away a large glass of red, and Janice's loud laugh could be heard coming from the direction of the drinks table. She had fetched herself a bowl of strawberries and cream and was pouring herself a Prosecco to go with it.

'We're staying overnight with Ronald,' said Matthew. 'He offered to put us up.'

'That was kind of him.'

They fell into silence again, Matthew inspecting his shoes, holding his bottle of beer awkwardly. Jess was wondering how she could politely disentangle herself when he leaned closer.

'I heard you lost someone recently you were close to. I'm sorry.'

'Who told you that?' she shot back at him.

He flinched. 'I'm sorry, I shouldn't have said anything. But Ronald mentioned it in the car. He seemed to think it was something I should know.'

Jess felt a bit miffed to be the subject of local gossip, but that sort of thing was only to be expected in a place the size of Rosedale Abbey. She'd known Ronald all her life and was sure he hadn't meant it unkindly. Perhaps he had sensed that Matthew was interested in her and had wanted to warn the younger man that she was still in mourning for her lost love. It wasn't really Matthew's fault.

'It was a few months ago now,' she said.

'You don't have to tell me if you don't want to.'

But Jess got the impression that Matthew would very much like to know more. She had no reason to dislike him, but he was coming on a bit heavy.

'Let's go and get some dessert,' she said. 'I'm dying to try a slice of Janice's banana bread.'

CHAPTER 23

'What's wrong?' asked Becca as they drove away from Sleights after the interview with Brian Collins. Raven appeared even more morose than usual, driving in silence, his brow a field of deep furrows.

'I let Sean down. Just like the army did. When he needed me most, I refused to help.'

The tragic story that Brian Collins had told them about his brother seemed to have sent Raven over the edge, plunging headlong into an abyss of despair. But Becca was damned if she was going to put up with her boss wallowing in self-pity all the way back to Scarborough. 'You saved the man's life once. That doesn't make you responsible for what happened to him afterwards.'

Raven was having none of it. 'I turned him away when he came to me for help. That does make me responsible.'

'You're only human, Raven.'

That clearly wasn't what he wanted to hear. He set his jaw in a firm line, cutting off further debate.

Becca folded her arms crossly. Well, sod him. Let Raven be a martyr if he wanted. Some people just enjoyed being miserable. She had seen this dark side of him before, beating himself up over things most people wouldn't have given a second thought about. Heaping blame and responsibility upon his shoulders and refusing to talk about it.

Becca knew him better than most. As far as she was aware, she was the only one of his colleagues who knew about his time in the army. She was sure he had never opened up to Tony or Jess, revealing so much of his inner turmoil. She felt she had grown close to him since he'd arrived in Scarborough the previous year, dressed like a funeral director and with a face to match. But was Raven capable of truly being close to anyone?

As she clung on tightly to her seat, Raven taking the twisting road like a speed demon, she found herself wondering how much he shared with this Melanie person, the owner of Lulu, the King Charles Spaniel. He had only mentioned her once, but if she was regularly looking after Quincey for him, she was clearly an important person in his life. The cloying floral perfume that had hung in the car since yesterday had now mostly faded, but a lingering trace still remained. What was the precise nature of the relationship between Raven and Melanie? And how much did he reveal to her?

If anything.

'How certain can we be that the same person was responsible for murdering both victims?' she asked. 'The method of killing was different – in Dean Gibson's case, he was killed by a single blow from some kind of blunt object, whereas Sean Collins died from multiple stab wounds. Plus, no attempt was made to burn Sean's body or to destroy evidence. Could there be two killers, either working independently or together?'

Raven was silent for a minute before responding. 'Yet both victims were linked to RAF Fylingdales. Sean even spoke to Dean over the perimeter fence.'

'Could that be a coincidence?' Becca knew she was merely speculating. The murderer – or murderers – had left no physical evidence behind on Dean Gibson's body, and precious little had been recovered from the crime scene at Ravenscar. The ground had been too hard to leave footprints. So far, no clear fingerprints had been found on the Nissen hut, other than Sean's own prints. No hairs, no fibres, nothing.

The murder weapon, too, had been removed from the scene by the killer. There were no easy clues that would lead them to the murderer.

'Well, we know there's a conspiracy,' said Raven. 'So by definition, more than one person must be involved. So it's quite possible that we're looking for more than one murderer.'

'For sure.' But did that make the case easier to solve? Or harder?

A strange metallic sound came from the front of the car. A grinding, a rumbling, a thumping noise. Raven's frown grew even deeper.

'What's that?' asked Becca.

The clunking ceased, and then returned. Louder this time. Much louder.

Phwump. Crunk. Shlam.

'Is that the engine?'

Raven eased his foot off the power, and the car seemed to recover. 'I don't know. I think it'll be–'

The car gave an almighty scrunch and lurched in the road. Red warning signs lit up the dashboard like a house on fire. The car lost all power and slewed to a crawl.

'Bollocks!' said Raven, jerking the steering wheel to pull the vehicle to the side of the road. He switched his hazard warning lights on, reached down to release the bonnet catch, and stormed out of the car, slamming the door behind him.

Becca watched him from the passenger seat as he clomped his way to the front of the car and yanked up the bonnet. She had no desire to join him while he was in this mood. Better to let him cool off. And the engine too.

She checked her phone. Two bars. Just enough signal

to make a call. She wondered if Daniel, her blind date from the other night might have tried to phone her while she was out at RAF Fylingdales. But there were no messages.

She swung the car door open and went to check on Raven. He was poking furiously at the engine and muttering to himself, but it was obvious he didn't have a clue what he was doing. They could have used someone like Brian Collins right now. He seemed to know his way round the inside of a car engine.

'It's never broken down before,' Raven declared, as if the car had dishonourably violated the terms of some gentleman's agreement.

'Getting on a bit though, isn't it?' said Becca. 'What is it, eighteen years old?'

'It's been well looked after,' he protested. 'Anyway, it's not as old as Jess's car.'

'Jess's car is a deathtrap,' she pointed out.

Eventually Raven straightened up and admitted defeat. 'I'm going to have to call for help.'

Becca looked up and down the road. They were halfway between Sleights and Scarborough on the A171. There wasn't a building in sight. The nearest village was just a pub and three houses. 'I assume you have breakdown cover?'

Raven shook his head. 'I've never needed it before.'

'First time for everything.' Becca eyed the car meaningfully. 'And in this case, maybe not the last.' She pulled out her phone and called the garage that normally serviced her own car. Miraculously they were still open. They were willing to come out to help, but not so quickly on a Saturday evening, and not too cheaply either. She broke the bad news to him. 'Two hours minimum, and it's going to cost you.'

'How much?'

'An arm and a leg.'

Raven shrugged. 'What choice do I have?'

'None.' She was glad he'd seen sense.

They sat down on the long grass at the side of the road,

resigned to a long wait. It was a beautiful evening, the heat of the day beginning to cool, the roadside like a wildflower meadow, full of colour. The sky was deepening, turning pink as the sun slowly sank toward the horizon.

Becca's phone vibrated with an incoming call. Daniel. She walked a short distance from Raven and answered it. 'Hi.'

'Hi,' he said. 'How are you?'

'Good.'

She wanted to say, *I was thinking of you just now*. But that might have given him the wrong idea. It wasn't a good look for a girl to appear desperate.

'Just wondering if you're free this evening?' he asked. 'We could go for a drink. Maybe get some fish and chips. Eat them on the seafront.'

She smiled. Sweet of him to suggest something low key after the full-on partying of the double date. Fish and chips on the seafront sounded fantastic. Relaxed and informal. They could talk and get to know each other a bit better. They'd hardly spoken a word to each other on Thursday night, Ellie had done so much talking. It was a perfect evening for a stroll along the Foreshore, getting stuck into lightly battered haddock and crispy yet fluffy chips, all drenched in salt and vinegar. Her mouth began to water at the prospect. But she knew she could be waiting hours for the breakdown truck to arrive. She looked at her watch. It was already gone seven.

'I'd love to, but I can't make it this evening. I'm stuck with my boss by the side of the A171 waiting for a breakdown truck.'

She wondered if he would valiantly offer to come and rescue her, like a knight on his steed. But who was she kidding? This wasn't make-believe.

'Ah, that's a shame,' he said. 'Another time then?'

'Yeah, definitely.'

She ended the call and returned to sit beside Raven at the roadside.

He made no reference to her phone call. Instead he

asked, 'What did you make of Brian Collins's claim that Sean was a conspiracy theorist?'

Becca nodded slowly. 'It tallies with what Sean told you, doesn't it? That wild claim he made about some kind of enemy plot.'

'Traitors,' said Raven. 'You think he was simply delusional? He believed in it enough to seek me out. He believed in it enough to try to get inside RAF Fylingdales at night.'

Becca shrugged. 'I don't know. But if he believed in all kinds of other conspiracy theories, then perhaps this plot was just another of those.'

'Makes sense,' said Raven. 'Except that conspiracy theories don't get you killed. Not unless they're real.'

Becca's thoughts shifted back to the body in the Nissen hut. The homeless man, living rough in a derelict World War Two shelter. The knife wound to his chest. 'Sean's murder might just have been a random attack.'

Raven swung his face towards her, piercing her with his dark eyes. 'Do you believe that?'

'No.'

They sat in silence, each locked in their own thoughts as the sun slowly set. Becca wondered what Daniel might be doing now. Eating fish and chips alone by the seafront? Or meeting someone else instead. If only Raven's BMW hadn't conked out...

'I suppose it is quite old now,' Raven mused. 'The car, I mean.'

It seemed her boss's train of thought was moving in tandem with her own. But was he reading more into the situation than just a broken-down car? Raven had his own troubles, both mental and physical. The limp in his leg. The trauma he had suffered in Bosnia and that he so resolutely refused to discuss. His recent divorce.

The dents and scratches that spoke of a life long-lived.

'Well,' said Becca, 'all cars develop problems when they're...' She trailed off.

'Old and decrepit?' said Raven. 'Like their owners?'

She chose her words with care. 'I guess you could call your car a classic.'

He laughed, the lines around his eyes and mouth deepening in the late evening light. 'That makes two of us. An old war vet and a classic car. We'll both be on the scrap heap soon enough.'

They were sitting close together, their shadows long on the grass. Becca studied his profile. A strong nose and brow. Firm jaw, accentuated by dark stubble with just the slightest salting of grey. His eyes were bright and sharp, with a playful glint that belied his age. He held his head with confidence and ease. Despite their twenty-year age gap he was still a supremely attractive man. Melanie was a lucky lady.

Raven kept his gaze fixed firmly on the horizon. 'That bullet. I suppose it was one of the defining moments of my life.'

God, his thoughts were all over the place this evening! Becca guessed it was the discovery of his old war colleague that had triggered it. The death of a friend was a lot for anyone to process. Especially if, like Raven, you held yourself personally responsible.

For a while he said nothing more and Becca wondered if that was it. She didn't want him to shut down on her now that he'd brought up his war service voluntarily for the first time. She waited, uncertain what to say to keep him talking, but it was Raven who picked up the thread again.

'In one instant, everything changed. That's how it is with the biggest changes. They come with no warning. There was life before the bullet, and life after it. It sent me onto a whole new trajectory.'

Becca allowed her thoughts to drift to the defining moments of her own life. The car accident that had put Sam into a coma. The instant of his reawakening. The moment he told her he was leaving for Australia. Raven was right. Your life could change completely in a single heartbeat.

'Ultimately,' she said, 'that bullet brought you back to

Scarborough.'

Raven's stern mouth broke into a smile and he turned it on her. 'I suppose it did,' he said. 'I suppose it did.'

★

To Raven's relief, the breakdown truck arrived sooner than expected, at just after half past eight. But there was no question of the mechanic, who introduced himself as Dave, fixing the car there and then.

'No idea what's wrong,' he declared after a cursory inspection of the car's innards. 'But I bet it'll be a right bugger to fix.'

'Is that your expert opinion?' said Raven caustically.

'Yeah,' said Dave. 'These ancient BMWs are a right pain. I'll need to take it back to the garage. And we don't carry parts for them either. They're far too specialist. It's going to cost you a bob or two,' he added in dour Yorkshire tones.

'I expect it will,' said Raven, his dislike of Dave growing by the second.

'Might be better off trading it in for a newer model,' advised Dave as he lowered the ramp at the back of the truck. 'Not that you'll get much for this old heap.'

Raven bit back the words that were on the tip of his tongue. He would never trade in his old car for a new one. It had plenty more good years ahead of it, he was sure.

'You and the lass can hop in the cabin with me,' said Dave, once the M6 was securely loaded onto the back of the truck.

'That's very kind of you, Dave,' said Becca with a smirk directed at Raven. 'Thanks so much for your help.'

'Yeah, no problem.'

They clambered into the front of the truck, Raven offering the window seat to Becca.

'So what do you reckon about England's chances of winning the second test next week?' said Dave as soon as they'd set off.

Raven turned to Becca, trying to convey with a single glance his complete and utter lack of interest in all things cricket.

She gave him a wink. 'Not so good, Dave. What do you think?'

'Reckon you're right. It's going to be a washout. We'll have to wait until Yorkshire play Lancashire for a real bit of excitement.'

'It'll be the Wars of the Roses all over again,' said Becca.

If any irony was intended, it was lost on Dave. 'The White Rose versus the Red Rose. You could be right there, love. Well, at least we were born on the right side o' the Pennines, eh?'

Raven closed his eyes, filtering out Dave's inane chatter. He didn't open them again until they reached Scalby on Scarborough's northern fringe.

'Where d'you want me to drop you off?' asked Dave.

'Peasholm Gap would be good,' said Becca.

'It's on my way.'

The breakdown truck stopped close to Becca's flat, and Raven decided to get out too. He didn't think he could take any more of Dave's banter.

'I'll take the car back to the garage,' said the mechanic, 'and you can phone on Monday to talk about repairs.'

'Will do,' said Raven.

He was aware that the incident had totally ruined Becca's evening. He'd only partially overheard her phone conversation at the roadside, but he'd heard enough to deduce that a romantic plan had been well and truly scuppered. He felt bad about that. She deserved some happiness in her life.

'Sorry about messing up your evening.'

'Don't worry about it.'

'See you tomorrow, then.'

She walked to her apartment block and Raven set off in the direction of Quay Street. On the way he called Melanie to say sorry for ruining her day too. First the callout to

Ravenscar, then the breakdown on the return from Sleights. A total fuck up.

But Melanie dismissed his apologies. 'Don't worry about it,' she said, sounding as cheerful as ever. 'It's not so late. I'll bring Quincey home now.'

'I don't want to put you to any more trouble.'

'No trouble at all. I'll be with you in ten minutes.'

Raven put on a spurt to make sure he'd be home by the time she arrived. The walk up North Marine Road and down the steep hillside on the south side of the headland was further than he'd realised. The red Volkswagen Golf was already turning into the car park at the end of Quay Street as he reached his front door.

'Perfect timing,' said Melanie when she arrived at the house, Lulu in her arms and Quincey bounding along the pavement in front of her.

The dog seemed inordinately pleased to see Raven, a welcome he didn't deserve. No amount of bad dog ownership on his part seemed to dampen Quincey's adoration of him. He knelt down and gave the animal a guilty hug, allowing Quincey to slobber all over him with his tongue. When he straightened up, Melanie was standing by his front door.

'Would you like to come in for a coffee?' asked Raven.

'I'd love to. In fact, I threw some ingredients into a bag and brought them with me.' She held up a Marks and Spencer carrier bag. 'I thought you might not have eaten, what with your car breaking down and everything.'

Raven hesitated for just a second. Could this be one of those moments he had told Becca about, when your life could turn on a dime? If it was, there was no knowing which direction it would go. The only thing to do was to go along for the ride. 'That would be wonderful.'

Melanie's smile widened. 'Let's go inside and start cooking then.'

She soon took charge of preparing the meal. It was the first time Raven's new kitchen had been properly put through its paces, and Melanie enthused over the induction hob and the shiny new appliances. 'This won't take long,' she said. 'Why don't you go and freshen up?'

He headed upstairs, taking advantage of the opportunity to have a quick shower and change his shirt. By the time he returned, the dogs were stretched out on the living room sofa and Melanie had rustled up a fabulous smelling meal.

'That looks amazing,' he told her and was rewarded with a dazzling smile.

Quincey and Lulu chewed contentedly on some doggy treats while Raven and Melanie sat at the table together. Tagliatelle with wild mushrooms in a truffle sauce. It was an impressive meal to conjure up on the spur of the moment. Melanie was clearly a fantastic cook. She had even brought chocolate desserts that were rich and velvety and melted in your mouth. 'I baked them myself,' she told him. 'They're very bad for you. Far too much cream and sugar.'

'They're delicious,' said Raven.

She didn't ask him about his day, and it was wonderful to simply relax in her company. There were no questions about police work or his time in the army or the trainwreck of his marriage. Nothing for him to fend off or clam up about. When he brought two coffees over to the sofa, it seemed perfectly natural that Melanie would curl up next to him, the dogs at their feet. They drank their coffees in companionable silence, then Raven took her hand and led her upstairs to his bedroom.

CHAPTER 24

The first thing Becca did when she got up on Sunday morning was trip over Liam's trainers. He had left them, together with a pair of smelly socks, lying around between the bathroom and the living area. It was almost as if he'd done it deliberately. Except that Liam never did anything with purpose and planning.

He and Ellie had been out when Becca arrived home the previous evening so she'd had the entire place to herself. She had considered calling Daniel to let him know she was back earlier than anticipated if he was still on for a fish supper, but had decided that what she most wanted was a quiet evening in by herself. Perhaps Dr Felicity Wainwright's advice was right after all, and living alone was the secret to happiness. She'd popped a ready meal into the microwave and enjoyed a guilt-free couple of hours curled up on the sofa, catching up with the latest reality TV and a talent show before getting an early night. Bliss.

With a sigh, she scooped up her brother's trainers and socks and deposited them by the front door. Having Liam around the flat was just like being back home. Worse, since her mum wasn't around to tidy up and do his dirty laundry for him. If he imagined Becca was going to cook him breakfast like Sue did then he had another think coming. And if for some reason he thought that Ellie was the kind of girl who would wash his socks and iron his shirts he was destined to be badly disappointed.

Fortunately there was no sign of either Ellie or Liam this morning. With any luck they wouldn't surface until gone noon.

She popped a couple of slices of bread in the toaster and checked her emails on her phone while waiting for the kettle to boil. She was surprised to find one from Holly Chang marked *urgent*. She opened it at once and read it quickly.

It seemed that the CSI team had made a significant discovery the previous day at the old radar station in Ravenscar. Holly had sent the email to both Raven and Becca and was clearly expecting a response. Had Raven already replied to the message but failed to copy Becca in? It was a distinct possibility. But it was equally likely that he hadn't yet seen it.

The toast popped up and Becca quickly spread it with margarine and strawberry jam. She splashed boiling water into a mug for her tea. Then she called Raven.

'Hi, Becca, what's up?' He sounded sleepy, almost as if he'd been enjoying a lie-in. Unusual for Raven. Even on Sundays he was often to be found at work, especially if there was a big investigation running.

'Have you seen the email from Holly? She's expecting a response.'

Raven stifled a yawn. 'Haven't checked my emails yet. What's it about?'

Becca felt herself growing irritated by his lack of engagement. Irrational, since it was Raven's day off and she had no claim to his time. But she had come to expect more dedication from her boss, above and beyond the call of duty. It was what he seemed to demand from everyone else.

'Holly doesn't say exactly, just that the CSI team made a significant discovery.'

At the other end of the line, a woman's voice called something in the background. It was muffled, but sounded like 'Lulu, come here sweetie!'

Becca almost dropped the phone in surprise. 'What was that?'

'Nothing,' said Raven.

But it wasn't nothing. If Becca wasn't mistaken, it was Melanie. And if the new woman in Raven's life was at his house at nine o'clock on a Sunday morning, then dog-minding wasn't the only thing she was doing for him.

There was the sound of a door closing and then Raven spoke again. 'Okay, I'll take a look at the email and give Holly a call. I was just about to go into the station anyway.'

'How are you getting there without your car?'

'Um, I hadn't really thought…'

'I'll come and pick you up,' said Becca. 'Half an hour?'

★

Raven made sure that he was waiting outside his front door when Becca's Honda Jazz nosed its way into Quay Street. He'd had no time for breakfast but Melanie had promised to cook for them both later when he got home. She had just taken both dogs for a morning walk along the beach. He was quickly coming to depend on her, and had even given her a key so she could let herself back into the house. Last night had been enjoyable. Not earth-shattering, but warm and tender and satisfying. He could easily get used to having Melanie around. She was an uncomplicated, domesticated sort of woman, and the fact that she was so keen to look after Quincey was a real bonus. Lisa would never have allowed a dog inside the house in case it dropped hairs on the carpet, or worse.

Becca drew the Jazz to a stop on the narrow, cobbled street. He opened the passenger door and squeezed himself into the little car.

'You can move the seat back if you want more room,' she said.

He pulled the lever and shifted the seat back as far as it would go, but his knees were still up close to his chin. The car was ridiculously small.

How long until the M6 was fixed and ready for collection? Dave's remarks had been discouraging to say the least. And it was only Sunday. The mechanics wouldn't even have looked at it yet.

'Is Melanie looking after Quincey again?' asked Becca.

'That's right.' He wondered what she'd made of a woman being in the house. Becca was no fool. She'd obviously guessed what was going on. But why should that matter? Becca was his sergeant. It was none of her business who he slept with.

They arrived at the station to find DC Tony Bairstow already at his desk. Raven had read Holly's email before leaving home but it had been frustratingly vague, only hinting at an important discovery of some kind. The CSI team leader had clearly expected him to respond immediately and would probably be in a bad mood because he hadn't. Maybe she'd been making a point of contacting him at an unsociable hour, a habit he was normally guilty of. Or perhaps she was daring him to call her back on a Sunday morning and risk her wrath.

Mind games. There was no chance of him outwitting Holly Chang. Whichever way he played it, she would get the better of him.

'Does anyone know what this cryptic message from CSI means?' he asked.

Fortunately, Tony had the answer. 'Sir, the team found this at the back of the old radar building.' He picked up a metal object and deposited it on a table at the front of the room with a clunk. 'It was well hidden. They had to crawl right into a corner to find it.'

Raven couldn't imagine Holly Chang crawling into a tight space in the corner of a derelict shed. Presumably the youthful – and somewhat more athletic – Erin or Jamie had done that. He leaned in for a closer look at the object.

It was a black steel cash box, about six inches in length, with a handle on the lid and a lock at the front. Raven slipped on his gloves and tried the lid. Locked, obviously.

'Where's the key that was found on Sean's body?'

Tony passed him an evidence bag. Raven unsealed it, removing the brass key with care. It was still stained red with dried blood. He tried not to think about that as he slipped it into the lock.

It turned with a click and Raven opened the box. Inside was a single memory stick. There was no label or marking but whatever was on it was important enough for Sean to have locked it inside a hidden box.

He passed the stick to Tony. 'Fire this up and let's see what we've got.'

Tony slipped the memory stick into his computer and ran it through a virus scanner before accessing the data on it. 'There's lots of stuff on here, sir. Look.'

Raven and Becca leaned over Tony's shoulder as he scrolled through the list of files on the memory stick. Most of them appeared to be saved emails. Their names gave nothing away.

'What's that one?' asked Raven, pointing at a JPEG file.

Tony clicked on it and a map appeared on the screen, showing the outlines of buildings, the positions of roads and other features.

'It's a plan of RAF Fylingdales,' said Becca. 'There are the checkpoints and the perimeter fences. There's the command centre, the power station and the radar itself. It's precisely the sort of map that someone planning an attack on the site would need.'

'Open up some of these emails,' said Raven. 'I want to see who was sending them, and to whom.'

Tony did as he was asked. The emails were brief and appeared innocuous but looked as if they were written in code. They made references to *The Shire* and *Mordor*. Frustratingly, the email addresses themselves were anonymous and the communication was between two people calling themselves *Gandalf* and *Frodo*. But Raven didn't believe for one minute that this was a harmless conversation between a couple of Tolkien fanatics. Gandalf, whoever he or she was, was clearly giving the orders. Frodo was charged with destroying the ring because Frodo had access to Mordor. But the map hadn't been of Middle Earth. It had been of RAF Fylingdales. If Gandalf was the mastermind, then Frodo was the traitor on the ground.

Was this proof that Sean Collins's conspiracy claims were true?

Raven mentally ran through the people he'd encountered at RAF Fylingdales. Flight Lieutenant Mark Jones with his less-than-perfect service record. Major Nicole Anderson who'd had an affair with a man employed to defend the site – a man who had ended up dead. The MOD police chief, Sergeant Gary Murphy who nursed a king-sized grudge against his superiors. Even Wing Commander Fitzwilliam-Brown. Could one of them be Gandalf or Frodo?

'I looked into protests at RAF Fylingdales, like you asked me to,' said Tony.

'Anything interesting?'

'You could say that.' Tony dug out his notes. 'The protests have been led by a Dr Aaron Blake, a lecturer at Teesside University.'

'I studied at Teesside,' said Becca. 'I remember Dr Blake. He was a very political activist, always organising marches and protests.'

'Do you think he could be this Gandalf?' asked Raven.

Becca shrugged. 'It might be worth interviewing him.'

'Who else has been involved in these protests?'

'There have been a number of arrests,' said Tony. 'I've got a full list of names here. But two names stood out. Janice Sillitoe and Matthew Whelan. They were on the walk with Jess when the body of Dean Gibson was found.'

Raven whistled. 'Now there's a coincidence.' He remembered clearly the middle-aged woman who thought she recognised him. He had a less clear picture of Matthew but recalled a youngish chap without any strong distinguishing features or much of a personality. Mind you, it was often the quiet ones you had to watch out for.

'What do you reckon?' asked Becca.

'I think we have enough proof now that an attack of some sort is planned. Two murders: one of a security guard and one of a man who had inside knowledge. What we don't have is any names or specifics. Tony, can you go through all the documents on the memory stick? See if you can break the code and work out what they're talking about. We need names and dates.'

'Right, sir.'

Raven picked up his phone and dialled the number that Flight Lieutenant Mark Jones had given him. A landline number. Raven hoped that someone would pick up if Jones wasn't around on a Sunday.

He needn't have worried. The call was answered almost immediately. 'Flight Lieutenant Jones speaking. Who is this?'

'DCI Raven here. There's been a development. Could you put me through to Wing Commander Fitzwilliam-Brown?'

'I'll take a message. The wing commander is busy at the moment.' Jones sounded stressed himself. His reply was crisp, leaving no room for argument.

'He'll want to speak to me when he hears what I have to say.'

'Let me be the judge of that, Raven.'

But Raven wasn't about to accept a refusal and rely on his message being passed up the chain of command. 'You made a mistake in your career once before, I hear, Jones. Don't make another one!'

His words had the desired effect. After a brief hesitation, Jones caved in. 'I'll put you through, but this had better be urgent.'

Raven waited for his call to be transferred. Before long the voice of the wing commander boomed down the line.

'Fitzwilliam-Brown speaking. What is it, DCI Raven?'

Raven was grateful for the wing commander's no-nonsense manner. If his hunch was right, there was no time to lose. 'We've uncovered evidence that strongly suggests an attack on RAF Fylingdales may be imminent.' Raven briefly outlined the contents of the memory stick and the circumstances of its discovery. Fitzwilliam-Brown listened without interrupting.

'You don't need to tell me we've got a problem,' he said once Raven had finished speaking. 'A group of protesters has gathered outside the main gate right now. If this is a cover for something more serious, you have my authority to act accordingly.'

'Thank you,' said Raven, but the wing commander had already hung up.

CHAPTER 25

The morning after the summer barbecue always involved a lot of clearing up, but Jess didn't mind. It had been a good party, one of the best they'd given, everyone said so. The guests had eaten their way through hundreds of burgers and kilos of sausages and drunk gallons of wine, beer and fizzy pop. Not the healthiest of days, to be sure, but one of the most enjoyable. She swept the ashes from the barbecue into a bucket and carried them over to the compost heap in the corner of the garden.

'Hi there, do you need any help with that?'

She spun around at the unexpected voice behind her. 'Matthew, I wasn't expecting to see you here today.'

He shrugged his shoulders. 'Janice left early to go back to Goathland, and Ronald went to church, so I thought I'd come over and make myself useful. It was a great barbecue, by the way. Thanks for inviting me.'

'I'm glad you enjoyed it.'

They walked back towards the barbecue area. A few empty glasses and dirty plates were still lying around. The family's Golden Retriever was doing a good job of clearing up bits of dropped food.

'I think we're nearly done inside,' said Andrea, emerging from the kitchen. She looked from Jess to Matthew, a huge smile spreading across her face. 'Why don't you two go for a walk or something? I can finish off here.'

Jess wished her mum wouldn't be so transparent in her desire for Jess and Matthew to spend time alone together. She was worse than Janice and Ronald. 'Are you sure, Mum?'

'Of course, now off you go. Make the most of the good weather.'

'Sounds like a great idea,' said Matthew. 'Are there any good walks around here?'

'Sure. We could go up Chimney Bank.' If Matthew really was interested in her, the walk up the incredibly steep hill that started in the village and climbed up to the old iron ore kilns at the top of the valley would test his commitment.

'Lead the way,' he said.

They set off up the hill, keeping well over to the side of the road in case of cars or cyclists careering downhill with a death wish. If your brakes failed on the way down Chimney Bank, there was no way to stop other than by crashing into the overgrown verge at the side of the road.

Jess had walked the route hundreds of times and her heart and lungs were well used to the challenge. Matthew, despite being a keen walker, was obviously struggling. He did his best to keep up the pace, but he couldn't disguise his puffing and panting. At a hairpin bend in the road, Jess took pity on her companion and paused so that he could catch up. Even though they were only halfway up the slope, the views over Rosedale Moor were stunning and always had the power to lift her spirits.

'You okay?' she asked.

Matthew wiped beads of sweat from his upper lip with the edge of his T-shirt. 'I'm not as fit as you, clearly. But great views.'

'Wait till you get to the top,' she said, setting off again. 'It's even better up there.'

Fifteen minutes later they were at the summit, standing in front of a row of stone arches, the old iron ore kilns from the nineteenth century.

'It feels as if we're on top of the world,' said Matthew, looking down at the patchwork quilt of fields, woodland and moor spread out before them.

Jess was reminded of the last time she'd been here. Then, she'd brought a book of poems by Edgar Allan Poe. She'd sat alone at this very spot reading *The Raven* with its haunting *Nevermore* refrain. She had been in the very early stages of grief, and the pain had been almost unbearable. She had wondered if coming back here would reignite those feelings, but she found she was able to enjoy the views without stirring up those painful emotions.

She was moving on, she supposed, and time was working its healing magic. Somehow that felt worse than if she'd broken down in tears.

'Shall we go right to the top?' suggested Matthew.

'Sure.'

They climbed up above the kilns and sat down on a limestone slab at the very highest point, looking out at the valley below. From here it really did seem as if you could see the whole world.

'You know that body we found at Lilla Howe?' said Matthew after a while.

'You know I can't talk about an ongoing investigation,' said Jess.

'I realise that, but I was just wondering...'

She turned to him, the wind blowing her long hair across her face. 'What?'

'Janice said yesterday that the victim worked for the MOD police at RAF Fylingdales.'

'So?'

He turned to look at her. 'Do you think he was killed by a protester?'

Jess frowned. 'What makes you say that?'

Matthew averted his gaze. 'Oh, nothing really. It was just an idea.'

Jess waited to see if he would say more, but he lapsed into silence, gazing out across the distant hills. The sun was rising, growing stronger with every passing hour, but Jess shivered despite its warmth.

CHAPTER 26

'Organise a couple of squad cars,' Raven told Tony, 'and send them over to RAF Fylingdales. They've got protesters at the gate. I'm sure the MOD Police are capable of securing the site, but if there's any connection between the protest and our double murder investigation then I want our lot on hand.'

'Will do,' said Tony, picking up the phone.

'Becca, are you happy to drive us over there?'

'Happy if you are.'

'Good. Let's go.' He really wished he had his BMW back, but Becca's car was the next best option.

'One more thing,' he told Tony as he was heading for the door. 'Anything you've got on this Dr Aaron Blake, send it to my phone before I lose my signal.' Going out onto the moors was like stepping back in time to an age before mobile phones and the internet. Nice enough for a quiet weekend away, but hopeless when you were in the middle of a murder investigation and needed to stay in touch.

He squeezed himself back into Becca's car and they set off out of Scarborough, taking the Scalby Road at a sedate pace. The Jazz wasn't just cramped, it was far too slow for Raven's liking. They trundled along, Raven wanting to push his right foot to the floor, but knowing that it wouldn't help.

They hadn't got far when his phone buzzed with an incoming message from Tony. He read it through then told Becca what it said. 'This Aaron Blake person has a police record for violence at protests.'

'How violent?'

'Damaging property and carrying a knife.'

'Sean Collins was killed with a knife,' Becca reminded him.

'True.'

'Blake was something of a rabble-rouser on campus. Some students worshipped him. I thought he was a bit of a narcissist.'

'Dangerous?'

'Potentially.'

'Do you think he could be Gandalf from the emails?'

'It's possible,' said Becca. 'I suppose the Tolkien connection might appeal to an academic.'

They were now clear of Scarborough and driving north on the open road. Becca changed up a gear.

'Does this thing go any faster?' asked Raven.

'I'm driving as fast as the speed limit allows and is compatible with road conditions and safety.'

'Sure,' said Raven. 'But does it go any faster?'

She did accelerate a tad when the road straightened out. She was a good driver, Raven had to acknowledge that. It was just that he wasn't a good passenger. He hated not being in control. He needed to get over himself.

Before long, his mobile phone signal faded to zero. The moors rolled out before them, as empty and barren as always. As they approached RAF Fylingdales, the protest at the main gate became visible. It was impossible to drive through the throng of people and so Becca pulled off the main road, parking on the grass verge.

The road leading to the outer checkpoint was blocked

by a group of protesters waving placards and chanting in unison. MOD police officers had thrown a protective cordon around the entrance to the base, standing in line, their Heckler & Koch submachine guns slung across their chests. They looked ready to use them.

The situation was brimming with tension and could explode at any moment. Raven was pleased to see that the two marked police cars he had requested had already arrived and were parked opposite the protest. Four uniformed officers had joined the line of MOD police and were attempting to defuse the situation by speaking to protesters.

But there was another vehicle present that made Raven's heart sink. The team from BBC *Look North* was setting up cameras and microphones, and the presenter, Liz Larkin, was having her face powdered by a young woman from the makeup department.

Liz and Raven had history. And not of the good kind.

'Looks like we've got company,' said Becca, turning off the engine. 'Liz will be thrilled to see you.' Raven noticed an edge to Becca's voice. Perhaps she disliked the habit the journalist had of giving all her attention to Raven and ignoring other members of his team. He didn't much care for it either.

He gritted his teeth and got out of the car.

Liz scented his arrival with the nose of a trained bloodhound. She made a beeline in his direction. 'Chief Inspector Raven! What perfect timing!' She laid a hand on his arm and leaned in close. 'We're just about to start filming. Perhaps I could ask you a few questions?'

Her perfume assaulted his nostrils, something rich and musky. The scent was much more seductive than the floral perfume preferred by Melanie, although Raven pushed that thought to the very furthest corner of his mind.

'I'm not here to make a statement.' His purpose was to speak to Dr Aaron Blake, the man who might potentially be Gandalf, and he had no intention of being waylaid by the pushy news presenter.

'Are you sure?' said Liz. 'Our viewers would be delighted to hear your interpretation of events and whether this protest is in any way related to the recent murder of an MOD policeman from the base.'

'Is that the angle you'll be pushing?'

'I don't push angles, DCI Raven,' she told him indignantly. 'I report the facts objectively.'

'Keep telling yourself that.'

Liz scowled, an expression that sat badly on her fine-featured face. 'If you feel that way, you should definitely give an interview to ensure balance. I'm giving you the chance to put your points across.' She stared into his eyes and cocked her head to one side, challenging him to respond.

Raven turned his back on her.

'Please, Chief Inspector...'

He went to join Becca, leaving Liz Larkin with a look of thunder on her face. Perhaps he ought to have said something bland on camera to placate her. Now she would say what she liked and there was nothing he could do to stop her.

Becca had been watching the encounter, but now she turned to indicate someone in the crowd. 'Look, there's someone over there we know.'

Raven soon saw who she was pointing at. Janice Sillitoe, the retired teacher from Goathland who had been on the walk with Jess when the body of Dean Gibson was discovered. Tony had said she was a regular at these protests. She was standing in the front row of demonstrators, leading the chants with gusto.

'What did Tony say she'd been arrested for?' he asked Becca.

'Destroying or damaging property. She tried to cut her way through the perimeter fence using wire cutters.'

'Nice old lady.'

Raven and Becca went over to her.

'Ms Sillitoe,' said Raven. 'Perhaps we could have a word?'

Janice was dressed for the weather, with a wide-brimmed cotton hat over her grey curls. She cut an imposing figure, her nose as sharp as an eagle's, her back as straight as a rod, her mouth set in firm resolve. She was carrying a hand-painted banner that read, *Say No to Nukes*. She paused in her chanting, giving Raven a frosty look. 'Ah, it's the chief inspector. Are you here to arrest me?'

'Why?' said Raven. 'What have you done?'

'Nothing yet, just exercising my lawful right to protest.'

'Well, perhaps we could go somewhere quieter to talk?'

'I don't think so,' said Janice. 'I like it here at the frontline.' She brandished her placard and shouted in the face of one of the MOD officers. The man gave Raven a pained look.

'Well–' began Raven.

Janice turned her attention back to him. 'Actually, I was hoping we might bump into each other again. After our encounter at Lilla Howe I remembered where I'd seen you before. There was a Tom Raven at the school where I used to teach in Scarborough. I never forget a name.'

Miss Sillitoe. Of course.

Raven was horrified to realise that this woman had been the games mistress at his school. She'd mainly taught the girls netball and hockey, but occasionally she'd made the boys do cross-country runs and had been far tougher than their usual male teacher. He recalled being sent out into the cold and the wet, the boys' howls of protests going unheeded.

'Small world,' said Becca with a look of amusement on her face. 'How nice that you two know each other.'

'Isn't it?' said Raven, trying to force a smile.

The mood of the demonstrators was turning angrier. The chants grew louder, the verbal abuse of the police more aggressive.

'Are you sure you want to be here, Ms Sillitoe?' said Becca. 'There could be trouble.'

'Trouble?' boomed Janice. 'My dear, I'm counting on trouble. If there isn't any, we won't get any attention. I was the one who called the team at BBC *Look North*. It's my job to get the word out.'

'Perhaps you could help us, then,' said Raven. 'We want to speak to Dr Aaron Blake. We understand he's the organiser of this protest.'

'That's him over there,' said Janice, pointing to a man with untidy shoulder-length hair and a scraggly beard. 'But he won't talk to you. He doesn't talk to the cops.'

'He may not have any choice,' said Raven.

'Thanks for your help, Janice,' said Becca. 'And stay safe.'

Stay safe. Raven didn't much care whether Janice stayed safe or not. If she got into a scuffle, it would serve her right for all the misery she had inflicted on teenage boys over the years. Then again, Janice of all people would give as good as she got. She'd be the last one standing after everyone else had given up through exhaustion or boredom.

Raven approached the man she had indicated. He was positioned at the front of the crowd, his gaze levelled on the line of MOD police and the distant radar installation they protected. There was a messianic fervour to his expression, as if he were leading his people to the promised land. 'Dr Blake?' Raven produced his warrant card. 'DCI Raven, Scarborough CID. Could I have a word?'

'Sod off!' shouted Blake. 'I'm busy!' The lecturer resumed his angry chanting.

'Don't make me arrest you,' warned Raven.

'What for? I'm not doing anything wrong. This is a free country. The last time I looked, citizens had the right to protest peacefully.'

Raven glanced around him. The demonstrators were growing more belligerent with every passing minute. They were only just on the right side of peaceful protest. The crowd was pushing forward against the MOD police, who had now been joined by the police from Scarborough as they sought to hold people back from the gate. He hoped the situation wouldn't descend into chaos before he had time to interview Dr Blake.

'I'm not interested in your right to protest,' said Raven. 'I'm investigating two murders, and your activities have brought you to our attention. I have some questions for you. I just need ten minutes of your time.' He didn't add that, depending on the answers Blake gave, he might find himself in the back of a police car being taken away for further questioning.

'Five minutes,' offered Blake, stepping away from the crowd. 'Then I'm back on the protest. Can I ask you a question, DCI Raven?'

'Go on.'

'Who do you think this country's real enemies are?'

Raven sighed. He had neither the time nor the inclination to discuss politics with an idealogue. People like Blake never changed their views, they just sought every opportunity to push their opinions onto others. He was saved from having to answer when Blake, who clearly enjoyed the sound of his own voice, jumped in.

'If you're thinking it's the Russians or the Chinese, then you've swallowed the propaganda. Our enemies are the powers that control nuclear weapons.'

Against his better judgement, Raven couldn't help himself from responding. 'If I'm not mistaken, that includes Russia and China.'

A thin smile appeared on Blake's face. 'The Americans are to be feared as much as the Russians or the Chinese, and trusted as little.'

Raven, who had worked in close contact with US forces in Bosnia, couldn't agree with Blake's assessment, but knew this wasn't the time or place for an argument he was never going to win.

Blake took advantage of Raven's silence and pressed on with his case. 'The true enemy is the military–industrial complex in all its forms and in all countries, in particular those with nuclear arsenals.'

'Isn't it the job of RAF Fylingdales to protect us from a nuclear strike?' asked Becca, joining in the debate for the first time.

Blake's eyes gleamed with the shine of a zealot. 'Don't you see? RAF Fylingdales exists to detect a potential nuclear strike. That makes this base itself a target. North Yorkshire would become the frontline in a global war. And if the Americans have the capability to detect a Russian nuclear launch, then they can respond to it. The result would be mutually assured destruction.'

'So we'd be better off not knowing if the Russians launched an attack?' said Raven. 'Is that what you're saying?'

'What I'm saying is that if we can't see the strike coming, then our nuclear weapons are no longer a deterrent and we might as well get rid of them.'

Raven didn't follow Blake's logic, but the lecturer had a way of speaking that made him sound convincing. He had used that skill to persuade someone as forthright and opinionated at Janice Sillitoe of his cause.

Out of the corner of his eye Raven spotted Sergeant Gary Murphy on the periphery of the protesters, a look of deep loathing on his face. He had clearly recognised Dr Aaron Blake amid the crowd. The number of protesters seemed to have swelled and they were now standing only a foot or two away from where Blake was making his case about nuclear Armageddon. Fortunately, Liz Larkin had become embroiled in an exchange with some of the protesters who had blocked her way through the crowd. She shot a look of frustration in Raven's direction.

'Right,' said Raven to Blake. 'You've asked your questions. Now you can answer mine. Last Tuesday, the body of an MOD police officer was found at Lilla Howe. Do you recognise the name, Dean Gibson?'

'Should I?'

'I didn't ask if you should. I asked if you did.'

'Well, then. No, I don't.'

'What about the name, Sean Collins?'

Dr Blake tugged mischievously at his beard. 'Wasn't he a pop star in the eighties?' It was clear that the lecturer intended to cooperate as little as possible with the police.

'Can you account for your movements on Friday night and the early hours of Saturday morning?'

Blake gave Raven a cold look. 'I know my rights. I'm not obliged to answer your questions. Not unless you plan to arrest me.' He glanced over his shoulder to where Liz Larkin was attempting to extricate herself from a protester who clearly had a lot to say. Raven knew he had only seconds before the interview with Aaron Blake would become the subject of a live TV broadcast.

'What does the name "Gandalf" mean to you?'

Blake laughed. 'Gandalf? It sounds like you've been reading too much fantasy fiction.'

'Is it your codename?'

'Is it, hell!'

'Do you know of anyone who uses that codename?'

'What, apart from that old man with the long beard and walking staff over there?' Blake pointed into the crowd, a smug look on his face.

Raven knew that unless he arrested him, Blake would give him nothing. But what justification did he have for arresting the leader of a lawful protest? There was no direct evidence to link the sociology lecturer with an impending attack on the RAF base.

Just then the crowd surged forward and Raven felt a shove. Blake stepped back and disappeared from view.

'Becca?'

Raven glanced around for his partner, but before he could spot her a fist connected with the side of his face. He couldn't see who had thrown the punch but he staggered to the side, seeing black dots in his field of vision and feeling the warm trickle of blood from his nose.

Shouts and cries rang out as the protesters pushed against the line of police, forcing them back behind the gate. Raven stumbled, and he feared he might fall and be trampled in the melee.

A strong hand grabbed his arm and pulled him to his feet.

'This is not the time or the place to be conducting police interviews,' growled Sergeant Gary Murphy in Raven's ear. 'I'm taking you inside for your own safety.'

Raven looked around again for Becca, but she'd vanished.

CHAPTER 27

For once, the MOD sergeant dispensed with the usual security protocols and took Raven straight to the command centre where operations were in full swing. The building was situated next to the radar itself, which was enclosed within its own inner fence and protected by a third checkpoint.

In the operations room at the heart of the windowless and air-conditioned building, RAF personnel in army fatigues were seated at their desks, silently monitoring a suite of computer screens. Each display showed a circular map of the northern hemisphere covering Europe and the Middle East, most of Asia, North America, Greenland and North Africa. Dots of various colour – none of them representing nuclear missiles, Raven hoped – crawled across the maps, each leaving a trail in its wake. The atmosphere inside the operations room was one of intense concentration as the "eyes" of RAF Fylingdales closely observed the skies over much of the world.

Raven remembered their motto. *Vigilamus* – We Are Watching. He hoped they were also paying attention to the situation on their own doorstep.

'Don't worry about your colleague, Sergeant Shawcross,' Murphy assured Raven. 'She's safe.'

They had left the situation outside the gate in turmoil, with some of the protesters hurling bottles and stones at the police, who had retreated to a position behind the main gate. There had been several arrests, and the violence had now abated. But with the combination of demonstrators determined to stir up trouble and the presence of armed police, there was always the risk of things getting out of hand. Raven wondered just how far Aaron Blake would push the situation, and whether he had plans for more than just a protest at the gate.

Was the demonstration simply a smokescreen for a more sinister operation?

He hoped Becca would have the sense to keep out of harm's way.

An RAF officer was making a verbal report to Wing Commander Fitzwilliam-Brown. 'Sir, we've completed a search of the radar. All clear. No suspicious objects detected.'

'Very good.' The wing commander began giving orders as he received further updates from his subordinates. Raven was impressed by the station commander's calmness under pressure. Here was a man who engendered respect.

Flight Lieutenant Mark Jones came over to Raven. He was dressed in green and khaki combat uniform instead of his usual blue-grey service dress. 'You look like you've been in the wars, Raven. Take a seat. I'll fetch the first aid kit.' All traces of the officer's boyish arrogance were gone and he seemed much more likeable as a result.

'Thank you,' said Raven. His vision had cleared now after the punch to his face, but his nose was still bleeding profusely, covering his shirt collar with red droplets.

The flight lieutenant supplied him with antiseptic wipes and tissues, and Raven held them to his nostrils, stemming the bleeding. It was surprising how much blood you could get out of a nose. He tried to wipe his shirt clean but succeeded only in smearing streaks of crimson all down his front.

A telephone rang at one of the desks and was picked up by a female RAF officer. She listened for a moment before raising her hand to attract the wing commander's attention. 'Sir, a call from Scarborough CID. They have new information which could be significant.'

Raven jumped to his feet. 'That must be DC Tony Bairstow. I left him going through the files on the memory stick that was found with the body at Ravenscar.'

'Put him on speakerphone,' instructed Fitzwilliam-Brown.

'Putting you on speaker,' said the officer.

Tony's voice came crisply over the line. 'Hello, sir, can you hear me?'

'Tony, Raven here. We can all hear you loud and clear. What have you got for us?' He looked to the wing commander, aware that he was probably breaching protocol by assuming command, but Fitzwilliam-Brown gave him an encouraging nod. In this situation they were allies and equals.

'I've been through all the computer files,' said Tony. 'In addition to the plans of RAF Fylingdales, I also discovered site plans for Beale Air Force Base in California, Cape Cod Space Force Station, Clear Space Force Station in Alaska, and Pituffik Space Base in Greenland. This goes much wider than the UK. It looks as if we're dealing with a possible international threat.'

'This is Wing Commander Fitzwilliam-Brown speaking,' said the wing commander for Tony's benefit. 'At the start of the day I alerted all the other bases to the heightened security risk due to the ongoing protest here. I am also working in close cooperation with the central command centre at Peterson Space Force Base in Colorado Springs. What you've discovered confirms that this was the right course of action. In view of this latest information, I will inform MI5 of the situation and instruct the security level at the base to be raised to its maximum state of readiness. I shall also inform my opposite numbers at the other bases. Thank you for your input. Do you have any further information that could help us understand the threat?'

'I can send you the data on the memory stick,' said Tony. 'As well as the site plans, there are emails between two individuals discussing the plot, but they're all written in code. I can't give you any specific details.'

'Please send that immediately,' said Fitzwilliam-Brown. 'Perhaps our chaps here can decipher the hidden meaning behind those messages.'

While the wing commander was talking, Raven was thinking hard. There was one person here at RAF Fylingdales who had been stationed at all the locations Tony had mentioned and who was closely entangled with the murder of Constable Dean Gibson. That person was Major Nicole Anderson of the US Air Force.

Raven knew he had been forbidden from speaking to the major again. But equally he knew he had to. The very fact that Nicole had gone to the trouble of setting a senior official at the US Embassy to keep him at bay showed she was willing to go to any length to avoid being questioned by the police.

He drew the wing commander aside and outlined his thinking. 'I need to speak to her again. Urgently.'

It was evident that the station commander wasn't happy about the proposal. But eventually he acceded to Raven's request. 'Very well. Flight Lieutenant Jones will escort you. And I want Sergeant Murphy to sit in on the interview too. Be mindful that Major Anderson is a United States citizen.'

Raven was already very much aware of that fact. But he readily acquiesced to the wing commander's conditions. This was the easiest way to get what he wanted, and the presence of the other two officers might well prove useful.

Especially if things turned nasty. If the major was somehow involved in a worldwide sabotage plot there was no telling what she might do.

'Come on, then,' said the flight lieutenant. 'There's no time to waste.'

★

'What is this, a delegation?'

When Raven arrived in the office of Major Nicole Anderson in the company of Sergeant Murphy and Flight Lieutenant Jones, she looked even less pleased to see him than at their first meeting.

Without waiting to be asked, Raven and Sergeant Murphy sat down opposite her. Flight Lieutenant Jones closed her office door and stood in front of it, feet apart, hands behind his back, ready to foil any idea she might have of making a run for it.

Raven knew he had to tread carefully. Not only was he about to go against his boss's explicit instructions and unleash a diplomatic shitstorm that risked ending his career. It was possible he was now sitting opposite the person calling themselves Gandalf or Frodo on the emails discovered in the possession of the murdered Sean Collins. If she was the mastermind of the sabotage plot or the person on the inside preparing to carry it out, then she would be doubly on her guard. And as a major in the US Air Force, she had the legal right to take refuge behind the Status of Forces Agreement and simply refuse to answer any of his questions.

But Raven needed her to talk.

'The last time we spoke,' he began, 'you admitted arranging to meet Constable Dean Gibson at a hotel in Scarborough for sex.'

Nicole narrowed her eyes. 'I made no such admission.'

Raven ignored her denial. 'At that time, I was investigating a murder. Now the stakes are considerably higher.'

Just as he'd hoped, his statement caught her off-guard. She glanced nervously at the flight lieutenant, and then back at Raven. 'What do you mean?'

'There have now been two murders connected to the security of this base. And evidence has been uncovered of a plot to sabotage RAF Fylingdales.'

Her eyes opened wider. 'I know nothing about any plot.'

'Not only that,' continued Raven, 'but there is a further link to the other bases making up the Solid State Phased Array Radar System: California, Cape Cod, Alaska and Greenland. All locations at which you' – he levelled a finger in her direction – 'have worked at, and of which you therefore have detailed, inside knowledge.'

The silence in the room crackled with tension. Raven was fully aware that he had just accused the major of possible treason. A crime that could carry the death sentence in the United States if she was found guilty. He expected her to refuse to respond to such an accusation. Instead, she exploded in rage.

'How dare you make such an absurd claim! It is my job to safeguard the project, not sabotage it. I've dedicated my entire career to this mission.'

Raven leaned back in his chair, assessing her performance. Gone was the bluster about international treaties and her right to silence. She was fighting for her life now.

'Tell me about your relationship with Dean Gibson.'

She sighed. 'Dean was a bit of fun, he meant nothing more to me than that. In my job, I tend not to stay in one location for very long. I don't have time to put down roots, and frankly I have no wish to tie myself down in a long-term relationship. But at the same time, a woman has needs. I'm sure you can understand that.'

Raven wondered if she had a man waiting for her at each of the bases where she'd worked, but that was none of his concern. 'Your relationship was purely sexual?'

'That's a very transactional way of putting it, DCI Raven. But yes, I chose Dean for his looks and his willingness to conduct a relationship on my terms. I had no wish to hurt anyone. There was no reason for his wife to find out. I made sure I was always discreet.'

'Apart from the cufflinks.'

She bit her lower lip. 'That was an indulgence. A whim.'

It was the closest she had come to admitting she'd made a mistake.

'When did you and Dean last see each other?'

Her eyes flickered, betraying a glimmer of emotion. Perhaps, despite her denial, her feelings for Dean had run deeper than she cared to admit. 'I saw him the Friday before we were due to meet. He told me he'd booked the hotel room. We were looking forward to spending some time together. But when I arrived at the hotel on the date we'd agreed, he wasn't there. I tried to call him, but there was no answer. I assumed he'd changed his mind or that something had held him up. I had no idea that...'

'What?'

'That he was dead,' she concluded.

'But perhaps he didn't change his mind,' suggested Raven. 'Perhaps you changed yours. Maybe Dean Gibson had outlived his usefulness for you.'

Nicole stared at him coldly. 'I don't know what you mean.'

'Did you really choose Dean solely because of his physical attributes? It seems a remarkable coincidence that out of all the eligible men you could have selected for an affair, you chose one so closely involved with the security of the base. Had you acquired all the information you needed from him? Or had he begun to suspect your motives? Is that why you killed him?'

Nicole's eyes narrowed to deadly slits. 'You're barking up the wrong tree again, DCI Raven.'

'Am I?'

'Absolutely. We've already been over this. I've told you far more than I'm obliged to, and I have raised this matter with the United States embassy in London.'

'So I understand,' said Raven. 'Do you think the ambassador would be interested to hear about your "special relationship" with a serving officer in the Ministry of Defence? A married man in fact.'

'There's no law against conducting such a relationship.'

'No, but it might blot your clean record, especially since Dean Gibson's murder forms part of an ongoing investigation into a possible terrorist attack.' Raven gave her a reassuring smile. 'But don't worry. I've got better things to do with my time than spread gossip. Let's try a different angle. Do you know of a man called Sean Collins?'

'No.' Her expression didn't change at the mention of Sean's name. But perhaps she was simply getting better at hiding her reactions.

'Sean Collins used to be a soldier in the British Army. He was a patriot. He gave his life trying to protect this country from its enemies.'

'I'm sorry to hear that, DCI Raven, but I've never heard of him.'

Raven cast a glance over her neatly ordered desk. It was just as immaculate as her own carefully pressed uniform and tightly bound hair. 'During your liaisons with Dean, did he ever mention a security incident that took place at the perimeter fence of the base?'

'No.'

'Are you sure? A couple of weeks ago, Dean encountered an intruder during a night patrol. Did he never mention it to you?'

'Dean and I never talked about work.'

'Really?' Raven wondered if that could be true. What else might the down-to-earth MOD officer and the ambitious major have found to talk about during their illicit get-togethers? What interests could they possibly have shared, other than a desire to get into bed together? 'Let's talk about your work. What precisely is your role here?'

Nicole's jaw tightened. 'That's highly classified information.'

Raven looked to Jones for guidance, but the flight

lieutenant gave a firm shake of his head. The subject was clearly off-limits, but that made Raven even more curious to delve deeper. 'I find it interesting that a US officer is assigned to work here at RAF Fylingdales. This isn't a US Air Force base, is it?'

The major's eyes were cold. 'I work alongside my British colleagues in an advisory capacity.'

'Do you? Or are you here to keep an eye on them, rather like Flight Lieutenant Jones has been told to keep on eye on me.'

'Raven,' warned Jones, 'please don't say something you'll regret.'

But Raven knew he would regret remaining silent more than causing a diplomatic row. 'It's almost as if the Americans don't trust their British counterparts.'

Major Anderson gave him a thin-lipped smile. 'My government subscribes to the view that trust isn't necessary as long as there is oversight.'

'You're saying you can't trust the Brits to do their job properly?'

'I didn't say that. I said we don't rely on trust.'

Raven turned back to the flight lieutenant, who was looking increasingly uncomfortable. 'What about you, Jones? Do you trust her?'

Jones folded his arms across his chest. 'Allies don't have to trust each other. We simply have to work together effectively. Our goals are the same. And so are our enemies.'

'Teamwork,' said the major, nodding in agreement.

'Yet what if one member of the team goes rogue?' pressed Raven. 'What if the enemy is within?'

The major's face was impassive. 'That is why we watch, DCI Raven. We watch the enemy and we watch each other. And now, if you'll excuse me, I have important work to do. I'm sure I don't need to remind you, Chief Inspector, that according to the terms under which US military personnel operate in this country, any investigation into my conduct would be under the jurisdiction of the United States military court.'

She stood up to make it clear that the interview was over.

CHAPTER 28

The sun was high in the sky and beating down hard on the Bank Top kilns. 'Perhaps we should go,' said Jess. Although she loved it up here, she was ready to walk back down the hill and return to the embrace of her family. She didn't see them so often now that she had moved to Scarborough, and she wanted to make the most of her visit to Rosedale Abbey.

But Matthew showed no sign of wanting to leave. He kicked off his trainers and leaned back on his elbows against the close-cropped grass. 'I like it up here,' he said.

A lone sheep wandered over and stared at them for a few moments before deciding it had better things to do and went back to its nibbling.

After a moment or two Matthew returned to the subject of their earlier conversation. 'It wouldn't surprise me if a protester had killed that MOD policeman, you know.'

'What makes you say that?' Jess was starting to feel a little unnerved by Matthew's continued interest in the investigation. Although it was natural for people to be intrigued by a police inquiry, especially a murder, Matthew just didn't seem to be able to drop it. His behaviour bordered on the obsessive.

'Well, I mean, they're asking for it, aren't they?' said Matthew.

'Who are asking for what?'

'The whole lot of them.' Matthew made a sweeping gesture with his hand. 'The RAF, the MOD, the whole military machine. Anyone involved with Britain's so-called nuclear deterrent.'

Jess turned away. She had no desire to get involved with him in a discussion about the rights and wrongs of nuclear weapons. She'd known about his interest in environmental affairs, but he'd never before expressed his political views to her so forcefully.

But Matthew reacted as if she'd encouraged him to continue. He sat up and looked earnestly into her eyes. 'People think that RAF Fylingdales is there to keep us safe, but really it only increases the risk. Think about it, if the Americans see a missile coming, or even if they think they do, they'll fire at Russia, and we'll all be blown to smithereens. It's time to dismantle all these ballistic missile early warning sites. We should never have let things get this far.'

Despite the growing heat of the day, Jess shuddered. 'And so you think that makes it okay to commit murder?'

'I didn't say that.'

'Then what's your point?'

He brought his knees up close to his chest. 'Forget it. I hoped you'd understand, that's all.'

Jess studied his face, trying to work out what was going through his mind. Did he know something about the murder? In which case, why didn't he just spit it out?

She was saved from having to continue the conversation by the buzzing of her phone with an incoming call. She checked the caller display and was surprised to see DC Tony Bairstow's name. She and Tony had become good mates working together. But why was he calling her now?

'I have to get this,' she told Matthew. She stood up to

take the call and moved a short distance away from him. 'Hi, Tony. What's up?'

'Just thought you might like to know what's been going on in the last couple of days,' said Tony. He sounded excited, quite unlike his usual calm self.

'Tell me.' It was obvious that something major had happened while she'd been taking a short break in Rosedale Abbey.

She listened in astonishment as Tony told her about the body of the former soldier being found at Ravenscar and the suspected plot to sabotage RAF Fylingdales and possibly other sites in North America and Greenland.

'I had no idea,' said Jess. 'You should have told me sooner. I'd have come back into work if I'd known.'

'We only learned about the sabotage plot this morning,' he explained. 'Anyway, we still don't know much except that the people behind the plot are using codenames. They call themselves Gandalf and Frodo.'

'As in *The Lord of the Rings*?' Jess had read Tolkien's epic work as a teenager, spending hours in her bedroom, lost in Middle Earth.

'Exactly,' said Tony. 'I've only watched the films myself, but even I recognised those names. Raven thinks Gandalf is the mastermind behind the plot and Frodo is the person charged with carrying it out.'

Jess was itching to tell Tony she would come back to work immediately. She had wasted enough time on this hillside already.

But Tony hadn't finished. 'And another interesting thing turned up. Two of the people on that walk with you have previously been arrested.'

Jess dropped her voice to a whisper. 'Arrested?' She cast a sideways glance at Matthew, who was still sitting where she had left him, watching her as she spoke on the phone. She stepped further away from him, out of earshot.

'Yes,' continued Tony. 'They took part in a protest at RAF Fylingdales and were arrested on suspicion of causing criminal damage. I recognised their names when I was looking into demonstrations at the base.'

'Who?' breathed Jess. She shivered as a cloud passed over the sun, causing a sudden breeze to blow over the exposed moorland. Matthew was about twelve feet away, still watching her intently.

'Janice Sillitoe and Matthew Whelan.'

'Oh,' said Jess in a small voice. She turned away from Matthew and cupped her hand over her mouth. 'Do you think one of them could be Gandalf or Frodo?'

'It's a possibility,' said Tony. 'The boss is up at RAF Fylingdales right now. There's a demonstration going on as we speak.'

'Is everything all right?' Matthew was suddenly right behind her. She hadn't seen him stand up nor heard him approaching.

Jess spun round. 'Yes, it's just someone from work.'

Matthew frowned. 'About the murder?'

Jess said nothing but gripped the phone tighter in her hand. She waited to see if he would say any more, but he took a step back from her and looked away.

She turned her attention back to Tony. 'Thanks for calling. I have to go now. But if you speak to Raven, tell him I'm coming in.' She ended the call.

She was about to pocket her phone, then changed her mind and held onto it. Dialling 999 in the middle of the moors might be fairly pointless since a squad car would take so long to reach her. But it might deter Matthew if he tried anything.

She regretted now that she'd agreed to go for a walk with him to this isolated spot. Her imagination was in freefall. Could Matthew be Gandalf? The person behind the plot to sabotage RAF Fylingdales? Why did he keep asking questions about the murder of Dean Gibson?

He stuck his hands into his pockets, looking disgruntled. 'Bit mean of them to phone you on your day off.'

'I don't mind,' said Jess. 'I've told them I'm going in to work.'

'Why don't you just say you can't?'

'Because I enjoy my work.'

'Really?' He gave her a sulky look. 'Hasn't it ever occurred to you that you're on the wrong side? You know, that you're just helping to prop up a rotten system? You could jack it all in, do whatever you wanted to.'

'Like what?'

'Join the opposition. Put yourself on the right side of history.'

'Is that how you see me?' she asked. 'On the wrong side of history?'

He put out a hand towards her and she instinctively took a step backwards. Adrenaline rushed through her system. *Fight or flight.* She was fitter than him and could outrun him if she had to. And she knew this place like the back of her hand. She could lose him and find a place to hide among the old kilns. Or run back down to the safety of the village.

But fighting sounded more appealing than fleeing.

She was a trained police officer and had faced more dangerous individuals than Matthew. She decided to confront him.

'Where were you on Friday?' she demanded. Tony had told her that the body of Sean Collins had been discovered on Saturday morning and that Friday evening was the most likely time of his murder.

'Why?' Matthew looked puzzled.

'Just answer the question.'

He shrugged. 'I was in Goathland all day working on my thesis.'

'And what about later? Did you go out?'

'Is this a police interview? Are you interrogating me?'

'I can arrest you if you prefer.'

He gave her a confused look as if this might be a joke. But when it became clear she was serious, his face turned pale. 'No, I didn't go out on Friday. I cooked myself a meal, opened a beer and watched a film. I was in bed by eleven thirty.'

'Can anyone verify that? Was Janice there?'

'Janice? No, she went out on Friday. She was at a dinner, although they call it a wake, organised by the Lyke Wake Club.'

'Where was that?' asked Jess.

'At the big hotel in Ravenscar,' said Matthew. 'Why, has something happened?'

CHAPTER 29

Becca wasn't best pleased to be left outside the gates of RAF Fylingdales when Raven was ushered inside for his personal safety. She had no idea what he was doing and couldn't call him because there was no mobile phone signal, as usual.

One of the uniformed officers waved her over to his car. 'Ma'am, we've got DC Tony Bairstow on the radio, asking to speak to DCI Raven or yourself.' He handed her a walkie-talkie.

At least some technology still worked out here. Becca took the device and spoke into it. 'Hi Tony, what's up?'

'I called Jess to update her on what's been happening and she just phoned me back. She said she tried calling you but couldn't get through.'

'She wouldn't be able to,' said Becca. 'I'm outside the RAF base. What did Jess want?'

'She said she'd been with Matthew Whelan and she asked him about Friday night. He told her that Janice Sillitoe was in Ravenscar on Friday evening attending a dinner, or a wake as they call it, of the Lyke Wake Club.'

'Janice?' said Becca. 'At Ravenscar?' She looked across

at the group of protesters. Janice was one of the loudest and most militant among them, tirelessly waving her placard and chanting her slogans. All those years as a games mistress on the hockey pitch had given her formidable stamina and a voice to match. For a moment, Becca pitied the young Raven, at the mercy of this single-minded woman.

Could Janice have wielded a knife and thrust it into Sean Collins's chest? Becca didn't doubt it for a second.

'Jess also said that Janice knew the first victim,' said Tony. 'Apparently Janice volunteers at the school where Laura Gibson teaches. She met Dean Gibson at school events.'

'Did she?' Becca's mind was quickly turning over the facts. They all seemed to point in the same direction. 'Janice is outside the gate right now,' she told Tony. 'I think I need to speak to her. Thanks for calling.' She handed the two-way radio back to the uniformed officer.

She watched Janice for a moment, wondering if this indomitable woman was hiding behind the codename Gandalf.

Becca knew that Janice would never admit to anything if questioned casually. She would have to be arrested and taken into custody, but Becca couldn't do that on her own with all these protesters around. She would never be able to get Janice into a police car without causing a ruckus. In any case, she wanted Raven to be present when Janice was questioned, and that meant getting her inside RAF Fylingdales.

She approached a pair of armed MOD police and explained what she had in mind.

The two officers looked glad to be doing something useful rather than just standing around having abuse hurled at them. Within seconds they had extracted an astonished Janice from the throng and brought her to Becca, who informed her that she was under arrest on suspicion of murder. Accompanied by the MOD police officers, Becca and Janice were led inside the base.

But the other demonstrators weren't going to stand by and watch one of their own – and an old woman at that – be taken away. The incident was the spark needed to ignite the tinder-dry mood of the gathering.

Behind her, Becca heard the protest erupt into a full-scale riot.

*

Raven heard Janice Sillitoe protesting at the top of her voice before he saw her.

'Get your hands off me! This is an outrage! I have the right to take part in peaceful protests. I shall be writing to my MP about this.'

He was on his way back to the command centre in the company of Flight Lieutenant Jones and Sergeant Murphy, having been sent packing by Major Nicole Anderson. Now it sounded as if he was going to have another belligerent woman on his hands. He turned to see Becca coming around the corner followed by two MOD policemen leading a clearly furious Janice by the arms.

'What's going on?' he asked Becca.

'A word, in private.' She beckoned him into an empty meeting room nearby. It was much like the office where they had first been introduced to the station commander, except that this room was windowless. Becca shut the door behind them. 'I've arrested Janice and brought her in for questioning.'

'Why?'

'Long story. But Jess has found out from Matthew that not only did Janice know Dean Gibson through his wife Laura, but on Friday evening, she attended a wake of the Lyke Walk Club.'

'A wake,' said Raven. He remembered what Ronald had told him about the club's arcane practices. 'That's what they call a dinner.'

'Yes,' said Becca. 'But guess where the wake was held.'

Raven hazarded a guess. 'Ravenscar?'

'Precisely.'

He mulled over the facts and was forced to concede that the web of connections made Janice a suspect in the two murders. 'Do you think she could be Gandalf?'

'Don't you? She's got it in her. You saw her at the demonstration. She's pretty terrifying.'

'I won't dispute that,' said Raven. At first glance, the old woman might seem an unlikely evil mastermind, but Raven recalled how brutal and merciless she'd been at school, how she'd made the boys do cross-country runs in freezing weather, how she'd bellowed at slackers, how she'd been nicknamed "the dragon". If she'd bought into Dr Aaron Blake's arguments, how far would she go to achieve the ultimate aim of dismantling the UK's nuclear deterrent?

Through the closed door, he could still hear her making a song and dance about her "wrongful" arrest and demanding to be allowed back outside.

'Let's see what she's got to say for herself,' said Raven, heading back to the corridor.

'Chief Inspector,' bellowed Janice as soon as he emerged from the meeting room, 'I have been brought here under false pretences and I insist that you allow me to return to my position on the frontline.'

'The frontline?' said Raven. 'That's an interesting choice of word, Janice. Do you see this as a battle between opposing sides? A war, even?'

'Absolutely, I do. A war of right against wrong.'

Interesting. Aaron Blake had come across as an extremist, but this retired schoolteacher from Goathland was working hard to outdo her mentor. And if she saw this as a war, did that mean she was prepared to kill the enemy?

'You did say you were hoping for trouble,' said Raven, 'but perhaps this wasn't the sort of trouble you were expecting.' He turned to address the flight lieutenant. 'Is it all right if we use the meeting room to interview Miss Sillitoe?'

'No problem.'

After the two MOD police officers had shown Janice into the room, Raven dismissed them. 'Thanks for your assistance. We'll handle this from now on. From what I hear, you're needed outside.'

They left the room, leaving Janice alone with Raven, Becca, Sergeant Gary Murphy and Flight Lieutenant Jones. Strictly speaking, Raven was within his rights to dismiss the latter two, but it would be more efficient for them to hear everything that Janice had to say. And who knew, it might not hurt to have them to hand if she became rowdy.

'You'll have been read your rights by my colleague, DS Shawcross,' he told Janice, 'so you'll be aware that it may harm your defence if you do not mention when questioned something which you later rely on in court.'

'I have nothing to hide,' declared Janice.

'That's good.' Raven studied the woman seated opposite him at the conference table. She had lost her placard, but none of her belligerent attitude. She held herself erect, regarding him with a haughty glare. In a way, he was reminded of Major Nicole Anderson, even though the two women came from opposite sides of the Atlantic Ocean and were decades apart in age.

Difficult women. Raven had spent his whole life dealing with them.

'It has been brought to my attention that you knew the man whose body was found at Lilla Cross. Dean Gibson.'

'Yes,' said Janice. 'I've never denied it.'

'Did you know that he worked for the MOD police and was stationed at RAF Fylingdales?'

'Of course I did. Goathland's a small village. Everyone knows everyone.'

Raven imagined that Janice knew more than most. He could see her poking her long nose into everyone's affairs. Might she even have ingratiated herself with Laura Gibson in order to reach her husband?'

'But I had no idea that the body we found was Dean's,' Janice continued. 'How could I? It was burnt beyond recognition.'

'Apart from the metal bone plate that enabled us to identify him.'

Janice shrugged. 'I don't know anything about that.'

'How well did you know him?'

'Quite well, but I liked his wife better. I didn't approve of his job, and I made no secret of it. I've never hidden my opinion of RAF Fylingdales and the UK's Trident submarines.' She levelled a malevolent look at Jones and Murphy, the current representatives of the system she abhorred.

'The two of you argued about it?' queried Raven.

'I didn't say that. I try to get along with my neighbours.'

Raven tried hard to imagine that, but found himself struggling with the notion.

'In the last week,' he continued, 'there have been two murders connected with RAF Fylingdales. Let's start with the most recent one.'

'What?' said Janice. 'Two murders?'

Raven nodded to Becca to take over the questioning.

'Can you tell us where you were on Friday night, Janice?' she asked.

'Friday night? Well, I was in Ravenscar. I attended a wake of the Lyke Walk Club in the Raven Hall Hotel.'

'In this context, a *wake* means a *dinner*,' explained Raven for the benefit of Jones and Murphy.

'It was our midsummer wake,' confirmed Janice.

'What was on the menu?' asked Becca.

'By tradition we have witches' broth, hare stew with rowan jelly, crab apple pie, and funeral biscuits.'

'How appropriate,' said Becca, 'given that a man lost his life that evening.'

For the first time, Janice lost her composure. 'What do you mean? Who?'

Raven studied her face, trying to work out how much she really knew. But Janice's expression had quickly closed again. She was good at this game.

Becca continued her questioning, steadily applying the

pressure. 'The victim was Sean Collins, formerly Private Sean Collins of the Duke of Wellington's Regiment. He was found dead at the old World War Two radar buildings in Ravenscar, just a short distance from the hotel where you were celebrating, if that's the right word.'

'I've never heard of this Sean Collins,' said Janice.

'So you say, yet he was also associated with RAF Fylingdales, and you just happened to be in Ravenscar on the night he was killed.'

Raven leaned his arms on the table. 'Do you believe in coincidences, Janice?'

She regarded him defiantly. 'If you're going to start making outlandish accusations, I think I need a lawyer.'

But Raven didn't have time for the kind of delays that getting a lawyer out to RAF Fylingdales would involve. 'Gandalf,' he said. 'What does that name mean to you?'

Janice shook her head. 'A fictional wizard? What does that have to do with anything?'

'Do you know anyone who uses that name as an alias?'

'Certainly not.'

'What about Frodo?'

She folded her arms across her chest. 'Are you just going to play silly games now?'

'Janice,' he said, 'we are investigating not only two murders, but also a threat to national security. If you know anything about this at all, and you remain silent, you could be in very serious trouble indeed. Do you understand that?'

'What I understand, DCI Raven, is that you don't have any evidence against me, and that this is a violation of my civil rights. I've every mind to pursue a claim against the police for wrongful arrest.'

'Janice,' said Becca, 'We need you to provide an alibi for the entire evening you were at Ravenscar. I presume that won't be a problem?'

'Not at all. As I said, I was there for the wake.'

'And who can confirm that?'

'Why, Ronald Fairchild was with me. We went together.'

'Was Ronald with you the whole time?'

Janice shifted in her seat and wouldn't meet Becca's eye. 'Well, no, now you mention it. He did pop out for a short while between courses. But the other members of the club will confirm I stayed behind.'

Becca gave Raven a sharp look. They were both thinking the same thing.

'Where did Ronald go?' asked Raven.

'I'm not sure. He didn't tell me what he was doing, just that there was a job he needed to take care of.'

'And how long was he gone?'

'Oh, about half an hour, I suppose. He was back in time for coffee.'

Becca leaned forwards. 'Does Ronald have any history of protesting against RAF Fylingdales?'

'Oh yes,' said Janice, full of admiration. 'He was quite the radical back in the day.'

CHAPTER 30

'Penny for them?'

Jess looked up in surprise. 'Oh, hello Ronald, I didn't see you there.'

Having walked back down Chimney Bank in silence, she and Matthew had gone their separate ways. What more could they say to each other? She had all but accused him of murder, and she could see the hurt and confusion in his eyes. At the edge of the village, he'd told her he was going to the pub for a beer. He hadn't invited her to join him, but even if he had she would have refused.

Their short-lived relationship was well and truly over, if you could even call it a relationship. He was barely more than an acquaintance. She hardly knew him at all.

She had set off for home feeling quite upset. Everything seemed to be going wrong at the moment. Her grand attempt to complete the Lyke Wake Walk had ended disastrously, turning into a murder investigation. She had wanted to complete the walk in order to open a new chapter of her life, one in which she moved forward confidently alone. She hadn't been ready for a new relationship, and yet her hopes had been raised when

Matthew showed interest, only for those hopes to be dashed when he turned out to be completely wrong for her.

What was the accusation he had levelled at her? Being on the wrong side of history. If anyone was on the wrong side, it was Matthew Whelan.

Not to mention being a totally spineless wimp.

Matthew might brag about protesting against nuclear weapons, but he was all words and no action. If he'd really had the courage of his convictions, he would have been with Janice, who was almost three times his age, and the other protesters outside the RAF base right now instead of hanging around Rosedale Abbey, lamely trying to hit on her.

She was glad to be rid of him.

Ronald had just emerged from the graveyard next to the church of St Mary and St Laurence. It was the church where he had officiated until his retirement. He always went to the Sunday services, and often visited the churchyard to lay flowers at his wife's grave. The russet-and-grey stone church and the trees and headstones that surrounded it were one of the touchstones of Jess's childhood. A place as familiar to her as her own hands.

She stopped when she saw Ronald coming out through the iron gate. It was good to find a friendly face.

'You look as if you could do with cheering up,' he said. 'Got time for a cup of tea? Keep an old man company?'

'Yes, why not.'

They walked back to his house on the village green together.

Ronald had lived in the house for as long as Jess had known him. She wasn't sure when she had first got to know the vicar, but he had been a family friend for as long as she could remember. Her mum and dad had probably known him even before she was born. That was the way it was in Rosedale Abbey, and she felt a tug in her heart, that familiar twitch that would always keep her coming back no matter how far she might roam. If her mum had got her way, she would never have left the village in the first place.

'You go and sit down,' said Ronald. 'Make yourself comfortable. I'll put the kettle on.'

Jess went into the front sitting room where she had sat with Raven a few days earlier. It had been strange bringing her boss to this place. Raven belonged to the new life she had chosen for herself, whereas Ronald embodied the past, the unshakeable core that would always be a part of who she was. She supposed that every adult had to go through the same transition, of leaving the security of home in order to discover their true self. For Jess, the journey had been a rough one and was still a work in progress.

People like Matthew, she supposed, were simply obstacles to be steered around. Or perhaps they were signposts, helping her discover what she wanted by showing her what she didn't want. If that was the case, he had done her a big favour.

She didn't sit down immediately but stood browsing Ronald's bookshelves, which always looked so enticing. She loved the smell of old paper and the look of old books. Ronald's collection was particularly intriguing.

His interests were eclectic, ranging from the obvious religious and philosophical works – the writings of CS Lewis being a particular favourite – to classic nineteenth- and twentieth-century fiction. She remembered coming here when she was a girl and being delighted to find Lewis Carroll's *Alice in Wonderland* books. The vicar had patiently explained to her that they were not just silly books about a little girl called Alice, but also very clever writings by a professor from Oxford. He had read some passages to her and told Andrea that Jess was welcome to borrow any book she liked from the collection.

Ronald appeared in the doorway bearing a tray with his best crockery. 'I do find that tea and biscuits can cure most of life's ailments, don't you?'

Jess smiled. One of the books on the shelves wasn't properly aligned with its neighbours and she reached up to push it back into place.

But something stayed her hand. She paused and took

the book off the shelf instead. It was one of the books she had borrowed from Ronald and read many years ago as a young teenager.

The Fellowship of the Ring by JRR Tolkien.

She flicked through the pages and the book fell open to a chapter entitled *The Shadow of the Past*. Gandalf was talking to Frodo about the Ring, and part of Gandalf's words were underlined.

All we have to decide is what to do with the time that is given us.

Suddenly the book felt very heavy in her hands.

'Ah, yes,' said Ronald from behind her. '*The Lord of the Rings*.'

Jess felt as if she'd picked up a forbidden text and read something she wasn't supposed to see. She fumbled to put the book back on the shelf, but knew it was already too late.

Ronald put the tray down on the coffee table, then straightened up slowly. 'I can see you've found out my secret. I must say, it seems somewhat arrogant likening myself to such a powerful wizard, but I suppose it appealed to my sense of fun. You have to forgive an old man his foibles.'

Jess looked into the eyes of the old family friend, hardly able to process what he was saying. The mastermind behind the Fylingdales plot was Ronald. He had hidden his secret behind the codename Gandalf. Was he also a murderer?

She gripped the book tightly in her hands. It was hardly an effective weapon, but it was all she had. Her eyes drifted around the room. An iron poker next to the fireplace. A metal horseshoe hanging on the wall. A heavy candlestick on the mantelpiece.

Ronald followed her gaze. 'There's really no need to be afraid of me. You don't think I would hurt you, do you, Jess?'

Jess didn't know what to think. The certainties of her childhood were tumbling down before her.

'Let me make this easy for you.' Ronald sat down on the sofa and held out his wrists. 'I don't suppose you've brought your handcuffs with you?'

'No,' said Jess, 'but I can still arrest you.' She swallowed, gathering her courage to say the words she must. 'Ronald Fairchild, I'm arresting you on suspicion of…'

She paused. What exactly was she arresting him for?

'Since it's just the two of us here,' said Ronald, 'let me help you out. You could say "on suspicion of conspiracy to cause criminal damage" or "conspiracy to commit an act of terrorism" or even "murder".'

Jess's mouth felt dry. She could really do with that cup of tea but knew she would never drink it. Not here. Not now. She finished what she had started to say.

'Ronald Fairchild, I'm arresting you on suspicion of murder.' The word stuck in her throat. 'You do not have to say anything. But it may harm your defence if you do not mention when questioned something which you later rely on in court. Anything you do say may be given in evidence.'

'There, that wasn't so hard was it?' said Ronald brightly. 'I expect you'll want to call your boss. What was his name? DCI Raven. I liked him, I thought he was a decent chap.'

Jess stared at him in confusion. 'Why are you handing yourself in like this? I don't understand.'

Ronald gave a little shrug. 'At this point, there's nothing you can do to stop my plans from unfolding. My part in this drama is already done. Now it's up to my associate, "Frodo"' – he drew air quotes with his fingers – 'to do the rest. I always expected to be arrested eventually. In fact, I was rather counting on it. For the publicity, you understand. Not that I seek fame for some kind of personal glory but because I want to draw the attention of the British people to my cause. It's a necessary part of the story, you see. I'm sure Jesus knew he was going to be arrested in the Garden of Gethsemane.'

'But who is Frodo?' asked Jess. 'And what is the plot?'

'Ah, that would be telling,' said Ronald, tapping the side of his nose. 'You won't get that out of me. You wouldn't expect me to scupper my carefully laid plans, would you? You know me better than that, Jess.'

She stared at him coldly. 'I thought I knew you, Ronald. But I never really understood you at all.'

He seemed disappointed by her answer. 'A human soul is like a diamond. It has so many different facets. Turn it one way, it grows dull; turn it another and it sparkles in the light.'

Jess shook her head, unable to come to terms with the deluded maniac who had been hiding behind the mask of a kindly old man. 'I don't know how you could do this, Ronald. Murder, terrorism. They're against all the Christian principles you've lived your life by. If you disagreed so strongly with nuclear weapons, why didn't you just protest, like Janice?'

Her question seemed to ignite a flare of anger. 'Bah,' he said with a dismissive wave of his hand. 'I did protest in my younger days. I believed we could make a difference, that we could make the case for a change of government policy. But I learned that demonstrations are a waste of time. The only thing that will bring about lasting change is direct action.'

'But murder? How did Sean Collins fit into your plan?'

'He didn't fit,' said Ronald. 'That was the point. He threatened to reveal the plot and ruin everything. It was unfortunate, but Collins was a casualty of war. There is such a thing as a just war, you see. And in war there is always collateral damage.'

Jess had heard enough. She had stepped into the home of an old friend and found herself in the lair of a monster. Ronald had deluded himself into thinking he spoke reasonably, but his words were pure evil. She had to call this in.

She took her phone from her pocket.

'You do what you have to do,' said Ronald calmly. He lifted the teapot. 'Now, shall I pour?'

CHAPTER 31

Raven put the phone down with a clatter. A message had eventually got through to him via the switchboard at RAF Fylingdales. It was from Tony, who had spoken to Jess at Rosedale Abbey, reporting that the mastermind of the plot to sabotage the military base had been identified and arrested.

Ronald Fairchild.

The seemingly harmless old man who had talked so enthusiastically to Raven about the traditions of the Lyke Wake Walk was now waiting to be taken into custody. As well as admitting to planning and coordinating the conspiracy, he had also confessed to killing Sean Collins to prevent him revealing the plot to the police.

Sean, Raven reflected ruefully, had in fact already told him of the existence of the plot. He just hadn't revealed any details. If Sean hadn't been drunk and incoherent at the time, or if Raven had listened more patiently, all this tragedy could have been averted. Now the best that Raven could hope for was to prevent the plot from being carried out.

He called Jess's mobile using the landline at the base.

She answered immediately.

'Good work,' he said. 'Where are you now?'

'At Ronald's house. Waiting for a police car to arrive.'

'Are you okay?'

'Absolutely. Ronald didn't put up any resistance. He gave himself up and admitted what he'd done.'

Raven couldn't believe how calm Jess sounded given that she was alone in the presence of a killer. But Jess was made of stern stuff. 'What exactly has he confessed to?'

'He admitted to killing Sean Collins, and also to being Gandalf, and to organising the plot.'

'What about Dean Gibson?'

'He's refusing to say any more.'

'Has he given any indication what the plot actually is?'

'None. But he says we're too late to stop it.'

'Damn it,' said Raven.

'Oh,' said Jess, 'that's the police car outside now. I have to go.'

'All right,' said Raven. 'Take him back to Scarborough. He'll need to be interviewed by Counter Terrorism. You've done well, Jess.'

He hung up and turned to address the small group surrounding him – Becca, Wing Commander Fitzwilliam-Brown, Flight Lieutenant Mark Jones and Sergeant Gary Murphy. He briefly outlined what he knew.

Sergeant Murphy was the first to speak. 'The situation outside the gates is under control. No one has gained unauthorised entry to the base, and the perimeter is now sealed.'

'And I am happy to report that searches have been conducted at the other radar stations in the Ballistic Missile Defense System, and no explosive devices have been discovered at any of them,' said Fitzwilliam-Brown. 'Is it possible that this conspiracy is simply an elaborate hoax?'

'We can't take that risk,' said Raven.

'No,' agreed the wing commander. 'We absolutely cannot.'

'If the base's perimeter is secure,' said the flight lieutenant, 'but this man, Ronald Fairchild, insists that it's too late to stop the plot, then either a device of some kind must already have been planted, or else the saboteur is inside the base right now.'

'I want another search of the radar to be undertaken immediately,' ordered Fitzwilliam-Brown. 'Leave no stone unturned.'

'Very good, sir.' Jones left to carry out his instructions.

'The key question,' said Becca, 'is, who is Frodo?'

'Exactly,' said Raven. 'Let's think logically. Sean Collins was murdered by Ronald because he knew of the sabotage plot and wanted to reveal it. But how could Sean have learned about it in the first place?'

'Sean was a loner,' said Becca. 'The only person we know for certain he was in contact with was his brother, Brian.'

'Right, but how is Brian linked to RAF Fylingdales?'

'No idea,' said Becca, 'but I know who can find out.'

'Yes,' said Raven, immediately picking up on her line of thinking. He reached again for the phone and dialled an external number. He couldn't remember when he'd last made so much use of landlines and public phone boxes. It must have been about twenty years ago.

As soon as the call was answered, he switched it to speakerphone again. The others clustered around to listen, joined again by Mark Jones, who had just returned.

'Tony?' said Raven, 'I need you to tell us everything you can find out about Brian Collins. As quickly as you can.'

'Everything, sir?'

'We need to build a picture of his social circle. His work colleagues, his friends and family, people he hangs out with. Can you do that?'

'I can do my best, sir. Now?'

'If you don't mind, Tony.'

'Hang on.' They waited as Tony began his search, clacking away on computer keys. The diligent detective constable might sometimes come across as dull, someone best suited for routine and monotonous back-office work, but Raven had come to realise that the man was nothing short of a genius. No fact was too mundane, no piece of evidence too elusive to escape Tony's attention.

All he needed was time, and that was the one thing they didn't have.

'Anything, Tony?' Raven glanced at his watch. He had been in this bunker of a command centre for what seemed like hours. With no outside windows, it was impossible to tell what time of day or night it was. All he could see was the ranks of computer monitors – windows onto the unblinking eye of the phased array radar.

Tony began to relate what he had found. 'Brian Collins, resident of Sleights, married with two school-age children. His wife works as a hotel receptionist in Whitby. He studied Mechanical Engineering at Sheffield.'

Raven recalled the man's proficiency at maintaining his car, a skill that Raven sadly lacked. Brian had mentioned being an engineer when Raven had gone to see him. But what was his connection to the RAF base? It was starting to look as if there was no link at all and Raven was searching in the wrong place for a saboteur.

'No social media presence that I can see,' continued Tony. 'No involvement with the police at any time, either as a victim or a criminal.'

Raven hadn't really expected Brian to appear in the database of those arrested or charged. You could tell at a glance that Brian Collins was a law-abiding citizen. He probably hadn't even clocked up a parking ticket his entire life. Why were they even wasting time looking into his possible involvement in the plot?

'His current employer is VoltMatrix Engineering, whose head office is in Birmingham.'

'Birmingham?' queried Raven. 'That's a long way from where he lives. Does the company have an office closer to home?'

'Just a moment, sir. I'm looking at their website now.

Ah yes, there it is. They have a division based in York.'

York. That made more sense. But it still wasn't a connection. They probably needed to widen the net and consider the RAF and MOD staff who worked at the base. But that might run to hundreds of individuals.

'Wait,' said Sergeant Murphy. 'I know the name of that company. We have regular visits from them. I've seen their vans on site.'

Flight Lieutenant Jones clicked his fingers. 'They have the maintenance contract for the power station here.'

Raven felt his heart pounding. He looked to Becca, who nodded. This was it.

'Is this man present on site now?' asked the wing commander.

Sergeant Murphy picked up another phone and dialled an internal number. 'Hi, Bob, Gary here. Quick question. Is Brian Collins in today? He is? Right, keep an eye on him but don't do anything that might spook him! We're coming over.'

They all looked at each other. 'I think we've found Frodo,' said Raven.

CHAPTER 32

The manager of the power station met them at the entrance to the building. 'What's going on?' he demanded. He was wearing a hard hat and a short-sleeved shirt emblazoned with the logo of his company, VoltMatrix Engineering. His name badge read "Bob Dunford."

'Operational situation,' said Wing Commander Fitzwilliam-Brown, taking charge in his calm authoritative manner.

They climbed a metal staircase and entered a control suite where computer terminals stretched out across a long desk. Their screens showed power outputs, pressures, temperatures and a host of other real-time data. Behind the screens, large internal windows looked down onto the gas-fired power station itself – a giant assemblage of pipes, turbines, generators and transformers large enough to power a small town. Raven had thought the engine of his BMW was complicated enough, but this looked like something out of a dystopian sci-fi film. Even from this side of the thick glass viewing windows, the noise of the generators was uncomfortably loud. The floor of the building trembled with the steady throbbing of the turbines.

He had to raise his voice to make himself heard above the din. 'You need all of this to power the radar?' he asked Flight Lieutenant Jones.

'That's right. Two thousand five hundred solid state transmitters and receivers, each consuming a kilowatt of power. The whole system needs two-and-a-half megawatts to keep it running.'

The power station manager seemed keen to add his piece. 'Natural gas turbines, two thousand horsepower apiece, with diesel generators as backup. We keep these beauties running around the clock.'

'What would be needed to take the system down?' asked Raven.

The manager looked aghast. He eyed Raven suspiciously, clearly unnerved by the bloodstains on his shirt. Raven realised he probably looked more like an actor from a slasher film than someone who'd been involved in a minor altercation with an anti-nuke protester.

'Take it down? What on earth do you mean?'

'I mean, how would someone go about sabotaging it?'

'Who would do such a thing?'

'Bob,' said Sergeant Murphy, 'you confirmed to me that Brian Collins is in today. Where is he now?'

'I don't know. He clocked in at the start of his shift, but I haven't seen him since.' He turned to face the viewing windows. 'He must be inside the building somewhere.'

'What role does Brian have?' Raven asked.

'He's a maintenance supervisor. He manages the technicians looking after the gas and diesel generators and all the associated equipment. Pumps, compressors, switchgear and so on.'

'So he has access to all parts of the plant?'

'Of course.'

'We need to find him before he can do any damage,' said the wing commander. 'Sergeant Murphy?'

'Backup's on its way, sir. It should be here soon.'

The sergeant had radioed for support on their way to the power plant, calling a dozen of his men away from the protest at the main gate. It had been agreed that the demonstration was little more than a nuisance, possibly a diversionary tactic intended to distract attention from the real threat deep inside the base. It was conceivable that Dr Aaron Blake knew full well what was about to happen inside RAF Fylingdales which would explain why he had been so keen to waste time by engaging Raven in arguments about national security. Or perhaps he just liked the sound of his own voice.

Either way, the real threat was much closer to home and had been under their noses all the time. So much for the motto *We Are Watching*. What was the Latin for *We Are Sleeping?*

'Can we afford to wait for backup?' asked the flight lieutenant, casting a nervous glance at the turbine room below. The floor of the chamber was the size of a football pitch and the plant as tall as a block of flats. A handful of engineers could be seen moving around the labyrinth of pipework, carrying out their duties.

One of them might even now be preparing to strike.

'Let's start searching,' said Raven. 'We'll split up so we can cover more ground. Bob, you and Jones can come with me. Becca, you go with the wing commander and the sergeant.'

For once the station commander seemed content to take orders instead of give them. He gave Raven a curt nod of assent. 'Very well. Proceed.'

*

Inside the main part of the power plant, the roar from the generators was deafening. Bob had issued them with hard hats and ear defenders, though Raven doubted whether a hard hat would offer much protection if a bomb went off next to a gas-powered turbine. He pictured shards of hot metal and exploding gas ripping its way through the generator hall, leaving burning destruction in its wake.

No, he was pretty sure that hats would be of no help in that situation.

He descended a steep flight of metal stairs to the floor of the engine room, followed by the plant manager with Mark Jones bringing up the rear. At the bottom of the steps, walkways led off in several directions.

Banks of machinery towered overhead, and a tangle of colossal pipes stretched off into the distance. The air was thick with the stink of gas and oil. It was like being in the engine room of a vast ocean liner. Or the belly of some fire-breathing beast.

How were they going to find anyone in this place?

There was nothing for it but to get moving. Raven set off along the widest corridor, heat radiating from the columns of pipework on all sides. The thick steel tubes were painted a fiery red. No wonder Bob was wearing short sleeves. Already Raven's brow was prickling with sweat. When he wiped his forehead his hand came away wet.

He felt a tap on his shoulder and turned around. Bob was pointing down a side alley, mouthing, 'That way.' Perhaps he knew where Brian Collins was most likely to be working. Or had a hunch how the rogue engineer intended to carry out his plot.

Raven moved along the narrow space between the machinery, perspiration trickling down his back. He had the feeling he was headed to his doom. He was grateful for the white noise of humming equipment all around. It stopped him from thinking too hard about what the hell he was doing.

They rounded a corner and spotted an engineer in a black polo-shirt further along the walkway.

Raven immediately recognised Sean Collins's brother, Brian Collins. He signalled for the others to stop.

'It's him,' said Raven. He had to shout to make himself heard. 'What's he doing?'

The engineer was bent over a control panel fixed to the wall. It looked like the nerve centre of the entire system –

a tangle of multi-coloured wires and switches. Lights blinked and flashed in red and green along the panel. A tool bag lay open on the floor at his feet and he was holding some kind of wire cutter. It appeared that the plan involved a low-tech method of sabotage. Crude but effective, it negated the risk of smuggling an explosive device into the high-security RAF base.

Bob gave a sharp intake of breath. 'What the hell does he think he's up to? He shouldn't be messing about with those switches. Those are the controllers for the high voltage switchgear. If he breaks them, he'll shut the whole power off. The radar will be blind!'

'At least he doesn't have a bomb,' said the flight lieutenant. 'Let's take him!'

The engineer had his back to them and hadn't heard their approach over the din of the generators. Raven began to make his way slowly towards him. If he could get close enough without being seen...

'Hey!' yelled Bob. 'Don't you dare cut those wires!'

So much for stealth. Raven's plan had been blown out of the water almost as soon as he'd formulated it. Collins jumped at the sound of the plant manager's shout and his eyes went wide as he saw Raven approaching. He turned his attention back to the cables, fumbling with the cutters.

Raven began to run, but before he could get far, he heard the unmistakeable click of a gun slide being pulled back and released, ready for firing.

He turned around slowly and saw the flight lieutenant holding a Glock 17 semi-automatic pistol, the standard-issue side arm of the RAF, in his right hand.

'Hands above your head! NOW!'

Raven raised his hands. 'Take it easy, Mark. Don't do anything stupid.'

Jones jerked the pistol to one side in irritation. 'Not you, Raven! Him!' He aimed the gun at the engineer.

Collins stood frozen, a look of raw fear in his eyes.

'Drop the cutters!' bellowed Jones.

The wire cutters trembled like a leaf, but Collins held

onto them grimly.

Raven took a step towards him. 'Drop them, Brian!'

Collins seemed to come to a sudden decision. His hand stopped shaking. 'Don't come any closer or I'll cut the cable!' He was standing right next to the open control panel, the jaws of the tool around a dark brown cable.

'Bloody hell,' said Bob. 'That's a live wire. If he cuts that, he'll go down as well as the radar!'

'Don't do it, Brian,' urged Raven. 'Think of your family.'

The engineer's face was a picture of confusion as conflicting emotions played across his features. But he held on tight to the wire cutters. 'Tell him to drop his gun,' he pleaded, nodding in the flight lieutenant's direction.

'Lower your gun, Jones!' called Raven. An armed confrontation wasn't helping the situation one jot. Nor was the incessant din of the power plant. He wished these damn turbines would be silent for a minute. He could barely hear his own thoughts.

Jones shook his head, the gun still levelled at his target. 'No way. I'm not taking any chances. He has to drop the wire cutters before I lower the gun.'

Raven looked from one man to another. Stalemate. It looked like it was up to him to defuse the standoff.

He advanced cautiously, his palms raised and open, making no sudden movements, until he was close enough to the engineer to talk without having to shout his head off. 'It's all over, Brian. Ronald has been arrested. He's confessed to being Gandalf. We know that you are Frodo' – Raven watched as the man's eyes confirmed the truth of it – 'it's time to turn yourself in.'

Raven hoped his words would have a calming effect, convincing the engineer that his goal was futile, but they seemed to do the opposite. A look of defiance spread across Brian's face. 'I'm not doing this for Ronald. I'm doing it for my brother.'

'Sean?' Raven knitted his brows together in puzzlement. 'I don't understand. Why?'

The question seemed to fill the saboteur with renewed vigour. 'Because this country let him down. He was only eighteen when he was sent into a war zone, and what did he get for his trouble? A bullet that put him out of action and ruined his life forever. He was never the same after he returned from Bosnia, and what did the army do to help him? Nothing! He was thrown on the scrap heap like a broken piece of machinery.'

Raven eyed the open control panel. 'And how will cutting that wire help him?'

'Ronald said it was payback time. He told me the country didn't deserve my loyalty, and the armed forces weren't to be trusted. He explained how places like RAF Fylingdales are a threat to our national security. Why should I support anything run by the military after the way the army betrayed Sean?'

'I understand why you feel that way,' said Raven. 'Your brother deserved so much better.'

'Too right he did!'

Raven fell silent, rueing the day he had turned away from his old friend when he was at his most vulnerable. He wished he could wind back the clock and do it again differently. But who didn't wish that from time to time?

'Grab the wire cutters, Raven!' yelled Jones from behind him, but Raven ignored him. He edged closer to Brian so that the others wouldn't hear what he had to say.

'I let your brother down too, you know. A couple of weeks ago, Sean came to me and told me he had discovered a conspiracy. He asked for my help in stopping it. I didn't believe his story and I refused to help. But I should have trusted him. If I'd listened properly to what he had to say, he'd still be alive now.'

Brian's expression was unreadable. The news that his own brother had sought out Raven's help didn't seem to have come as much of a shock. Nor did the fact that Sean had asked the police for help in preventing the sabotage plot.

'Sean shouldn't have gone to you. He misunderstood

what I was trying to do. When I explained the plan to him, I thought he would be pleased. Instead, he accused me of being a traitor.'

'You showed him the messages between you and Ronald?'

Brian nodded.

So that was how Sean had got hold of the site maps and emails that were found on the memory stick.

Raven felt pity for the man standing before him, about to throw everything away. His family, his freedom, his country. Maybe even his own life. He could see how Ronald had manipulated him, had played on his vulnerabilities and used him for his own nefarious ends.

'Your brother was treated badly by the army,' Raven said, 'but he was treated even worse by Ronald.'

Brian shook his head angrily. 'Sean didn't even know Ronald.'

'Maybe not, but Ronald knew about him. And he knew what Sean intended to do.'

'What do you mean?' A flicker of doubt crossed Brian Collins's face.

'Ronald murdered Sean to keep him quiet and stop him revealing the details of the plot.'

Anger flashed in Brian's eyes. 'You're lying! Ronald would never do a thing like that. He's a man of peace! A man of God!'

'He's already admitted it and we have him in custody, under arrest for murder.'

'But...' Brian looked close to having a nervous breakdown. Sweat trickled down his face and the hand holding the wire cutters was shaking uncontrollably. The blade of the tool dug into the cable, drawing a spark that lit up the inside of the control box.

The roar of the turbines seemed to grow louder, but it was probably just the blood in Raven's head.

'Your brother was proud of you,' he told Brian. 'When we were in the army together, he was always talking about you. He said he wanted to set a good example so that his little brother could look up to him.'

Brian's face crumpled. 'And I did!' he wailed. 'I only wanted to do what was right for Sean. I wanted to make him proud of me. That's all I ever wanted.'

'Make him proud now, Brian. Give me the wire cutters.'

Brian hesitated and seemed on the brink of obeying, but as he glanced up, his eyes widened in a startled look over Raven's shoulder.

Raven turned and saw the flight lieutenant bearing down on them, his hand outstretched, the Glock ready to fire.

'Didn't you hear what the DCI said?' shouted Jones. 'You're a bloody disgrace, putting the safety of this country in jeopardy. You should be hung, drawn and quartered as a traitor.' He advanced on the terrified engineer, his finger on the trigger of his weapon.

'No!' shouted Raven. 'Put that down!'

But the RAF officer was beyond reasoning. He marched right up to the engineer and held the gun to his head. 'I'll count to three!' he shouted. 'One, two...'

A shot rang out, deafening in the enclosed space, even above the scream of the turbines.

Brian Collins cringed, dropping the wire cutters in terror. But he wasn't the one who had been shot.

Flight Lieutenant Jones let go of the pistol, letting it clatter to the floor. He tottered in confusion, his hands reaching out to steady himself. But his left leg crumpled and he toppled over, clutching at his limb in agony.

Sergeant Gary Murphy was advancing along the corridor, his Heckler & Koch MP7 submachine gun braced against his shoulder. Becca and Wing Commander Fitzwilliam-Brown followed closely behind.

Raven reached down to retrieve the Glock and the wire cutters.

But both Brian Collins and Mark Jones had ceased to be a threat. Murphy lowered his weapon and Becca came forward to put Brian in handcuffs.

'You see,' growled Murphy at the engineer, 'we're actually here to protect you. Although you don't deserve it.'

The flight lieutenant was writhing on the floor in a slowly spreading pool of blood.

'Bloody hell,' said Bob. 'It's a health and safety nightmare.'

'Go and fetch a first aid kit,' Becca told him. 'And then call an ambulance.'

The wing commander had less sympathy for the fallen RAF officer. He stood over him, his hands clasped firmly behind his back. 'Flight Lieutenant Jones, I am relieving you of your duties with immediate effect.'

CHAPTER 33

'No,' said Raven, finding himself once again in the welcome quiet of the radar command centre. 'Ronald Fairchild didn't murder PC Dean Gibson.'

It was a mercy to be out of the power plant at last, the hellish din of the machinery no longer assaulting his eardrums. The shriek of the turbines was still in his head, however, tormenting him like a chorus of banshees. It felt like it would never leave him. His sweat-drenched shirt was glued to his skin, slowly chilling his bones in the frigid air conditioning.

'What?' asked Fitzwilliam-Brown. 'I don't understand.'

Raven hated to disappoint the station commander. A moment earlier, the RAF officer had shaken his hand, congratulating him and Becca on foiling the plot and saving the radar from being taken offline. The would-be saboteur had been led away by Sergeant Murphy, and an ambulance had taken Flight Lieutenant Jones to the Daniel Cook University Hospital in Middlesbrough. The demonstration outside the base had ended with no further arrests and no casualties.

Unless you counted Raven's nose and his bloodied shirt.

They were just collateral damage.

'Ronald was the mastermind behind the conspiracy,' he explained, 'and he did kill Sean Collins. But he couldn't have been behind Dean Gibson's death. He has a cast-iron alibi for the time that Dean's body was burned.'

He looked to Becca to see if she had worked it out too.

She nodded, picking up the thread. 'One of our own detective constables can vouch for him. Ronald was in Rosedale Abbey on the night that the body was burned. He was with the other walkers, prior to them setting out from Osmotherley to do the Lyke Wake Walk. They were the ones who discovered the body.'

Fitzwilliam-Brown looked exasperated by the news. 'Then who on earth is the culprit?'

'Well, I have an idea about that,' said Raven.

*

At the Coach House Inn in Rosedale Abbey, Matthew drained the last of his pint. The beer was good, and the surroundings pleasant, but he couldn't spend all day drowning his sorrows and wallowing in misery. It was time to head back to Goathland. In fact, the sooner he could leave North Yorkshire and return to Newcastle the better.

His fieldwork for his PhD on the effects of climate change on the peat moorland was almost done. He'd enjoyed his time lodging with Janice and getting involved in some of her many causes and campaigns. She was a kindred spirit in some ways, although she could be fierce at times. Back at uni in his shared student accommodation, he had never bothered to keep the kitchen clean and tidy, but in Janice's house, he made sure to wash up his dishes after every meal and to fold the tea towel neatly back onto its rail after each use. As for the bathroom... leaving the toilet seat up once had landed him in massive trouble.

No doubt about it. Janice could be a dragon if you got

on her wrong side. He wouldn't miss her that much.

It was Janice who had introduced him to Jess. Matthew had been well up for the challenge of the Lyke Wake Walk. Janice had talked about it several times before he'd been invited to join the group, and he'd been excited to discover that a girl his own age would be tagging along and it wouldn't just be crusty old Ronald accompanying them.

But the walk had turned into a total disaster.

He'd been attracted to Jess from the outset, and she had seemed to like him too. She'd been a little cool when he'd followed up with a phone call, but his persistence had paid off with an invitation to the barbeque at her place. He'd really hoped to get to know her better, maybe even to go out on a proper date without Ronald and Janice and all of Jess's family watching over them.

Yeah, that hadn't worked out.

When he'd finally got her alone, she had virtually accused him of murder! That's what you got when you tried to date a policewoman, he supposed. He wouldn't make that mistake again.

But now he was stuck in Rosedale Abbey. No car, no bus service in the middle of the moor, obviously – it really was time for him to move back to the city – and he'd missed his chance to catch a ride with Janice hours ago.

He went up to the bar and asked the barman if he could recommend a local taxi firm. The cost of a private taxi from Rosedale to Goathland would be a killer, no doubt, but he could hardly go back to Jess's place and ask her for a lift.

'We always use this lot,' said the barman, handing Matthew a card with the name and number of a company. 'They're based in Pickering. They're usually reliable.'

'Cheers,' said Matthew. He went outside to make the call, then perched on the stone wall surrounding the pub garden to wait for his ride. He turned his face to the sun, enjoying the warmth.

Just over twenty minutes later, a red Ford Galaxy pulled up. The taxi driver wound down his window.

'Matthew Whelan?'

'That's me.' Matthew opened the front passenger door and hopped inside.

The driver was a local, judging from his accent. A moorlander, as Matthew liked to think of them. They could be a bit in-bred and narrow-minded.

This one was quite rough-looking. Shaven head, grey stubble, a tight-fitting tee revealing gym-toned biceps and a wealth of tattoos. He stank of sweat, despite the best efforts of the pine tree-shaped air freshener that dangled from the rear-view mirror. Matthew wished he'd sat in the back of the car.

'Where to, mate?'

'Goathland, please.' Matthew did up his seatbelt. The roads around Rosedale were hair-raising, as he'd learned to his cost, riding in Janice's car.

'I've got a sister who lives in Goathland,' said the taxi driver, pulling onto the main road. He drove past the Abbey Tea Rooms and turned right by the Milburn Arms Hotel. 'I'm Gavin, by the way.'

'What does your sister do?' asked Matthew, more to be polite than anything. It was going to take a good half hour to reach Goathland so he might as well make conversation. It would take his mind off the morning's emotional trauma.

'She teaches at the primary school there.'

'Oh,' said Matthew, 'my landlady volunteers at that school. Your sister probably knows her. Janice Sillitoe? She used to be a PE teacher in Scarborough before she retired to Goathland.'

'Maybe,' said Gavin, a touch gruffly. He fell silent.

Suit yourself, thought Matthew. *Miserable sod.*

He fixed his gaze out of the side window, hoping that the conversation was over. They had left the village of Rosedale Abbey now and were taking a road straight over the moors, not a sign of human habitation for miles around. In the distance, a single tree dotted the horizon. Other than that, nothing.

He had loved the unspoiled nature of the bleak landscape when he'd first moved to Goathland. It had felt like a true wilderness and he'd thought of himself as an explorer in the desert or the Antarctic. Lawrence of Arabia. Captain Scott. Now he was growing bored of its flat emptiness. He was glad he'd be gone before winter returned. It could be bloody freezing when the wind gusted across the barren moor.

'You're not from around here,' said Gavin.

Matthew dragged his eyes away from the view. 'No. I grew up in Tunbridge Wells. That's in the south of England,' he added for the benefit of the taxi driver, in case the guy was as thick as he looked. 'But now I'm a PhD student at Newcastle.'

'Oh, yeah. What're you studying then?'

'Geosciences. I'm researching the effect of climate change on the peat moorland.'

'Okay.'

The taxi driver didn't display any enthusiasm for the subject, but Matthew was used to that. When he'd started his studies, he'd engaged with people and tried to excite them about his work, to make them understand its importance. These days, he couldn't be bothered. He'd learned that most people just didn't care. He'd tried to explain it to Jess, but even she'd been only half interested.

'I was out on the moors the other day with a group of walkers doing the Lyke Wake Walk,' he told Gavin, 'but we didn't get to the end because we found a man's body at Lilla Cross.'

He didn't know why he'd said that. He'd been hoping to avoid the subject of the murder. It had brought him nothing but grief so far. But thinking about the moors had led naturally to mention of the walk and the discovery of the body.

'Bloody hell, you found what?' The taxi suddenly swerved in the road.

Matthew grabbed the door handle to brace himself, half expecting the car to plunge headlong into the ditch at the side of the road, but the driver righted the vehicle before it could come to any harm. He continued on driving as if nothing had happened.

'What the hell?' said Matthew.

'Sorry, mate. Grouse in the road.'

'A grouse?' The big red birds inhabited the moorland in large numbers and were often to be spotted dashing across the road. But Matthew hadn't seen any grouse from where he was sitting. Certainly none close enough to warrant the kind of driving that could get them both killed. He was really starting to regret getting into this taxi. Perhaps he should have phoned Janice, or gone to Ronald and asked for a lift. He stared at the road ahead, keeping his mouth firmly closed. With any luck, the conversation was now well and truly finished. He certainly had no intention to discuss either dead bodies or moorland again. In fact, he would be more than happy to finish the journey in silence.

But it seemed that Gavin was a lot more interested in the discovery of a man's body than he had been in the effect of climate change on peat bogs. 'A burnt body, you say? I think I might have heard about that on the news.'

'Did you?' Matthew wasn't sure he'd mentioned the man's body being burnt, but perhaps that was one of the details the police had released to the media. He couldn't remember now, being so closely connected to the case himself.

The driver kept his eyes firmly fixed on the road and didn't look at Matthew. 'So did you, like, speak to the police?'

Matthew sighed. It seemed that he had little choice other than to tell this guy as much as he knew. 'Yeah, we did. We were the ones who called 999. In fact, one of the women in our walking group is a detective with Scarborough CID. Her boss is in charge of the investigation.'

Despite everything that had happened between them, Matthew felt a deep pang of longing as soon as he mentioned Jess. He had really liked her. He'd been sure she liked him too. Until she accused him of murder.

'This friend of yours, the detective,' said Gavin, 'she probably gives you all the inside gossip on what the police are up to.' He turned to Matthew and gave him a matey smile, encouraging him to open up and spill the beans. But there was something cold about that smile that left Matthew feeling anxious.

'Not really,' he said. 'She's not supposed to talk about her work.'

'Course not,' said Gavin quickly. 'But do they know what happened to the poor bugger? Dean Gibson, I mean.'

'Dean Gibson?' Matthew was pretty sure he hadn't mentioned the name of the dead man. He couldn't recall any of the news reports giving the victim's name either, and Jess had said something about the police holding it back because of the military connection. So how did Gavin know the victim's name?

The taxi driver must have realised what he was thinking. He gave Matthew another grin. 'News travels fast in a place the size of Goathland.'

'Yes, I suppose it does.' Janice was certainly a prime source of village gossip, and no doubt she'd told her friends everything she knew. It was too good a story to keep to yourself. Although how did the taxi driver know what went on in Goathland? Matthew remembered him saying that his sister taught at the village school. That would be it.

But then he had an uncomfortable thought. What if this guy's sister was the wife of the murdered MOD policeman? There couldn't be that many teachers at Goathland school, the place was so tiny. What was the name of the victim's wife? Laura, Janice had told him. Laura Gibson. Was the taxi driver her brother?

If that was the case, why didn't he just come out and say so?

'I don't think they know who did it,' Matthew said guardedly. 'I mean, they haven't arrested anyone as far as I know. But they think the murder might be connected to a terrorist plot.'

This time the driver stamped on the brakes and brought the car to a screeching halt in the middle of the single-track road.

He swivelled in his seat and turned to Matthew, his eyes bulging. 'A terrorist plot? What the fuck?'

The man was wound like a tightly-coiled spring. His tattooed arms were taut and his knuckles white as he gripped the steering wheel.

Matthew drew away from him as much as he could. Which wasn't nearly far enough, in the closed confines of the taxi.

What the hell was going on?

The landscape had changed now, open moor giving way to woodland. The road rose and fell, twisting and turning as the trees closed in around them, plunging the car into shadow. It felt like being in a forest clearing from a dark fairytale, fleeing from the big bad wolf.

Except that the wolf was with him in the car.

Gavin killed the engine and a dreadful silence closed in.

Matthew reached for his phone. There was no time to make a call, but he started tapping out a panicky message to Jess. His thumbs were all over the place and the words came out garbled and autocorrected beyond all recognition. Would she understand it? He wasn't even sure he knew what was happening himself.

But he had a very bad feeling about all of this.

There was one tenuous bar of signal on his phone. He pressed send just before it blinked out to zero. Had the message gone? There was no time to think about that now. He made a grab for the door handle, hoping to get out and make a run for it. Where to? He would worry about that once he was out of the car.

But as he tried to escape, a meaty hand seized hold of his collar and dragged him back to his seat. Fingers closed around his phone and yanked it away, sending it spinning into the footwell of the car with a clunk.

He opened his mouth to protest, but his abductor spoke

first. 'You're going nowhere. Sit there and don't move a muscle.' Gavin pulled out a switchblade and snapped it open. The edge of the knife glinted silver in his fist. 'Now, tell me everything you know.'

CHAPTER 34

Jess's phone pinged with an incoming message. She checked the screen and frowned in annoyance. Matthew. Why on earth was he messaging her now? Did he still think he was in with a chance? Dream on. She shoved it back in her bag.

A police car had just arrived from Scarborough to take Ronald away. She let the two uniformed officers into the house and showed them into the front room where Ronald was patiently waiting. He lifted his eyes to hers forlornly, as if he had only now begun to think through the consequences of his actions and realise the magnitude of what he had done. It was a bit late for that.

'Goodbye, Jess,' he said to her as the officers escorted him to the front door. 'I wonder if I might ask a favour?'

'What is it?' She motioned for the policemen to let him speak. This was painful to her. She may have apprehended a murderer, but her family had just lost a friend. A piece of her childhood had been ripped from its roots, the memories sullied, a host of clamouring questions in place of solid ground. It would take time for her to process what had happened.

'Please do let Janice know what's happened to me. I wouldn't want her to worry. And,' he gestured back at the living room. 'Do help yourself to any of my books that you like the look of. The Lewis Carroll collection, perhaps? I remember how much you enjoyed reading them as a child. I don't suppose I'll be allowed to take them with me where I'm going.'

She couldn't bring herself to say anything, afraid she might embarrass herself by bursting into tears. She merely nodded and watched him walk meekly to the police car.

The car drove off and she was left alone in the house. The silence seemed deafening. How was she going to break the news to Janice?

She picked up her phone again, in need of distraction. The message from Matthew was still there, waiting for her attention. She couldn't just delete it without reading it, otherwise she would never know what he had to say. She tapped it open and stared with incomprehension.

In tax with killjoy. Need hello now

What on earth was that supposed to mean?

In tax? Did he mean taxi? But who was the killjoy? She studied the second sentence. Need hello now. It sounded urgent, but why did he need her to say hello to him? Was he hoping she would call him up and tell him everything was good between the two of them?

Fat chance.

She shoved the phone back into her bag and returned to the sitting room.

So many books on Ronald's shelves. He probably wouldn't be reading them again. She didn't know how long he would spend in jail for the terrorist offences, but murder alone carried a mandatory life sentence. A man of Ronald's advanced age would likely die in prison.

She lifted the antique volume of *Alice in Wonderland* from its shelf and turned to the table of contents. As a girl, even the list of chapters had made her giggle. They had such silly names. *Advice from a Caterpillar. The Mock Turtle's Story.* The whole book was nonsense from start to finish.

Much like Matthew's message.

In tax with killjoy. Need hello now

What could he possibly have meant? She scooped up her phone again and stared at the words once more. A horrible thought began to take shape in her head. What if killjoy meant killer?

In taxi with killer. Need hello now.

Hello didn't mean hello, it meant help!

Oh my God. There was only one taxi driver she knew who might plausibly be a killer.

Gavin Wilcox, the brother of Laura Gibson. The man who had tried to assault Raven at the Gibson's family home.

Jess's mind began to process the logistics of times, dates and alibis, but she shut that train of thought down quickly. She didn't have time to work through it now. She needed to act.

Even though Matthew's text was a jumble of words, one part of the message was crystal clear. He had managed to share the GPS coordinates of his location. She tapped her phone and saw he was at a place called Key Green, just north of Goathland.

She tried calling Raven but there was no answer. Still out of range, no doubt. Instead, she called Tony and asked him to get a message through to Raven as soon as possible. She also requested backup to be sent to Key Green. 'It's close to Egton Bridge on the Wheeldale Road.'

'Got it,' said Tony. 'And where are you now?'

'On my way to the Land Rover.' She ended the call before he could dissuade her from leaving.

*

A phone rang in the command centre and was handed to the wing commander. He listened, frowned, then passed the handset to Raven. 'It's for you, again.'

'Raven speaking.'

'Sir, Tony here. I've just had a call from Jess. She's received a message from Matthew Whelan. It's a bit garbled apparently, but she thinks he's in a taxi with Gavin Wilcox, and that Gavin is a killer.'

Raven relayed the information to Becca, who narrowed her eyes in puzzlement. 'Gavin Wilcox? We ruled him out. His alibi was solid. Could Jess be mistaken?'

'Possibly, but maybe there's something we overlooked.'

Tony's voice came across the line again. 'So, as I said, the message was confusing, but Matthew sent his location and Jess is heading there now.' He paused. 'I hope I didn't do the wrong thing, sir, but I requested an Armed Response Unit to be sent out.'

'No,' said Raven, 'you made the right call. If this is a hostage situation, we can't take any chances. Where is the location?'

'Key Green, sir.'

'Where's that?'

'Ten minutes north of Goathland.' Tony gave Raven the details.

It was just as he expected – the middle of nowhere again. 'How long will Jess take to get there?'

'It's about twenty minutes from Rosedale Abbey and she set off five minutes ago.'

'And how long for the ARU?'

'They're coming from Scarborough. I've been told to expect them in forty-five minutes.'

'That's too long.'

Jess, though competent, was a junior officer. She didn't have the experience to handle a hostage situation alone. And a lot could go wrong in half an hour. Raven pictured the shaven-headed taxi driver with his muscled arms and quick temper and didn't like what he saw.

'We're on our way now.' Raven handed the receiver back to the wing commander. 'How long is it from here to Key Green?'

'About fifteen minutes,' said Fitzwilliam-Brown. 'Ten if you really put your foot down.'

'Come on, then,' he said to Becca. 'Let's find out how fast your car can go.'

CHAPTER 35

The Jazz sped quickly along the moorland road, skirting the edge of Goathland and turning left at the old grey church by the Mallyan Spout Hotel. Becca seemed to know where she was going, taking them along a straight road that went on forever across the monotonous expanse of the moor.

Raven longed to be behind the wheel of the M6 but knew she was driving the Honda as fast as it would go. He held his tongue, confining himself to a quick glance at his watch. They'd already been driving for seven minutes, and this road just stretched on and on, as straight as a bullet.

'Not too much further,' Becca assured him.

The road eventually turned and began to descend, becoming narrower as it wound its way downhill. Left and right it weaved, crossing old stone bridges and passing the occasional cottage or farm. What kind of people lived in these isolated places? In winter, they might be snowed in for weeks.

Trees sprang up along both sides of the road, hemming them in. If they met a tractor, Raven didn't know how they would squeeze past.

And then it happened.

The car came to a halt, facing an enormous agricultural vehicle that blocked the road ahead. The driver of the combine harvester, or whatever the contraption was, gave them an apologetic shrug through the window of his cabin. There was no way he was turning that monster around.

Becca twitched the car into reverse and crept backwards. The behemoth advanced slowly, a green metal giant, almost filling the entire width of the road.

'The nearest passing place was about a hundred yards back,' said Raven. 'This is going to take forever.'

'Hang on,' said Becca. 'I think there's a quicker way.'

She edged back a few more feet, angling towards the verge. She beckoned to the other driver, who looked puzzled, but manoeuvred his vehicle onwards.

'There's no room to get past,' said Raven.

Becca turned the steering wheel and reversed a little more, tucking the car into the very edge of the road. The passenger wing mirror almost scraped against a tree. She waited as the driver of the farm vehicle inched forward, its raised metal arms and threshers looking like the mandibles and claws of some gigantic insect.

The gap between the two vehicles narrowed to about a centimetre, and then widened. With a burst of diesel fumes and a toot of his horn, the driver of the massive harvester sped on his way.

Becca slung the Jazz into gear and set off again. 'Just as well we brought my car today,' she remarked.

Raven said nothing.

They climbed a hill, the engine of the little car whining in protest, and Raven wondered if they would make it to the top. The ground dropped away on one side, revealing views stretching out for miles. It would have been a picturesque route if he hadn't been so wound up.

He fought hard not to look at his watch again. Yet eventually they made it to the place Tony had described.

Key Green.

'Is this it?' Raven looked around. 'There's nothing

here.'

'Not a lot,' agreed Becca.

Apart from a farmhouse and a cottage, there were no buildings of any kind. And no cars in sight.

'Damn it, where are they?' asked Raven. He pulled out his phone to call Tony, but the display showed no reception. Of course. What had he expected?

'I'll keep going,' said Becca. She pulled the car up to a T-junction where the road joined another on a steep hill. Looking down the hill, Raven caught a glimpse of red between the trees.

'That way.'

The splash of colour soon resolved itself into the shape of a red Ford Galaxy and Becca halted in front of it. 'Twelve and a half minutes,' she remarked proudly.

'Not too shabby,' conceded Raven.

A driver and passenger were visible inside the stationary vehicle. Beyond it, further down the hill, Jess's Land Rover was just rattling into view. As expected, the Armed Response Unit was nowhere to be seen.

'They should be here in about thirty minutes,' said Becca. 'Shall we wait?'

'Sod that,' said Raven. He got out of the car before Becca could protest. 'You stay here.'

Although Tony had called the ARU, there was no reason to believe that Gavin Wilcox was armed. All the same, Raven approached the Ford Galaxy with caution. Through the car's windscreen, he could see two men. Gavin Wilcox in the driver's seat, a terrified-looking Matthew Whelan sitting beside him in the passenger seat. Raven signalled to Jess to stay in the Land Rover. She had played her part, alerting him to the situation. Now it was up to him to finish things off.

He sauntered up to the driver's side of the Galaxy and saw that Gavin was holding a knife. Not an ideal setup for a hostage negotiation, yet having encountered the taxi driver before, he felt he had the measure of the man. Gavin Wilcox might be reckless and dangerous, but he wasn't entirely unhinged.

Raven tapped on the window. 'Open up, Gavin. Let's talk.'

The driver ignored him.

'Wind your window down,' called Raven. 'An armed response unit is on its way and will be here in about' – he checked his watch – 'twenty-five minutes, so why don't we sort this out nicely before the rough boys get here.'

With a buzz, the window wound down a couple of inches.

Raven took that as a good sign. He didn't need Gavin to open the window all the way. In fact, the glass would keep him from getting too frisky with that knife.

In his peripheral vision he noticed that both Becca and Jess had got out of their vehicles and were watching closely. Why wouldn't people just do what he asked them to? It would make life so much easier.

'How are you, Matthew?' called Raven. 'You doing all right there?'

The young man nodded nervously. His face was ashen white, but he appeared to be unharmed. Raven hoped that things would stay that way.

'Why don't you let him go?' he suggested to Gavin. 'He's not involved in any of this. Let Matthew go and I'll come and sit with you instead.'

Gavin shook his head. 'I like him here with me. He makes me feel safe.' He cast a nasty glance in Raven's direction. 'I don't fancy having you in the car with me.'

Raven smiled innocently and spread his hands. 'You don't need to worry about me, Gavin. Like I said, it's the boys with the guns you need to be thinking about. They're always itching for a chance to use their toys.'

'They won't shoot if I've got a hostage with me.'

Raven shrugged. 'Let's see if we can avoid putting that to the test, shall we? Why don't you tell me about your brother-in-law? You knew that Dean was having a secret affair with an American officer.'

'I already told you that.'

'And you didn't like the way he was treating your sister.'

'Would you?' growled Gavin.

'Of course not. But was killing him the only solution?'

Gavin's face crumpled with the impact of Raven's words. 'Dean was an idiot! There was no need for it to go the way it did. He got himself killed!'

'Why don't you tell me what happened, Gavin?'

The taxi driver pulled a sour face, but Raven knew that few people could resist the urge to fill a silence with words. And he was willing to wait. He had plenty of time.

Twenty-four minutes, to be precise. A lot could happen in that time.

Gavin seemed to be wrestling with his emotions. 'I'd known for a while that Dean was cheating. I told you I saw him and that American woman leaving a hotel in Scarborough. And then, when he told Laura he was going on a training course, I guessed it was just a ruse. So I followed him in my taxi and stopped him. I told him the game was up and he had to end the affair, but he got rowdy. He wasn't having it.' He shot a glance in Raven's direction, then quickly looked away. 'I hit him. I didn't mean to kill him, but he bled to death right in front of me. There wasn't time to call an ambulance.'

'And then what?'

'I hid his body in the boot of his car and went back to work. I waited until Monday evening, then drove his car out to Lilla Cross and burned his body to get rid of the evidence. I dumped his car in Whitby.'

'Did your sister know about this?'

'Of course not. I did this to protect her. I couldn't tell her that I killed her husband!'

Raven waited to make sure that Gavin had finished his confession, then shook his head. 'Nice story. But it's not true.'

'What do you mean?' said Gavin angrily. 'Course it's bloody true.'

'No,' said Raven. 'Let me tell you what's wrong with it.

First of all, we checked your movements that day with the taxi firm. Just like you told me, all your pick-ups and drop-offs are logged electronically. At the time Laura says she saw Dean drive off, you had already picked up your first passenger and were well on your way to Leeds Bradford airport. You didn't return to Pickering until two hours later.'

'I—'

'Secondly,' said Raven, 'if you'd driven Dean's car to Lilla Cross and then on to Whitby, you'd have been stranded there. You needed some way to get back to your own car. You needed help, Gavin.'

Gavin glared at him, bristling with fury but knowing he'd been defeated.

'So here's what I think really happened,' said Raven. 'Laura didn't see her husband driving away on Monday morning. She couldn't have done, because he was already dead.'

The grim set to Gavin's jaw told him he was right.

'It was a smart move to burn Dean's body,' Raven continued, 'because that made it nigh on impossible to pin down the time of death. The only reason we assumed he was killed on Monday was because Laura told us he was still alive that morning. In reality, he had already been killed, probably on the Sunday, and his body hidden in the boot of his car.'

Gavin closed his eyes. 'Laura called me up late on Sunday. She was hysterical. I went straight round to her house. When I got there, she told me what she'd done. She'd guessed that Dean's story about going on a training course was a lie, and she'd confronted him. He admitted to having an affair, and in a rage she hit him with the hammer. She didn't mean to kill him.'

'And so you did your best to help her.'

'I calmed her down and told her what needed to happen. We wrapped the body in a sheet and hid it in the boot of the car, along with the hammer. Then we scrubbed the house from top to bottom. There wasn't time to dispose of the body properly, so we arranged to deal with it the following day. I had an early pick-up, and Laura went into school as normal. That evening, we drove the car to Lilla Cross and set the body alight. Laura drove on to Whitby and I followed in the taxi. We thought we'd covered our tracks.'

'You did,' said Raven. 'You might have got away with it if you hadn't pulled this stupid stunt today.' He looked over at Matthew, who was quaking in terror at his captor's revelations. Raven checked his watch again. 'We don't need to wait for the boys with their guns to get here, do we?'

Gavin shook his head. 'No.'

'Give me the knife.'

The window wound all the way down and Gavin handed over his weapon. He pressed a button and the central locking popped open. Matthew flung open the passenger door, stumbled out, and threw up by the side of the road. The stress and shock had clearly been too much for him.

Raven opened the driver's door and pulled Gavin out of the car, slapping a pair of cuffs on his wrists in the process. 'Gavin Wilcox, I am arresting you on suspicion of perverting the course of justice–'

The rest of Raven's words were drowned out by the sirens of the arriving armed response unit vehicles that swerved to a halt in the middle of the road, tyres screeching. Armed officers jumped out, their weapons at the ready.

Raven checked his watch. They'd got here a full fifteen minutes earlier than expected. That was good going.

He called to Becca. 'I'll finish off here. Tell them they arrived too late.'

CHAPTER 36

It was only a short drive from the scene at Key Green to Goathland. Raven and Becca arrived at Laura Gibson's house and knocked on the door. An ordinary door on an ordinary house in a quiet Yorkshire village. No one would have guessed what secrets it concealed.

To Raven's surprise, it was opened not by Laura but by Janice Sillitoe. She must have returned from her protest at RAF Fylingdales to spend some time with the grieving widow. Janice was nothing if not versatile.

She gave Raven a stern look, similar to when she had reprimanded him for slacking during the school cross-country run. 'What do you want now? Can't you leave poor Laura in peace? Or is it me you're after? You know, I could report you for wrongful arrest at the protest. I still intend to write to my MP about that.'

'You do that,' said Raven. 'But we're here to see Laura.'

Janice looked disappointed that Raven had chosen not to engage her in an argument about her arrest. She still seemed ready for a fight. An afternoon of waving placards and shouting at police officers clearly hadn't been enough to satisfy her desire for confrontation.

She continued to bar the way into the house with her tall frame. 'Have you found out who killed her husband at long last?'

'Yes, we have,' said Raven. 'May we come in?'

At that, Janice's belligerent attitude softened. 'Well, in that case, I suppose you can come in.' She stepped aside so that Raven and Becca could enter.

Laura Gibson was waiting for them in the lounge and must have heard every word exchanged at the front door. She rose to her feet as Raven and Becca entered.

'I think you know why we're here, don't you?' said Raven.

Laura nodded meekly.

'Your brother told us everything. At first, he claimed to have killed Dean himself, but I knew that couldn't be true.'

'Gavin's a good man, no matter what you might think of him. He's always done his best to look after me.'

Raven nodded grimly. Gavin had supported his sister in her hour of need, helping her remove her husband's body, clean away any telltale signs of blood, drive out to Lilla Cross and dump the car in Whitby. He had even offered his own confession to prevent her from being sent to prison. Few brothers could match Gavin when it came to family loyalty.

'There's one thing I still don't understand,' said Raven. 'Why Lilla Cross?'

A single tear came to Laura's eye and slid down her cheek. 'Because I loved him. Despite everything he'd done, I couldn't just leave his body by the roadside as Gavin suggested. Dean deserved better than that.' She turned her shining eyes on Raven. 'Dean and I often walked to Lilla Cross. It was the place where he proposed to me. He went down on bended knee and asked me to marry him. And so I knew I had to make my farewells there.'

She bowed her head meekly. It was hard to picture this mild and gentle schoolteacher striking her husband with a hammer so violently that his skull had fractured. But

Raven knew that even the most placid of people could be pushed too far. In a sense, it was Laura's deep love for her husband that had made her fly into such a rage on discovering his duplicity.

No one ever committed a murder because of indifference.

As Raven led Laura outside to a waiting police car, Janice stared at them open-mouthed, completely lost for words.

★

Raven and Becca drove back to Scarborough in silence. After the adrenaline rush of handling the demonstration outside the gates, saving the radar station from the sabotage attempt, and the stand-off at Key Green, the arrest of Laura Gibson for her husband's murder had been a bit of a downer.

The story was a familiar one. A wrecked marriage and shattered lives – the deadly fragments spinning out of control like shrapnel from a grenade. Dean Gibson had thought he could get away with infidelity but had paid for it with his life. His wife and brother-in-law would go to prison for their roles in the tragedy.

Only Major Nicole Anderson appeared to have escaped unscathed. No doubt she would move on to other postings and begin new relationships with other men. If there was any justice for the role she had played in the destruction of a happy family, it was that she would never know love.

'Thanks for driving,' Raven told Becca as she pulled up outside his house.

'You're welcome. Perhaps I could do more of the driving in future.'

'Perhaps,' said Raven. But they both knew that as soon as the BMW was back on the road, he would never voluntarily relinquish his place behind the wheel.

Raven's shirt was still covered in blood. He must look a right mess. He needed to get inside and clean himself up.

It had been a long day and he was exhausted. Yet he felt a strange reluctance to say goodbye to Becca. They had been working together so closely that he had broken one of his own golden rules and had come to regard her as a friend.

His closest friend.

No, second, he corrected himself, after Barry the builder.

'Would you like to come inside for a mug of tea?' The invitation was spontaneous. Raven hadn't known he was going to make it until the words were out of his mouth, but as soon as he'd said them it seemed the right thing to do.

Becca's face lit up. 'That would be love–' But she didn't finish what she was going to say.

There was a sudden rap on the passenger window and the sound of dogs barking.

Raven turned to see Melanie smiling and waving at him through the glass. Both dogs were with her on a lead. She must have just returned from walking them. It had been such a long day that, to his shame, Raven had almost forgotten about her. He turned to apologise to Becca.

'Don't worry,' she said before he had time to speak. 'I'd best be off anyway. I'll see you in the morning.' She smiled at him but the smile didn't quite reach her eyes.

'Yes, all right,' said Raven. 'See you tomorrow.' He got out of the car and watched her drive away. He realised now that he had missed his opportunity to talk over the extraordinary events of the day with the one person who would best understand. But that was nothing new. Not talking about his experiences was what he did best.

Melanie didn't seem to notice his sombre mood. 'What perfect timing, Tom,' she trilled. 'I've just got back from taking Quincey and Lulu out for a run along the North Bay. Was that your sergeant? She seems nice.'

'Yes, that was Becca.' Raven bent down to greet Quincey who was as pleased to see him as he ever was. When was this dog ever going to learn that Raven was a lousy pet owner? He didn't deserve such unconditional affection.

'Well, let's go inside and put the kettle on,' said Melanie. She produced her own key and opened the front door as if she'd lived there all her life. Raven followed her into his own house, feeling a stranger.

He paused in the hallway. The house smelled different. He sniffed, detecting hints of vanilla combined with something floral. He noticed a small gadget plugged into an electric socket above the skirting board. It appeared to be the source of the rather overpowering smell.

'What's this?'

'Oh, just something to make the place smell nice.' Melanie threw her arms around him and planted a kiss on his lips.

Raven hadn't been aware that his home was in need of artificial perfume. He prided himself on keeping it clean and tidy, old habits from his army days. Even Quincey's addition to the household hadn't changed the cleanliness of the house.

'Come on,' said Melanie, leading him into the kitchen by the hand. 'Let me show you what I've been doing.'

Raven followed her with a growing sense of apprehension, a knot tightening in his throat.

'I've moved things around a bit,' she explained, a smile on her face. 'Don't you think it looks more homely now?'

Raven studied the changes she had wrought in his absence. A vase of cut flowers adorned the window sill. Spice jars that had previously lived in the cupboard were now on prominent display. Rice and pasta had been brought out of their cardboard packaging and placed into special glass storage jars on the worktop.

There was something missing.

Raven scanned the worktops that he had laid out with such painstaking care just the way he liked them. Objects had been moved at random, some brought out of the cupboards where he had stowed them away in minimalist style. And yet there was one item that was conspicuous by its absence...

'What have you done with my coffee machine?' he

asked.

Melanie laughed. 'Such a big, ugly contraption! But don't worry, I haven't thrown it away. After I rearranged all your cupboards I managed to find space for it at the back.'

She opened a cupboard door and showed him where she'd stashed his beloved Gaggia.

Raven leaned over the breakfast bar, his head in his hands. A vision of his ex-wife came to him. Lisa had tried to mould him into an image of what she thought he should be. And now Melanie was trying to do the same. He had to stop this before it went any further.

He took her hand and wondered how to break the news. Honesty, he decided, was the best policy. He owed her that much at least.

'This isn't going to work,' he told her.

The smile faded from her face like the colour from a summer sky at dusk. Her voice quavered. 'What do you mean, Tom? What isn't going to work?'

'Us. I'm not the person you think I am.'

'What on earth is that supposed to mean?'

Raven felt terrible. He didn't want to make her cry. 'It's not you,' he explained. 'It's me. You're a lovely person, Melanie, and you've been very kind looking after Quincey. I did enjoy our night together. But I'm just no good at sharing my space with someone.'

Melanie's eyes swam with tears. 'I thought–'

He squeezed her hand. 'I know you did, and I'm sorry.'

'Perhaps we could do things differently,' said Melanie. 'I could give you more space. A little more time, perhaps, and you'll be ready to–'

Raven cut her off before she could finish. 'I think it would be better if we called it a day.'

Quincey trotted over and sat by his side in what he took to be a show of solidarity. Man and dog. Dog and man. Together. Alone.

Melanie withdrew her hand. 'Well,' she said briskly, 'thank you for being honest with me.' She slid the door key onto the worktop. 'Lulu? Where are you, girl?' She scooped up her dog and left the room, shutting the door behind her with just a touch more force than was strictly necessary.

Raven breathed a sigh of relief. 'Did I do the right thing?' he asked his dog.

Quincey gave a single loud bark and wagged his tail.

Raven reached down and patted him. 'It's you and me now, boy. Just you and me.'

He looked in the cupboard for the Gaggia and removed it carefully from the corner where Melanie had hidden it. God, he desperately needed a strong coffee.

★

Becca drove around the headland and along the North Bay, heading for home. She had finally met the elusive Melanie. She'd seemed nice enough, even though her taste in perfume was a little overpowering. She was older than Becca had pictured, but then Raven was late forties. A man his age couldn't afford to be too picky.

Becca was sorry not to have gone inside for a brew with him though. It would have been good to wind down by chatting over the events of the day. She could have done that in the car, she supposed, but the drive back from Goathland had been too soon to begin putting things into perspective.

She'd never seen inside Raven's house and was curious about how he lived, especially after all the work he'd had done on the place. She'd quizzed Liam once or twice about the changes Raven had made to the old house, but Liam's info all came second-hand from his builder, and could never be relied upon.

Nothing her brother said could ever be relied upon.

She parked the car and went up to the apartment. Even before she opened the door she could hear voices and laughter. The kitchen was a mess. Ellie and Liam were attempting to cook a recipe from a cookbook. Neither of them knew what they were doing. Ingredients were strewn all over the worktop. Dirty pans were piled in the sink. Liam was wielding a large meat knife he was almost certainly not qualified to handle.

Becca dodged around the kitchen, making sure the island unit stood between her and the knife.

'Oh, hi,' said Ellie. 'How was your day?' She giggled and Becca noticed the wine bottle and the pair of half-empty glasses that stood next to it. Liam definitely ought not to be handling that knife in his current state.

'Good,' said Becca. It was too much trouble to explain that she and the team had seen off a terrorist threat to the UK and made multiple arrests in connection with two murders.

'Do you want to join us?' asked Liam. 'We're making seafood risotto with braised asparagus. Or something like that.'

'Um...' Becca was hungry but she didn't want to spend the evening playing gooseberry with Ellie and Liam. Or dodging that knife. Her phone buzzed in her pocket and with relief she saw it was Daniel. 'Oh, I need to take this call,' she told Ellie. 'You two just carry on without me.'

She went into her room before answering. 'Hi, Daniel. I've just got back from work.'

'Working on a Sunday, as well as Saturday? Your boss really does drive you hard.'

'Something came up. I don't usually work weekends.'

'Well, now that you've finished, would you like to go out? I'm just finishing up in the office myself. We could meet in, say, half an hour?'

'For fish and chips?'

'I was thinking of something more upmarket.'

Becca didn't need any further encouragement. 'I'd love to.'

He suggested a restaurant not far from her apartment.

There was no time for a shower. She changed quickly into something comfortable, not bothering to agonise over her outfit the way she had on the double date and went out.

They arrived at the restaurant at the same time.

'Is this what you call upmarket?' she asked.

Daniel grinned. 'These things are relative. Compared with fish and chips out of a cardboard box, anything's upmarket. But we can go somewhere more expensive if you prefer.'

'No, this is fine. Let's eat.' Becca's stomach wasn't prepared to wait.

The restaurant was an unpretentious Italian place that did good pizzas and pasta dishes. Just what she needed after her day out dashing about the moors. The waiter showed them to an outside table beneath a red and white canopy.

'Wine?' suggested Daniel.

'Why not?' She wouldn't be driving again that evening and could afford to relax and enjoy herself.

Daniel ordered a bottle of Chianti, and they settled back to study the menu.

'We didn't really get a chance to talk properly last time,' he said after they'd both ordered.

'No,' agreed Becca. 'It's hard to compete when Ellie and Liam get started.'

Daniel laughed. It was a pleasant sound, warm and genuine. 'I tried contacting you a couple of times earlier today but I couldn't get through.'

'I was probably out of range,' said Becca, taking a sip of her wine.

Daniel looked puzzled. 'I thought everywhere had a phone signal these days.'

'Not in the middle of the moors. And especially not around RAF Fylingdales.'

'Wow, what on earth do you do for a living?' he asked. 'Don't tell me you work for the military. You're not a sergeant major are you?'

Becca laughed. 'No, although you're not a million miles away. Hasn't Liam told you what I do?'

'When I asked him, he refused to say. He said I should

ask you.'

Becca hesitated. Telling people she was a police detective sometimes put them off, as if they thought she would report them for speeding on the motorway or failing to pay a parking ticket. But Daniel had to find out sometime. 'I'm a detective sergeant with Scarborough CID.' She waited to see his response, fearing the familiar souring of the face she had seen so often before.

Daniel, however, looked impressed. 'Well, in that case, it's possible we might run into each other professionally sometime.'

'Why do you say that?'

He raised his wine glass to her. 'I'm afraid I work for the opposition. I'm a criminal defence lawyer. I sit on the other side of the table during police interviews.'

'Oh.' That was the last thing Becca had expected him to say. Defence lawyers could be the bane of detectives' lives, often infuriatingly advising their clients to answer "no comment" to every question put by the police. It would be easier if he was an accountant or an estate agent or something.

'You're disappointed, I can tell. My mother was too, when she found out that I planned to study Law. She'd always wanted me to go into a respectable profession like being an actor or a rock star.'

Becca laughed. 'You're funny. Do you crack jokes like that during police interviews?'

'I find that most police officers lack a sense of humour.'

'That's what we usually say about lawyers. Perhaps we should try to see more of each other when we're off duty.'

He smiled. 'Like now?'

'Like now.' She sincerely hoped they wouldn't encounter each other in a professional context. But in a place the size of Scarborough, it was a wonder they hadn't done so already.

Well, it was better to know your enemy. And she was starting to get to know Daniel.

The waiter arrived with their food. A pepperoni pizza

for him and spaghetti carbonara for her. Calories, sure. But she had earned them today.

'Bon appétit,' he said, picking up his knife and fork.

She smiled back at him. 'Bon appétit.' She'd worry about their respective jobs later. For now she was going to enjoy the food and the company.

'So,' he said, cutting a slice of pizza, 'do you think you could get to like spending time in the company of a lawyer?'

Becca studied his face, taking in the warm, upturned smile. The bright, intelligent eyes. The strong jaw and laughter lines.

She gave him an enigmatic smile. 'No comment.'

CHAPTER 37

The end was in sight. The pale blue line of the sea far in the distance beyond Stony Marl Moor. They had covered around thirty miles so far. Ten more to go. Jess had found another group of walkers to join, and this time she was determined to make it to the end of the Lyke Wake Walk.

This group comprised an experienced leader, Michael; a retired couple from America who were hiking their way around the British Isles; and an undergraduate student from Edinburgh, a girl called Harper. They got on well together. In fact, the American couple had already invited Jess to come to the States and join them on the Appalachian Trail in the Fall, although it sounded as if she'd have to take unpaid leave in order to walk the whole distance.

As they approached Lilla Howe, Jess felt a rising apprehension. Her nerves jangled, and she found her pace slowing the closer she got to the raised barrow.

Discovering a dead body left its mark, even on a police constable. And while Jess had now attended more than one post-mortem examination and counted herself familiar with Death, she didn't think she would ever quite grow used to it.

At least, she hoped she wouldn't.

She braced herself as she made the final ascent up the rocky slope, in the unlikely event that another body had been deposited at the foot of the stone cross. But the burial mound was clear of corpses, the charred topsoil the only visible reminder of the recent tragic events. In time, the remaining ashes would be blown to the wind and the land would recover. The moors were tough. They had stood for millennia and would last for many more.

She turned to look back at the distant pyramid of RAF Fylingdales, another human-made mound rising above the landscape. The scale of the radar station dwarfed the Bronze Age burial mound, but somehow she didn't think it would endure for quite as long.

She said nothing to her new companions about the grim discovery she had made at Lilla Howe, and after a brief stop to drink some water and nibble at energy bars, the group pressed on, keen to make it to Ravenscar before dusk.

They sang the verses of the Lyke Wake Dirge as they walked the last few miles, stumbling over the archaic words as they tramped across the heather moor.

> *This yah neet, this yah neet,*
> *Ivvery neet an' all,*
> *Fire an' fleet an' cannle leet,*
> *An' Christ tak up thy saul.*
> *When thoo frae hence away art passed*
> *Ivvery neet an' all,*
> *Ti whinny moor thoo cums at last,*
> *An' Christ tak up thy saul.*

Jess still had only the vaguest notion of what the dirge was about, but chanting it helped raise her spirits and take her mind off the physical challenge of the walk.

They eventually staggered into the bar at the Raven

Hall Hotel at five minutes to ten. Jess was exhausted, but euphoric. She had walked the entire distance of the Lyke Wake Walk in well under twenty-four hours. Forty miles, from Osmotherley to Ravenscar, qualifying her to become a member of the Lyke Wake Club.

She was now officially a Witch.

'Would you do it again?' Michael asked her, a smile playing on his bearded face.

Jess felt the heavy weariness of her arms, the agonised aching in her hips, her poor swollen feet whose soles were covered in blisters, and the total physical exhaustion that threatened to smother her like a pillow.

'In a heartbeat,' she said.

She ordered a pint of beer and collapsed into an armchair. Fifteen minutes later she was asleep.

*

The ghosts had fallen silent, no longer clanking their chains in the dark and dusty recesses of Raven's mind, waking him in the small hours, all bathed in sweat. They had ceased their mournful wailing, but it didn't feel like closure.

Perhaps closure was too much to hope for. To rid yourself of the murky past and sail blissfully into the clear waters of a bright future. The past was a part of him, perhaps the most important part. It was the journey that had brought him to where he stood now.

Where was that exactly? On a beach throwing a tennis ball for a dog to run after.

It was late in the day, but still light, and Quincey showed no sign of tiring. Raven threw the soggy ball again and watched his dog bound away after it across the sand. They were back on the North Bay, in exactly the spot where they'd been when Sean Collins made his reappearance in Raven's life.

Since the events at RAF Fylingdales, Raven had found himself thinking more and more about his old comrade.

Sean had been wounded in active service and on leaving the army had struggled to make a go of civilian life. That often happened with veterans, and Raven had struggled with the transition too.

War broke people. It was as simple as that.

But even though Sean had been broken by his experiences, he had died defending his country from those who threatened the security of the United Kingdom. In Raven's mind that made him a hero, even though his death would never be recognised as such.

Raven reached into his pocket and took out his own war medal. The Conspicuous Gallantry Cross. It had sat at the back of a cupboard for years, but he'd taken it out of its box recently and given it a shine with some polish. Hanging on a white ribbon bordered with narrow dark blue stripes and a central crimson stripe, the medal was in the shape of a silver cross on a laurel wreath with a medallion in the centre depicting St Edward's Crown. On the reverse were engraved his rank, name, unit, and the date on which the medal had been awarded. May 1994. A lifetime ago.

You could probably buy replicas on eBay for a few quid. But this was the genuine article.

What did it really signify?

He'd run away to the army at the tender age of sixteen to escape from his mistakes. And he'd fitted in well enough. What he'd done in Bosnia had felt like no big deal at the time, yet it had earned him this medal. That momentary act of bravery had ended his army career, and he'd never seen it as the action of a hero. Heroes were supposed to survive in one piece, not get carried out on a stretcher.

Leaving the army had felt like a defeat – just another in a long line of setbacks. But what if he was a hero like Sean, and what if that failure had been a stepping stone on the bigger path of his life? The idea was a novel one to him, but it gave him pause for thought. He found he rather liked it. The question was, where was he going next?

Trying to guess that was a fool's game. Better just to go

along for the ride.

The ghosts had fallen silent, but they were still there, treading quietly up and down the tangled corridors of his subconscious mind. He would never be rid of them, and why would he want to be? It was their home just as much as his.

Quincey dropped the tennis ball at his feet once more, bringing him back to more immediate concerns.

'Again?' he asked.

The dog looked up at him as if to say, 'Well, have you got any better ideas?'

Raven had none. 'One more time,' he said, bending to pick up the soggy, sandy ball. 'And then it's home to bed.'

⋆

Raven made sure he was back home in good time for Hannah's Skype call. Their online sessions had become a metronome, beating out a steady rhythm to his life, measuring it in terms of his weekly contacts with his daughter.

Without that connection he would be lost.

Her face appeared onscreen at the appointed hour, full of the casual optimism that came so easily to people of her age, no matter how tough they believed their lives to be. Her radiance was infectious, like a fountain of youth, and he quickly found himself beaming back at her.

He did his best to wipe the sickly smile from his face. *Come on. Play it cool.* No girl wanted to see her father grinning like a village idiot.

'Hi, Dad, how are you? What have you been up to?'

It was always her first question, yet the one he struggled with most. He allowed his mental eye to roam the rocky landscape of the past two weeks. How much of it was newsworthy, and how much merely a footnote to history?

'Not a lot,' he said.

She raised her eyebrows sceptically. 'Really? The internet says otherwise.'

He groaned, cursing Liz Larkin and her pesky news crew. The BBC cameraman had managed to capture the moment outside the gate of RAF Fylingdales when an anti-nuclear protester had landed a punch on his nose. The clip had made it onto YouTube and briefly gone viral before being eclipsed by the next sensation. If there was any compensation for his injury it was that Dr Aaron Blake had been arrested during the demo and charged with assaulting an MOD police constable. The university had suspended him from his teaching job, pending an inquiry into his behaviour.

'How is your nose now?' asked Hannah.

'It's absolutely fine.'

His car had been patched up too. An expensive repair, but one that had restored the M6 to its former glory and put him firmly back in the driving seat. He wouldn't be getting back into Becca's Jazz again if he could help it.

'Now, how about you?' he asked, seeking to draw a clear line under his five minutes of fame and shift the conversation away from his own troubles.

She drew her face into a mock frown. 'Oh, you know. Exams.'

'How are they going?'

'All done. Now I just have to wait for the results.'

'I'm sure you'll be fine.' Hannah had always done well at exams. She had her mother's gift for academic achievement and had luckily missed out on Raven's own bad genes in that department.

Her expression brightened. 'I'm really looking forward to my visit.'

'Me too. I've got the place all ready for you.' The date of her arrival was highlighted in his diary. He'd already made the bed in the spare room, and stocked up on the green tea she was so fond of.

'In fact, there's something I wanted to ask.'

'Sure, go ahead.'

'Would it be okay if I stayed a bit longer than planned?'

He could feel that silly smile tugging at his lips again,

and this time he gave into it. 'Stay as long as you like.'

'It's just that I applied for an internship with a firm of solicitors based in Scarborough. You know, while I work out what I want to do with the rest of my life.' She rolled her eyes in a parody of a young woman rolling her eyes. 'Well, I just heard that I've been accepted.'

His smiled widened further. 'That's fantastic news.'

'I'm going to be working for a lawyer called Daniel...'

She began to tell him excitedly about the summer she had planned. At her age, he'd had no plans, other than to put one foot in front of another and try not to topple flat on his face. He had stumbled his way along somehow. But Hannah would do better than him, he knew it.

She was bright and would go far.

It was getting dark outside. The longest day had already passed, although the heat of high summer was yet to come. It was funny how you could be basking in the sunshine even when autumn was well on its way. Like standing on a mountaintop, knowing that the only way was down.

He listened as Hannah continued to talk, but the darkening sky outside his window seemed to cast a shadow and he felt his mood slip.

He had left his own mountaintop behind some while ago, bidding goodbye to the clear skies and pure air that came with those rarefied heights. He was returning to earth, and the days were growing shorter.

When the Skype call was over and Hannah had made her farewells, he reached down absently and rubbed Quincey behind the ear. The dog gazed up at him, a sad longing in his eyes.

'It's just you and me, now, boy,' Raven reminded him. 'But don't worry. We'll manage somehow.'

*

Tony Bairstow was used to having packages dumped on his doorstep. Usually the delivery drivers who left them there had the good manners to ring the doorbell before driving off. Not this time. He nearly stumbled over the cardboard box that had been deposited on the step just outside his front door. He looked up and down the street to see who had left it, but there was no delivery van in sight. Whoever had left it here was long gone.

He bent down with annoyance to pick it up. The box wasn't heavy and he took it indoors to the kitchen table to examine it. No address or sender information. Strange.

Opening up the cardboard flaps, he was surprised to discover a helmet inside. He lifted it out and turned it over in his hands. It was a replica of a civil war helmet of the type worn by Royalist cavalry. Not a particularly good replica. The helmet was made from plastic and wouldn't fool anyone. He couldn't imagine any of his re-enactment friends wanting to be seen dead in such a thing. Had one of them sent it to him as a joke?

He reached inside and pulled out what appeared to be a packing note. Unfolding it, he began to read. The note was short but didn't make much sense.

Hello Tony,
I hear you like dressing up. Do you enjoy playing games?
I do.
Let's play a game in which I know the future.
You have to guess what's going to happen next.
Those are the only rules. Do you want to play?
Ironside

Tony read the note through three times before replacing it in the box with the helmet.

He liked playing games very much, but somehow he didn't think this was the kind of game he would enjoy at all.

STAINED WITH BLOOD
(TOM RAVEN #7)

A battle. A killing. An echo of history.

Scarborough Castle, high on the headland, is the picturesque backdrop for an English Civil War re-enactment. But the day takes a sinister turn when the town's MP is shot and killed in broad daylight. DCI Tom Raven is quickly on the scene, but the investigation is soon commandeered by a senior officer from Counter Terrorism, leaving Raven sidelined.

When cryptic letters are received, taunting the police, it becomes clear that democracy itself may be the target. The MP had received a number of credible death threats and suspicion quickly falls on a Russian tycoon with interests in the town. But the murdered man had many enemies, and the list of people wanting him dead quickly grows longer.

As more lives are claimed by a ruthless mastermind driving the narrative, only Raven stands between justice and an outcome stained with blood.

Set on the North Yorkshire coast, the Tom Raven series is perfect for fans of LJ Ross, JD Kirk, Simon McCleave, and British crime fiction.

THANK YOU FOR READING

We hope you enjoyed this book. If you did, then we would be very grateful if you would please take a moment to leave a review online. Thank you.

TOM RAVEN SERIES

Tom Raven® is a registered trademark of Landmark Internet Ltd.

The Landscape of Death (Tom Raven #1)
Beneath Cold Earth (Tom Raven #2)
The Dying of the Year (Tom Raven #3)
Deep into that Darkness (Tom Raven #4)
Days Like Shadows Pass (Tom Raven #5)
Vigil for the Dead (Tom Raven #6)
Stained with Blood (Tom Raven #7)

BRIDGET HART SERIES

Bridget Hart® is a registered trademark of Landmark Internet Ltd.

Aspire to Die (Bridget Hart #1)
Killing by Numbers (Bridget Hart #2)
Do No Evil (Bridget Hart #3)
In Love and Murder (Bridget Hart #4)
A Darkly Shining Star (Bridget Hart #5)
Preface to Murder (Bridget Hart #6)
Toll for the Dead (Bridget Hart #7)

PSYCHOLOGICAL THRILLERS

The Red Room

ABOUT THE AUTHOR

M S Morris is the pseudonym for the writing partnership of Margarita and Steve Morris. They are married and live in Oxfordshire. They have two grown-up children.

Find out more at msmorrisbooks.com where you can join our mailing list, or follow us on Facebook at facebook.com/msmorrisbooks.